KOKOPELLI

By

RICHARD W. ARMS, JR.

PREFACE

Grey against the western sky, more of a smudge than an outline much of he time, are the Chuska Mountains. Between them and the canyon stretch the rolling arroyo-cut wastes of the plateau, accented by ridges of sandstone, the layers of red and yellow seeming to be forcing their way upward through the levelness of the plateau. The ground is littered with angular pieces of black lava, a reminder of the region's fiery and violent past. Off in the distance, but closer than the mountains, are the jutting black spikes of basalt, the throats that remain behind from the ancient volcanoes that threw these pieces of lava across the landscape.

Northwest of the canyon itself the dry wash continues toward its eventual meeting with the San Juan River. The walls become lower as it approaches the badlands, the desolate area of twisted shapes, sculptured in black and white. There the sandy stream bed flattens and widens. The hills become lower. Looking to the horizon in this direction one sees the low but unmistakable shape of Sleeping Ute, the sacred mountain of the newcomers; the nomadic Indians who settled in the land abandoned by the Ancient Ones. He, the sleeping giant, lies on his side with his back to the southeast and his head to the north, as though unwilling to look toward the green mesas and canyons behind him, or the sere plateau at his feet; ignoring if he can the ghosts of those who left their pictures on the rocks and their cities in the desert, and who still haunt the land.

On the horizon to the south looms the symmetrical peak of Mount Taylor. From the canyon it looks deceptively small, since the canyon itself is more than a mile above sea level, and Mount Taylor is another mile higher than that. Even from the distance of seventy-five miles, as one gazes to the south from the rim of the canyon, however, it is an imposing feature against the clear sky of New Mexico.

To the east are the Jemez Mountains, the shattered remnants of a once towering volcano; now a ring of mountains rising above the Rio Grande. Yet even as a lingering corpse, the remains after a cataclysmic explosion in the distant past, they are awe inspiring in their grandeur. The center, the valley that was once the fiery throat of molten lava, now a grassy pasture for herds of cattle, belies the violence that blackened the skies ten million years ago.

High in these mountains, on the western ridge that runs down toward the Colorado Plateau, the snow stays until April. Then the clear skies and the warmth of the north-migrating sun finally prevail, and the top crust of snow begins to melt away. First it is just a few drops of water, filtering down toward the ground and running under the snow, but soon it becomes a trickle, and then a flood. Coursing into the streambeds, the cascade becomes a torrent, dropping downward toward the flat spaces to the west. Finally bursting into the openness of the high plateau, the water does as the first spring runoff has done for centuries; it sinks into oblivion in the parched sands.

As more snow melts, and the stream bed becomes saturated, the water finally makes its way across the plateau, and eventually into the canyon, on its way to its appointment with the Pacific Ocean. With it it carries a slim hope of life. The parched land is briefly treated to a stream of muddy roiling water. The cottonwoods drink in the moisture. The grasses suddenly come to life. They revel briefly in the yearly reprieve, and fill themselves with new life.

Soon it is over, however, and the sun takes back the gift, drying the sands and browning the vegetation. After that only the brief and violent thunderstorms of summer and the bitter blizzards of winter will bring occasional life sustaining moisture. So it is today and so it was then.

It is not a hospitable land, even now. A few paved roads arrow across the landscape, seeming to hurry one along to a less awesome and more welcoming region, one where there are gas stations and fast food outlets. Here the only sign of man is an occasional hogan, with its stack of pinon firewood, a pickup truck parked beside it.

One thousand years ago it was no more hospitable and inviting. It was as dry and harsh and forbidding as it is today. The rains in summer were few and unreliable, the snows in winter were often lacking. When either did come, they came violently and suddenly. Instead of giving the land a lifesaving drink the rains and snows tried to drown the land. Then, as today, only the hardiest plants could take root and flourish; only the strongest and best adapted animals could survive.

There were those, however, who chose this land for their home. They were surrounded by wetter, greener places, with game, food, water, yet they elected to live in the very center of this desolation; in the great canyon that divided the plateau across its middle. They were not hiding from enemies, they had none. They were not forced there by either man or nature since there was plenty of space for the taking, and no one to forbid it; they were not following a supply of food, the region had little to offer; they were not looking for good farmland, there was better close by in every direction. Yet they did settle in this inhospitable semi-desert.

That is not to say that they suddenly moved to the canyon and its surrounding bleakness. They had been there from time to time for ten thousand years before. They had eaten the berries, chased the deer and antelope, and caught the rabbits. They had even set up somewhat permanent homes in many places across the plateau. As they migrated, following the game animals as they moved or the berries as they ripened, they paused in the canyon and built shelters under the cliffs. Here they occasionally stored some of their food, that it might be there on their next trip through the region.

Then, at a time when Europe was still languishing in the dark ages, their civilization suddenly blossomed. Perhaps it was because their population had become too large to support a nomadic lifestyle. Maybe it was because the introduction of maize, which we call corn, from the Valley of Mexico had given a great boost to their agricultural sustenance, or maybe because they had reached the point of development to where they were specializing their societal duties and could support a move sophisticated organization. Perhaps it was a combination of some or all of these factors. But for some reason they moved from a nomadic hunter-gatherer society to a more sedentary agricultural society. They began to build permanent homes, and joined them together to form cities of stone. The walls rose five stores high. The rooms in each city numbered in the hundreds. They abandoned their nomadic lifestyle and planted crops. They developed a cohesive empire, far flung in its influence, but centered on the canyon. And all of this was done in as inhospitable a region as could have been found for hundreds of miles in any direction.

Within two hundred years they had developed the most imposing civilization the region North of the Valley of Mexico had ever witnessed; one that would not be surpassed for many centuries thereafter. Their cities were preplanned and carefully executed labyrinths of stone; each building block carefully formed and painstakingly laid in place. They spread out throughout the region and joined the central cities to the outlying villages by a network of roads; hundreds of miles of perfectly straight thoroughfares, radiating like the spokes of a wheel, and connecting the central cities to all parts of their vast empire.

They traded throughout a large part of the continent. Goods were imported from as far away as the Pacific coast and the Valley of Mexico. Food and pottery were exchanged with the surrounding tribes, and precious turquoise was brought from the mountains to the east. In a land of great distances, with neither beast of burden nor wheeled conveyances, they moved prodigious amounts of timber and stone to the canyon, in order to build their cities. In a land with little water they raised their crops to feed their people.

Then it all ended. The building stopped. The people started to move away. Within a short time the great cities were empty, crumbling in the sun. The cornfields were covered by the blowing sands; the dry weeds were stacked by the winds against the great walls of the crumbling cities. The roadways, left untrod, disappeared into the landscape. The empty rooms contained only ghosts; the great round ceremonial chambers, the kivas contained only memories.

Left behind, too, were the questions. No hieroglyphics were painted on the walls; no runes adorned the kivas. The few cryptic clues were to be found only on the canyon walls; pictures and symbols carved into the rock, and left over the centuries. No Rosetta Stone would be found to decipher these drawings. Only imagination and speculation could bring life back to the deserted cities.

And the questions that were asked, and continue to be asked, were not the right questions. The scholars and the tourists, the ranchers and the Indians, the surveyors, the hunters, the curious and the collectors; they each passed through, studied the ruins in their crumbling desolation, shook their heads in wonder and asked themselves why these people, these ancient ones, abandoned their homes.

With no written language, they left no explanation. Even the carvings and painted pictures on the canyon walls gave no clue. But the real question is the one that is not asked. Every visitor to the canyon puzzles over the sudden departure, whereas they should be asking the same basic question; why did the ancient ones choose to live here in the first place? The amazing thing is that these people were willing to fight to survive in such an inhospitable place when they were surrounded by many much more inviting locales. If we can find an answer to the primary question then perhaps the answer to the second question is easier to find. If the reason for the original amazing decision can be ascertained, then perhaps it was the removal of that reason that led to their abandonment of their magnificent cities.

No enemy lurked in the surrounding mountains. No climatic conditions could account for their choice of the barren canyon in the midst of a desiccated plateau to build their cities. No food supply lured them to the canyon bottom. Certainly it was not an abundance of building materials that tantalized them. We can only surmise that a unique set of circumstances, coupled with their singular customs and beliefs, could have set the stage for such a decision. If that is true, then perhaps a radical change in their customs, needs or beliefs could bring about a collapse of their civilization.

What follows is a possible scenario.

INTRODUCTION

We have never left the canyon. It was ours ten thousand years before you came, and it will be ours ten thousand years after you are gone. We came when there was no one here. We made it ours by making ourselves a part of it and only we have truly loved this land.

It is a bleak land, a dry land, which rejects lovers and stands aloof. It is not a land to be easily loved, and it tests its lovers. It distances itself from those who would love it, and asks for proofs of that love. And then it asks again, and yet again for those pledges of devotion. We, who you call the Anasazi, or the ancient ones, in our ceremonies, in our rituals, in our trials and sacrifices, attempted always to show our devotion to the land. But it demands so much as to make lovers into haters, and then it whimsically rewards the lovers with beauty and plenty, and rekindles the love that had become hatred, creating a yet deeper reverence and awe, and capturing the soul of the helpless worshipers.

That is why we are still here. We are in the land, we are of the land, we are the land. You build your roads on top of our land. You place signs and markers, and tell the tourists about our land. You explain our people in your pamphlets, your books, your tour guides, even in motion pictures and videotapes. Your campers pitch their tents, park their pickups, build their fires, and try to understand our land and our people. They climb our cliffs, gaze at our mesas, photograph our walls; they peer into our kivas and homes, and then they say they know about us.

You think we are gone, but we, the ancient ones, are still here. Our spirits are in the rooms and kivas. We still walk the roadways not your roadways but ours. In the nights we are on the mesa tops, watching the stars. During the cool of early morning we are in the corn patches, tending the crops. On the winter nights we are warming ourselves at the hearths, under the plaza, watching the smoke drift out the overhead openings. On that one day of the year when the sun goes all the way to the north, we sing the old songs for the crops.

Sometimes as I sit invisibly in the old kiva, and the tourists climb down to take their pictures, one will sit beside me. He will look up at the walls as they are, but he will see them as they were. There will be crossbeams and laths and brush and dirt; there will be a roof where no roof has been for eight hundred years. The crumbling walls will have a fresh coating of plaster, ready for the ceremony of the corn. He will know about the land and love the land as we love the land, and sometimes I think he knows I am there. He does not see me but I sense that he is aware of my spirit; of all our spirits.

It is for him that I tell our story. In his thoughts I have felt the questions. He knows of our land and he knows of our people. He is not a professor, classifying the fragments we abandoned, nor is he a student, sifting the sands for answers that will never be found in the sands. Yes, he has read the facts and the guesses, he has studied the pottery we left behind, he has gazed at the buildings we left crumbling in the canyon, he has climbed our cliffs and walked our ancient roads. But that is not why I will answer his questions. He has also sat alone on our mesa tops and contemplated the skeletons of our cities of stone below, and in his eyesight have materialized our people as they once were. In his imaginings he has felt the cold we felt in winter, he has burned with us in the withering sun of summer. He has known our hunger in the bad years when the crops wouldn't grow, and feasted with us in the good years, when the clay pots were full. He has walked the trails we walked, and felt the fears we felt, and now he wants to know why we are only spirits, roaming the canyon which was once our home. It is for him that I tell our story.

If I were able I would take him by the hand, and lead him back among the ruins. We would not start at the big towns; we would go north up the canyon to the old town, the most ancient town. We would sit together and face the wall of pictures, and I would then show him how to read our story in the rocks. And we would go in the early morning to the sacred kiva on the west side, and we would watch the ceremony of daybreak. I would call out all the other spirits so that he too could see them, and we would once again see the miracle of the sun. I would take him to the high pueblo where he could face in the direction of the gods, and show him the smoke on the horizon. We would go south to the homes of our ancestors and we would speak with them also. We would follow the roads to all parts of our empire, and he would understand what we once were.

I would tell him about The People. I would take him back to the beginnings to see our ancestors, and he would know why we were once great. I would lead him through the generations, and of the great men and the gods, and the reasons why we were strong. I would show him the pit houses and take him into the ancient caves. We would walk in the paths of the mammoth and the camel, and would see the huge herds as they roamed beside the melting walls of ice. He would carry a spear as our fathers carried their spears, and he would make the fine stone points as our grandfathers made them from the glassy rock. All these things would I show him, that he would know of The People.

All these things would I do if I were able. But, as I may not take him on this journey, only my thoughts will cross the centuries. I will tell him our story, the story of The People. I ask our gods to help me, so that he will understand.

CHAPTER ONE

He, the one we called Kokopelli, was a man, there can be no doubting that now. He seemed, at times, to be a god, and many of us thought he must have been returning to save The People. Yet, as you shall see, he was merely a man.

I will tell you of this single unique person. Just one man, yet in him is gathered the spirit of us all, and in his story is our story. When you know of his life you will know of all our lives, for in him has been concentrated the life and death of our people. His tragedy was our tragedy; his failure was our failure, and especially, his genius was our genius.

This is not just my story; it is a story of our people. It is a story that was told in the kivas for many years and then took its place with the ancient legends; a new story, but one to be told and retold, until it too would be ancient. It was carried to the new homes when the people left, and told to the children, that they might then tell it to their children. But then the people began to forget. The legends were told less and less as the people found themselves mixed into other tribes. The oldest legends were the best remembered and the most often recounted so they lasted the best and were adopted into the new cultures. But this, the new legend was allowed to die. It was a story for the generations, yet it is now a story that has been left untold for these hundreds of years. I will tell you the story, for I was there.

My story is true. It remains for you to see that truth and believe it to be true. You and I have sat together in the silence of the Great Kiva and you have asked the questions in a manner that I must answer you. But only in this way may I give you your answers. Listen and understand. Later, go if you will, to the walls of rock with the deeply etched pictures and you will know that my story is true, for the pictures in the rock are my witnesses.

I was a child when I was first told of Kokopelli. I had seen the drawings on the cliffs, and already knew well his form. In the round room of our clan the old woman would sit, in the honored place near the fire and tell us of the humpbacked flute player who filled such a unique place in the realm of the gods. As the smoke drifted upward toward the square opening over our heads, we would squat on the dirt floor, all the children of the clan, and listen to the raspy voice in its rhythmic recitation. Her hair was white and long, and her face, with its crisscrossed wrinkles, was like the grey clay in the arroyo bottoms after the sun has baked and cracked its surface. The old woman was our leader, of course, being the oldest woman of the clan. Her eyes were almost sightless, and her teeth were dark and rotted stumps, but her memory was clear, as she told us the legends of our ancestors. She would relate the history of our people; their migrations, their repeated failures and their occasional successes. She told of the gods and the Kachinas, of the destructions of the world and its new beginnings. But the story we all liked the best was the story of Kokopelli.

Even then I could imagine what he must have looked like, almost a locust in his bent over form; looking always at one from under his eyebrows, as his curved back forced his head over toward the ground. In the legend he played his flute so long that his back would never again be straight, and he went forever through the canyons, looking at the ground as he played the music no adults could hear.

So also was the man we called Kokopelli, although he once had a clan name just as the rest of us did. But his strange bent form that so resembled the god we had all been told of made this name inevitable. He was a strange man when he first came to the canyon, and a man who was too much like a god.

Where Kokopelli went people moved aside to give him room. When he spoke, the people listened. He stared out from under his heavy eyebrows, smiled in a way which held no mirth, nor even ridicule, but implied a knowledge, a vision, an understanding which made his listeners at once uncomfortable and yet transfixed them, demanding that they listen.

Perhaps we all hoped he was truly Kokopelli, returned to again save the people. He often seemed more a god than a man as he shuffled slowly from settlement to settlement, his head always pushed downward but his eyes always looking up, in a manner that seemed to tell us he knew an important secret. We were children, and he was already a man when he first came from the south. He came from the unknown. His strange shape, his piercing eyes, his knowing manner instilled a fear and a reverence. Added to this was his resemblance of the god of our stories, Kokopelli. Our fear, bordering on reverence, elevated him to a position of power.

It was in the hottest part of the summer that he came into the canyon. He came directly over the edge, not following the easier trail which circled more to the west, but coming directly down from the straight road which led from the land of the parrots. His feather robe was torn in many places and he shuffled slowly and wearily as he made his way over the edge of the mesa and down into the canyon. His sandals were worn, and his string bag, over his shoulder was empty.

We were setting snares to the south of the last cornfields when we saw him. Men who knew our trails did not approach the canyon in this way. It was, we were sure, a trader from the far country, bringing goods to barter, so we dropped our twine and sticks, and ran toward the tiny figure we saw making his way down the steep incline from the canyon rim to the flat floor below. As we approached him, however, and could see him better, our excitement began to ebb, and a caution took over. The man was not dressed in foreign clothes from the south, but in a feather robe such as we ourselves often wore in colder weather. But this day was not cold. He wore sandals, but one was flopping loosely where the bindings had broken. Over his back was a string bag, the sort often used by our people, but this bag was empty, and hung uselessly.

He moved slowly; more sideways than forward, bent over as though shouldering an immense load in the empty string bag. He was a figure we would have liked to laugh at, yet we felt, instead a foreboding, which stopped us at a distance. We were three small boys, looking up the trail toward the mesa top, at a grotesque man in tattered clothes, edging down the steep rocky path. He failed to notice us for some time, as he peered at the precarious footing, choosing his steps methodically.

When he finally arrived at the more level ground, he stopped, peered about from under his eyebrows, and then realized we were standing at a short distance, staring at him. It was then we knew who he must be. His hunched back and his strange appearance were too much like the pictures we had often studied, where they were pecked into the rocks. He could only be Kokopelli, returned to the canyon. The haunted look in his eyes, and his silent stare did nothing to dispel this impression, but only added to our apprehension and awe. Not knowing whether to run, we stood mutely and stared at him. He shuffled forward toward us for just three halting steps, opened his mouth, as if to say something to us, and then pitched forward into the sand, where he lay without moving.

Chapter Two

His first home was far to the south. There, where the red sandstone cliffs face the winter sun, and the wide valley stretches away to east and west, his grandfather, his mother's father, broke, formed and mortared with clay and sand, the rocks in the old way. He built the rooms against the face of the rock, that they would be protected from the north winds, and that they might gather in the rays of winter sun.

From the rooftop of the highest rooms the boy could gaze up and down the great valley. In the spring it would be light green with the new growth. In the dryness of summer it would be brown and grey and parched, and in the winter it would be alternate ripples of white snow and bare black ridges.

The houses looked small as they crouched below the towering pinnacles of sandstone. The red wall stretched away to the west as far as one could see, and, beyond the pass, also ran to the East until it seemed to meet the great mountain. The cliffs of stone were rounded, cut and indented. In places they seemed to be a row of boulders, lined up and fitted closely to one another. In other places they were a wall, straight and even, their unclimbable smooth surfaces blackened by the centuries, and streaked by the water that on rare occasions cascaded down from the mesa above.

The stone dwelling, which was his home, was built against the face of one of the smooth cliffs that curved upward and back, like a very steep hill of red sand. To one standing beside it, the massive smoothness of the cliff seemed to stretch upward only a short distance because it curved away as it got higher, but as one stood further away, it could be seen that the cliff was indeed very high. Near the top of the cliff was a massive overhang of sandstone, cut on both sides by runoff, and streaked black by the water. Cut, as it was, on both sides, and cracked underneath, and behind, it was a great slab of rock, threateningly suspended above the rooftops of the settlement.

The home of his clan consisted of eight square rooms, and one round room. The round room was actually built inside a square set of walls, and was below ground level. The other rooms clustered behind it, two wide and three deep, and then stepped back to a second story of two rooms, which pressed against the cliff face. The roof beams of the back rooms and the upper rooms were seated in holes that had been laboriously pecked into the smooth hard sandstone.

Just beyond the clan dwelling, if one went toward the east, three great caves penetrated the face of the cliffs. They were not deep caves, but recesses under an overhanging brow of rock. One could imagine that a great hand had scooped these caves out of the face of the cliff. Their immensity dwarfed the surroundings. The slopes of talus below the caves looked, from a distance, like small knolls, but proved to the climber to be large and steep. The cedars, which grew in the arroyos below the great openings, looked like small shrubs, so overwhelmed were they by the yawning holes in the rock. The rock above the caves was a bleached pink, while the recesses were a darker red, with black streaks reaching the sandy floor at the back of each cave.

On winter afternoons, if they were permitted, he and his friend Tokchii, a girl two years younger than he, from the Corn Clan, would climb up to the most easterly cave, and play there, under the overhanging roof. The low sun would warm the rock and reflect on the sand floor. It was a bright and pleasant place, protected from the cold winds of the north, and heated from the south. Here they would talk of the time when he would be allowed to enter the great round ceremonial chamber for his initiation into adulthood; of the long awaited day when he would be a man, and sit with the other men in the Great Kiva in the Main Pueblo.

They could look down from their high retreat and see the Pueblo, on the slope below them. It was not more than a quarter of a mile away, facing toward the valley; south, as was proper. The rooms were lined up across the slope, east to west, facing the central plaza; and another row of rooms formed an ell on the east side. Within the series of rooms were three round rooms, dwelling places for the three clans which made up the Main Pueblo; the Snake clan, the Corn Clan and the Kachina Clan. Then, off to the southwest, beyond the corner of the plaza they could see the Great Kiva; the kiva of all of the clans of the region. It was the kiva of many clans, not just those of the Pueblo. Scattered for many miles in all directions were small clan settlements, much like his home, but not always in such protected locales as the small cluster of rooms, nestled against the sandstone cliff.

The two children could see the large circle of the kiva from where they sat in the sun. It rose slightly above the surrounding land, but was, of course, mostly underground. In the center of the circular roof was a rectangular hole, and they could even make out the top of the ladder, protruding through the hole, from the great room below. In their imaginations they would see him descend that ladder, into the darkness of the chamber, and would see the circle of old men, chanting the ancient songs. The initiate would sit with them and hear the history of the people. He would listen to the playing of the flutes and the beating of the drums. He would take his place among the men of the tribe.

It was a day they talked of and dreamed of often. It would not come easily, they knew; he would have to work hard and show great bravery and strength before he could be called to the Great Kiva. His instruction, to that point, was the responsibility of the people of his particular clan. They knew he would spend many hours in the clan room, listening to the stories and learning them. He would have to memorize all of the chants and songs, and learn the sacred ways of speaking to the gods. Only then would he have the clan knowledge necessary to allow him to pass into manhood.

They also knew that the Great Kiva initiation was not the end of the process but the second beginning. He would then become the charge of the priests rather than the clan, and would learn the ways of the people; the sacred ways which had been passed from generation to generation since the Emergence. It would take years before he would be a fully qualified member of the tribe. The first step, though, would be the call to the Great Kiva, and the circle of elders. So they dreamed of that day as they sat on the warm sand at the front of the cave.

Tokchii, being only a girl, would never see the inside of the Great Kiva, of course. In fact, he knew that it was not really right for him to even talk to her about it, and when he had really been inside the Kiva and had been told the secrets, he would never be allowed to reveal them to any other person, even a man of another clan, much less a girl. But this child who went to the cave and sat in the sun with him looked at him with such awe that he got pleasure in talking to her about it. She seemed to anticipate his future as much as he did.

Being of the Corn clan, Tokchii lived in the main pueblo, in the Corn clan room. They had met at the dance of the harvest, and had become good friends, in spite of the fact that she was just a girl, and two years younger than he. Often, his other friends, the boys his age, would make fun of him because of the little girl who followed him everywhere, and he would then try to ignore her, especially in their presence. But, when the other boys were not around, he still liked to have her with him.

About as far to the East of his home as the first cave was to the west of his home was a wide break in the sandstone cliffs. It was the only place for many miles where one could easily pass into the valleys of the North. The small pueblo against the cliff was so close to this opening that the boys would always know when anyone was passing through. Travelers from the pueblos to the south, on their way to the great cities of the canyon, would pass within speaking distance of the stone homes. Often the youths would see these strangers, with woven bags full of trade goods slung over their backs. Many times they would hear them speaking but be unable to understand the words they used. The travelers carried many strange things he and his friends had never seen before, and wore clothing that was very different from their own.

Toward the rising sun was the Black Land. It stretched, crumpled and broken, from the base of the great mountain, and covered the older land to the south. It extended as far as a man could walk in two days; a jumbled expanse of broken, heaved, twisted and buckled lava. Little grew through the blocks of broken black rock except a few scraggly shrubs and some bunches of grass where a little soil had managed to accumulate. The deeper depressions held stagnant pools of rainwater, green and opaque; a breeding place for insects and a watering hole for the animals that managed to survive in the midst of the frightening barrenness; rabbits, snakes, lizards, an occasional deer, and many birds of all sorts.

The Black Land was forbidden. His father had so said. He had told the boy it was a land of evil and death, to which he might never venture. It was said that any man who went into the Black Land would never come back. For there was the place where the bowels of the earth had poured forth the hot black stones and covered the homes of men. Death had come with its beginning, and death was the fate of anyone who went back.

He could see the Black Land when he climbed to the rooftop of the upper rooms. Always a curious and wondering person, even as a boy, he would sit in the evening and ponder the light and shadows as the sun set to his right, and emphasized the ripples of black lava flows, many miles away to his left.

"Do not look in such a way toward the Black Land, my son"

"But father, I am only wondering what is out in the middle of the Black Land"

"Yes, and if that wondering were to become a desire? And if that desire were to lead you to the Black Lands? Would you then not bring misfortune on the clan? No, my boy, look not in such a way at the Black Lands, for there is only evil there. The gods have told us not to venture into the Black Lands, for they are the burned remains of the first world, pushed up into our sight. They are there to remind us of the evil which Sotuknang so despised that he destroyed all but a few of the first people, killing and destroying with fire, before creating the second world."

"Yes father", he would reply, but still he wondered about the black lands.

He was not then called Kokopelli, but by his clan name which was Paho, which means "Eagle Feather", for he was of the Eagle clan. Theirs was but a small branch of the main clan, and living far from the canyon of their leaders. They farmed the valley to the south, raising corn, squash, pumpkins and beans. The clan was a part of a larger farming community, centered upon the great kiva, and the rows of rooms to the north of it. Their allegiance, however, was to the clan and its leaders. It was for the clan that they raised the crops and it was for the clan that they guarded the gateway to the north. They were the outpost of the clan, and the providers of food for the leaders at the great canyon to the north.

Paho's mother had been of the Eagle clan, and had moved to the dwelling by the rock as a child. His father had been, and still was, a member of the Corn Clan, but had moved onto the dwelling of the Eagle Clan upon marrying into that clan. Therefore Paho was an Eagle, and would always remain, proudly, an Eagle. Were he to marry, he would move into the home of his wife, and adopt the customs and duties of that clan, but he would always retain his birth clan. He would always carry the proud name "Eagle Feather", an Eagle Clan name.

It was known that the eagle, with its ability to fly so high was our messenger to the gods. When our people prayed, the eagle would carry those prayers to the heavens. This meant that the Eagle, since the creation of the Fourth World, had held a very special place among the people. Its feathers were considered especially powerful, since they were the means of carrying those messages. Pahos, in the language of our ancient ones, were Eagle feathers; the sacred symbols attached to the most influential prayer sticks.So, it can be seen, the name "Eagle Feather" was an important one.

CHAPTER THREE

He was in his seventh year when he went with his uncle to the settlement on the mesa top. The story was repeated for many years in the kivas, as the people silently listened, wrapped in blankets and seated around the walls, lit by the glow of the fire in the center of the room. It had been decided that he should accompany his uncle, who was to visit the homes of his birth clan, many miles to the northeast. It was to be a journey of many days, since the distance to the far off mesa-top village was four days as a man walks. A small boy would make it a much longer trek.

It was in the coldest part of the year, just as the days were beginning to get longer and the sun started to go back toward his summer home. There were no crops to tend, no berries to gather, no water to carry. This was the time of weaving and of hunting. It was a good time to go. They would hunt as they went, looking for deer or antelope, as well as rabbits. He was too small, still, to draw a bow, and kill the larger animals, but he was fast and accurate with the thrown stone, which was often the best way to get rabbits.

It was cold and windy but the sky was clear on the morning they started. There had been a snow a few days before, which had blown before the wind, so that there were lines of snow gathered behind each ripple in the landscape, while the rest of the land was bare. Now, as the sky before them started to show just a touch of grey emerging from the blackness of night, they started to walk to the northeast, through the break in the sandstone cliffs. For a short distance they would follow the trail, which went between the walls; the trail that led north toward the Canyon of their people. After a short distance, however, they would enter the broad valley to the north, and have to leave the trail, turning to face into the biting wind as they angled toward their destination. The sun would be rising behind the great mountain by then, and they would set their direction by it. They could not yet see the great mountain since it was blocked from view by the bluffs and mesas which lines the edge of the valley, but they knew where it was, and knew they need only to pass to the left of it, and walk around its base until they reached a substantial arroyo coming down from the flanks of the mountain and draining toward the northeast. This would lead them to the river, which passed by the town that was their destination. Then they would need to move up the river until they came to the mesa, with the cornfields at its base.

All this they knew, yet neither of them had any knowledge of the trip except the stories that they had been told. His uncle had, of course, hunted in the valley to the north for many years, and had been to the great mountain, also. But the way to the mesa was not marked by a roadway, as were the many approaches to the Canyon and its cities. The roadways radiated outward from the center but did not, usually, connect one outlier with another. But the way was easy if one kept his eye on the location of the Great Mountain.

The sun rose palely before them as they turned off the trail. It gave no warmth yet, and the wind was in their faces, forcing the cold through the robes they wore. They wore sandals on their feet, and had wrapped their legs and feet in cotton cloth to keep out the cold. Still, the cold ground, the wind and the patches of snow soon made his feet numb and painful. He stumbled blindly behind his uncle, trying to keep up and not let his uncle know how cold he was. The wind in his face made him close his eyes unless he could get right behind his uncle, where the cutting cold gusts would be blocked off.

Nevertheless, he did not complain. He was making a trip such as none of his friends had made, even those who were older than he was, and he would not let anyone know he was cold or his feet were hurting. So he hurried after his uncle, who never glanced back at him, but just pushed forward into the wind and cold. They both had robes wrapped around them, warm and bulky. They were made of twisted and woven threads from the leaves of the yuccas, which grew everywhere. What made them warm was the turkey feathers, which were twisted into the threads, making a thick, downy fabric. His mother had woven this robe for him, in anticipation of the trip, and he wore it proudly. It was a robe such as men wore.

His uncle was of the Coyote clan, and was married to his mother's sister. Therefore, he now lived in the round room of the Eagle clan, the clan of his wife. He was a young man, and had spent all of his years in the settlement below the sandstone cliffs, even though he had been born at the village on the mesa top, their present destination. As a baby he had been brought to the new settlement by his family, who were spreading out, looking for new land on which to grow corn.

As they made their way toward the north side of the Great Mountain the shadow edge of the sun rising higher crept over the desert behind them, finally catching up with them and bringing a small amount of warmth. Soon, also, the wind died down, and the warmth of the sun began to penetrate through their robes, making him feel better. The wind was still chill in his face, and his feet still felt hard and remote, as though they belonged to someone else, but the sunlight in his eyes gave a promise of warmth to come, and he hurried after his uncle, toward the foot of the great mountain.

There was rabbit bush everywhere, so that they often had to push through it, scratching their legs. Scattered about were cedars, some twice as tall as a man, but they only dotted the landscape, without obscuring their view. Crossing the valley, the uphill sides if each roll in the undulating valley floor was bare and black, while each downhill side was covered by an inch or so of old snow, shiny and crystalline. It had snowed three days before, and the sun had been warm enough since then to melt off all the snow on the south facing slopes, but had not reached the shadowed protection of the north slopes. Bunches of grass poked up through the snow, and they tried to walk on them in order to keep their feet as warm and dry as possible.

Yellow sandstone ridges and bluffs made up the barrier, which ran to their right. They were not so high they could not be easily climbed and crossed, but the valley was tending to curve around them, to the east, so that it appeared they could follow the valley and work their way in the proper direction rather than start the arduous work of crossing ridges and draws. They knew that the time would come when they would have to do that, but they wanted to get as far as possible on level ground, first.

They had been walking for three hours, and were well up the valley when they first got a glimpse of the Great Mountain. A low spot in the sandstone bluffs allowed them a partial view to the southeast, and there it was, exactly where they expected it to be. The snow was heavy on the peak, and it thrust upward into the sky, with a prominent ridge making a line in their direction. The lower slopes were heavily forested, reaching downward until they were blocked off by the nearer hills. It always looked ghostly to the boy in wintertime. It seemed to float above the black lava beds at its base, like a mysterious island, but its ethereal quality also was a lure, calling him to come to it.

The great mountain was also visible from his home, as it was from all directions, for many miles. The people worshiped the mountain, as one of the sacred heights, dominating their land. In it were reputed to reside the spirits of the ancestors. It was the place they went at death, so that they could look back over the plateau, the canyon, the towns and villages, and see what their children and grandchildren were doing. He believed, as his people all believed, that the mountain would be his home in the next life. Therefore, the mountain was also a terrifying and foreboding place, looming over the surrounding canyons and mesas. It was fearful, yet it was appealing in its beauty and its mystery.

As they looked at the peak they could see wisps of snow, like spirits, blowing from the crest and disappearing into the sky.He wondered if he were seeing the ghosts of the mountain, rising up for a better view.

They trudged forward again, following the ridges to their right, and moving slightly uphill as they ascended the long slope of the valley. Ahead of them the valley narrowed into a canyon, cut into the black basaltic lava. They soon entered the canyon, and found themselves climbing much more rapidly, as the walls around them pinched together, blocking out much of the sunlight. They were now having to skirt great boulders and slides of rock as they worked their way to the head of the canyon. Cedar and pinon trees grew here, and occasionally, in the places where water must have collected in wet times, a profusion of brushy saplings blocked their path, making them push their way through, stumbling over the boulders in the dry streambed..

It was on the second day that they came across the roadway. They had spent the night, wrapped in their robes, at the head of the canyon, protected still by the high rock walls. They had eaten some of the cold cooked cornmeal that they had with them, and then crawled under a ledge, clear of snow, and slept. Then, as they worked their way eastward, below the slopes of the Great Mountain, the next morning, they had heard voices. Cautiously, they crept forward toward the source, knowing well what was ahead of them. They had heard the stories many times; the work gangs, often needing men; and they had no desire to become a part of them. They had been warned, before they left their village, of the fact they would be crossing one of the long, straight roadways, but they had not expected to reach it quite so soon.

He thought to himself that they would not want anyone as small and weak as he, but that they would certainly take his uncle if they were short of men. They climbed down into an arroyo, and found themselves well hidden by the high banks as they pushed forward, downstream. As they came closer, though, they suddenly could see the place ahead where the roadway dipped into their arroyo! There was no cover for them, here! Just then, the voices became louder, a chanting, rhythmic cadence, as the work group came nearer. Then, as he pressed himself into the sand at the edge of the arroyo, Paho saw them trot by, only feet from him and his uncle in their exposed location. They had not been seen.

Cautiously they crawled up to the roadway, and looked to the north and south. The men they had just so narrowly avoided were now well down the road to the south, still chanting and trotting in cadence, as they carried a monstrous ponderosa pine log between them. There were eight men in the party, four on each side of the log. It hung suspended from four cross poles, which they bore on their shoulders as they trotted along the broad roadway. The swath that they followed was absolutely straight, paying no attention to the terrain it crossed. They could see that all of the rocks and bushes had been removed and the rocks had been carefully piled along the side of the road. It was very wide, as wide as a tree is tall, and even the dirt had been scraped away, down to bedrock, in many places. Looking to the south the roadway met and surmounted a sharp rise, almost a cliff. Here steps had been cut into the sandstone rather than allowing the path to go around the hill and violating the straightness.

They crawled across the road and dropped down into the arroyo on the other side, bending low so as not to be seen. They quickened their pace then, and covered another mile before the stopped to rest.

"What would they have done if they had seen us, back there, uncle?"

"Perhaps nothing, it would depend upon whether they needed men, and if they thought us useful to them. They were a strong group, and in a hurry, maybe they would have ignored us, but we could not take the chance. On the other hand, they might have captured us and forced us into the timber carrying service."

"Would that be so bad?" he asked his uncle, "They are said to be the strongest of our people. They go where they wish, and have the best food. Whatever they want at the pueblos they take."

"They are not farmers." he said with finality.

"But they have all of the things the farmers raise, without working in the fields."

"They are not free." His uncle answered, "What they are told to do by the chiefs, they do. They have the best of food, and the pick of the squaws, true, but they pay a large price. They no longer belong to the land, because they do not work in it. They are owned by people, the chiefs, not by the land, and so they grow away from the gods and the ways of the people."

"But, are they not members of a clan? Do they not hear the stories of the people, and gather in the Great Kivas for the ceremonies? Do they not dance on the plaza?"

"Once they did all those things just as we do, and believed. Now they often take part but they no longer believe. They only believe in their own strength, their own power, the fear they bring to the people. We hide beside the road as they pass by because we fear them. We know that they could take us captive and force us to do their work, and no one would stop them. That power over others is their only god! Come, it is time to move on. No more questions."

On the fifth day, they were in the valley of the south-flowing river, which they called the valley of arrows, for the jagged peaks of black basalt, standing vertically up from the wide wash looked like arrowheads, pointing at the sky. The river itself was almost non-existent at this time of year. A muddy trickle in places, in others just disconnected pools, below the vertical walls of the riverbed. Twisted piles of brush, logs and boulders bore testimony, however, to the raging torrent, which must occupy that riverbed after a heavy summer downpour. They called this the Mud River, for it was always either low, whereupon one would sink to his knees in the mud while crossing it, or it was high and raging, a black torrent from the mud it carried. It was never without mud, no matter the season.

Ahead they could see the black arrowheads ranged before them, each the hardened and exposed throat of what had once been a volcano. They jutted up out of the valley; sentinels marking the way to the mesa-top village, which was their destination. There could be no doubt they had followed the instructions correctly, and were nearing the pueblo.

"Paho," his uncle said, "climb to the top of that ridge, and tell me what you see."

"Uncle, he shouted down," after having scampered easily to the top, "I can see some buildings of stone only about a mile from here, and there are corn fields all around them."

"Good, we are close, then. Do you see the mesa with buildings on its highest point?"

"Yes, now I do. It is just beyond the fields. I will come down."

CHAPTER FOUR

A cold wind blew across the mesa top, as they stood outside the largest kiva, awaiting admittance. Here, hundreds of feet above the valley floor, the clustered buildings, which made up the settlement, were afforded a view for many miles in all directions. Below them, to the south, were the fields and buildings they had seen as they approached the settlement. The valley structures were the living quarters for the people when they farmed those fields, so they consisted of many circular shaped sleeping and living rooms and just a few aboveground workrooms. The main storage rooms were, of course, on the mesa top. This was much like their home, where the central pueblo was primarily a safe storage area for their crops, and therefore consisted of a great number of above ground rooms but few underground round rooms, whereas the places where most of the people lived and worked, in the midst of the fields, consisted almost entirely of round rooms, the rooms in which they lived, securely, warmly, protected from animals, large or small.

The Coyote clan was the most powerful of the various clans that made up the remote farming outlier. It was the clan of his uncle, and the group they went to, seeking protection. They stood outside the entrance; the rectangular opening in the roof of the room, and shivered in the biting wind. The valley floor below them looked warm in the winter sun. Unlike the yellow sandstone mesa on which they stood, the cone of the adjoining hill, below them and to the south, was black. It was a small volcanic cinder cone, which had spread its ash over the valley eons ago. Its perfect shape and the indentation on the top made him wonder of it was not just waiting, to soon resume its activity. Then, looking beyond, it seemed that he was seeing other volcanoes just starting to erupt. Across the valley plumes of smoke were rising out of the ground, into the cold clear air. He knew, though, that they were only the homes of the people; the circular structures, hidden in the ground so that just the rooftop openings were evident. The fires within were producing the curls of smoke that dotted the valley.

Their arrival had not been the joyous homecoming they had envisioned. As they had neared the settlements they had been met by people who had seen them approaching, and had been closely questioned as to who they were and why they were entering the area. Unlike the attitudes at their home valley, the suspicion and fear was evident. Perhaps, he thought, this is because they are so far from the home canyon; so isolated. We are used to seeing travelers pass through our territory, traders on their way to the canyon. These people are much further from the center, and perhaps they have lost touch with the mother clans.

They had then been escorted to the mesa, and shown the approach; a narrow chasm, extending from the upper limit of the talus slope all the way to the mesa top. It was only wide enough for one person at a time to climb up to the village. As he had been climbing up through the narrowest and steepest part of the cleft he had looked upward, and seen that there were men with spears and bows watching him from the rocks over his head. It was, he realized, a very effective security system. The only other way to reach the top would have been from the other side, up a steep and exposed slope.

Then they had been made to stand in the cold wind for a long time, hearing low voices inside the clan room of the Coyotes, but unable to gather what was being said.

"Come! You may enter now." A louder voice, from within.

They climbed down the ladder, from the bright sunlight into the dark cavernous interior of the clan room. At first they were almost blind, but gradually they began to see that there were many people, seated on the hard packed clay floor around the perimeter, with their backs to the wall of stone. In the center a low fire smoldered, the coals being more than enough to supplement the heat generated by the closely packed people. Down here, they were out of the wind and insulated by the earth. The smoke spiraled upward through the doorway in the ceiling and fresh air entered from the opening behind a deflector to the north.

"How do we know you are who you say?" A voice, disembodied, came from a darker recess of the room. "Our son was taken away many years ago. We have not seen him or his parents, and do not even know if they still live. You may be from the Mother Canyon, coming to see if we have more grain to give. We have sent our tribute already, and have little enough left to live on. Perhaps you are sent to spy."

His uncle spoke calmly. "Were we to have come from the Canyon, would we have arrived from the South? Would we have been so poorly equipped, when the canyon has so much, taken from outlying villages like yours and mine? Would I have brought a boy on a spying assignment?"

"Only if you were very clever." An old woman mumbled, as she stared at them. "Only if you wanted to convince us of your innocence."

His uncle then reached inside his cloak, below his throat, and brought forth a pendant that hung from a leather thong around his neck. He stepped backward so that the light entering from the overhead entry was full upon him and illuminated that which he had in his hand. "Do they have such stones as this in the canyon?" he asked. "I have worn it since I was a child." It was a large flat piece of highly polished turquoise, oddly shaped in what could have been thought to be the form of a coyote. "My mother has told me that it came from the hills to the east, and that it was fashioned and polished in this pueblo; in this very room. Is there anyone here who would know this stone?"

The old woman who had challenged him before now rose and moved toward him. Her age and her air of authority made it evident she was the matriarch; the clan leader. She stepped close and peered through her old eyes at the pendant, then stepped back, nodded her head slightly. "This is truly the stone which I, myself, saw placed around the neck of the child. He is our son, returned. He and his companion will have places of honor at our fire. They will help us to celebrate the festival of the Coyote, for which they have come."

The next week was to be the midwinter festival, celebrated throughout the village and its surrounding dwellings. Every year for many centuries the people had held this festival in honor of the great gift of the Coyote clan. Shortly after the emergence into the fourth world and after some the clans had completed their migrations, the people were prosperous and living well. The crops of beans and squash and corn all thrived in the valley bottoms. The rains came when they were needed, and the cold of winter ended on time. But then came a year when the people had become complacent, and were living well, and they forgot to thank the gods for the good weather and the rains. They had enjoyed so much prosperity that they felt it would never end, and that they no longer needed the blessings of the gods. No corn meal was scattered to the wind, no dances of thanksgiving were offered.

That was the first year that the sun went too far to the south. Instead of turning back to the north as was usual, the days got shorter and shorter, and the nights got longer and longer. The people became fearful, then, and offered prayers of thanks, and spread lines of corn meal on the ground, pointing in the four directions. The sun then started to move back, day by day, toward its summer house, and the people were again happy. The next spring came late, of course, and the crops did not grow as well, but the people still had enough to eat, and the next year the sun turned north again as it always had.

For a few years after that the people observed the ceremonies, and the crops again were good. But again, they became satisfied and confident and they forgot to offer corn meal to the gods. And again, when the time came for the winter solstice, the sun did not turn back north, but continued to go away. The people offered prayers and dances, and spread corn meal, but this time it did no good. So it was decided that someone would go to the south, in search of the sun. Coyote, with his endurance and speed was chosen to make the trip.

When he had only traveled a short distance toward the land of the Parrot clan Sotuknang appeared to him, and said, "Your people have angered me. I will not send back the sun, and the land will freeze, and the people will starve."

Then Coyote pleaded for the people, but Sotuknang was adamant. Coyote tried to trick Sotuknang, but he was too wise to be tricked. Finally, he said, "I will offer myself to you, to do as you wish, if you will turn the sun back. I am the fastest runner, the smartest animal and the most clever, but I am not clever enough to win over you. Being smart, I should not have let the people forget to thank you for the prosperity. Therefore, punish me, not them, for I am to blame.

Then Sotuknang agreed, and said, "Yes, I will turn the sun back, and it will always turn back on the appointed day, as long as your people honor not just me, but you. I will not punish you, for you have shown me that you love my people, and are willing to be punished, that they should live. Truly, you are to be honored, for you are a servant of the people. Go now, and hold a great festival, that honors this agreement."

So it was that every year, soon after the sun turned back to the north, promising another spring, the people would gather to celebrate the festival of the Coyote. It was for this ceremony that Paho and his uncle had made their journey. His uncle was too young when he left the mesa-top settlement to remember the festival, but being of the Coyote clan it was to be his duty to now carry the spirit of the festival back to his home and his adopted clan, that they might also prosper from the return of spring.

On the morning of the next day, before the sun had risen, the four women of the pueblo who represented the clans of the directions rose to start the day of ceremonies. The Badger clan as the guardian of the North, the Parrot clan from the South, The Eagle clan representing the East, and the Bear clan guarding the West. They walked, each to one of the four corners of the mesa, in the cardinal directions for which their individual clan was responsible, and threw a handful of cornmeal into the air, that the early morning breeze could spread it to the four sides of their domain. They then began to sing the morning song, and watched the sun rise, before slowly shuffling back to the center of the settlement. Here the people had gathered, and joined into the song of the morning.

Great loaves of cornmeal had been prepared in the prior days, and these were then brought out, and ceremoniously offered to Sotuknang, that he might have a share of the year's harvest. These were placed on platforms erected on high poles in the center of the plaza. They would stay there throughout the day, so that Sotuknang could eat if he wished. Then began the dancing and chanting, led in turn by one clan after the other. Each clan desired to be heard and therefore protected by their gods. Throughout this the members of the Coyote clan did not lead, but did take part in the dances and songs. Whenever the others passed before the Coyotes they were careful, however, to look to the ground, and show respect.

Paho and his uncle were given places of honor, as guests, among the members of the Coyote clan. As the dancing went on, they saw that no one was allowed any food or drink. They danced in the bright coldness of the winter day, often with no protection from the weather. The men would bare themselves to the waist, and adorned only with necklaces of feathers, would dance until their upper bodies were beaded with sweat, in spite of the cold. Then they would retreat to a room with a fire, waiting a short time before emerging again to participate in another dance.

As the sun rose higher the people continued their dances, honoring the gods for the regularity of the seasons. Once again the days were starting to lengthen, and soon new life would come to the frozen and sleeping land. Sotuknang had kept his bargain, and now the people were fulfilling their part of the agreement, which had been made so many years ago by Coyote. Each dance had its song, and each song carried a message of thanksgiving. It would then be the duty of the Eagle to deliver the message to the gods. Paho thought to himself how lucky he was to be a member of the Eagle clan, entrusted with that duty. I will, he decided, be old enough soon to join the men in the Great Kiva. Then I will study the ways of the people, and be the leader, one day, of the Eagle clan.

It was late afternoon, when the tempo changed. What had been a solemn ritual gave way to a more joyous song. Then the people all gathered around the members of the Coyote clan, and their guests, carrying gifts of food and clothing, pots and blankets. Even Paho was given a finely woven shawl, made from the cotton which was grown far to the south. The thanks to Sotuknang and the other gods were ended, and it was time to give thanks to the Coyote. A period of dancing then followed, with the Coyotes reenacting the meeting and agreement of long ago. Then, as the sun set, just slightly further north on the horizon than it had the night before, the people all turned toward it, and sang the evening song.

Now, with the day ended, a boy was sent to bring down the loaves of cornmeal, which had been offered to Sotuknang. The members of the Coyote clan inspected them closely and conferred quietly. Finally the old woman who had spoken first in the kiva the day before stepped forward and announced that there was some cornmeal missing; the gods had eaten. Now, with the gods satisfied, it was time for the people to join with them and eat also. The loaves were divided among all of the people, and a great feast followed. Every person was allowed to eat some of the cornmeal, with the Coyotes being given the part closest to where the gods had taken their share. Other foods were brought forth, also, and everyone was able to break the fast, which had lasted the whole day.

The next morning it was snowing hard. Dry flakes swirled between the buildings and gathered behind the protection of walls. The valley below was a uniform whiteness. Paho and his uncle wrapped themselves in their feather robes, gathered the gifts they had received, accepted the food offered them for the trip, and started the long walk back to the settlement under the red cliffs.

Chapter Five

He awoke in a dim grey world. It had snowed more during the night, and the robe he had put over his head was weighted down with a layer it. He shook it aside, and raised his head to see where his uncle was. It was, he saw by the sun, already quite late in the morning, but his uncle was not there.

"Uncle," he said softly, "Where are you?"

It had snowed intermittently for the last three days; ever since they had left the mesa top village, and they had progressed slowly. The night before, knowing they were again nearing the roadway they had crossed before, they had decided to camp in a secluded hollow, and wait until morning before going across. They had carefully built a small fire, well hidden by rocks, and shielded by the depth of the ravine. It was better that others not know they were here. But now, his uncle was nowhere to be seen. He saw the place in the snow where he had slept, and looking beyond, saw a trail of footsteps leading to the south.

"He has gone to look for firewood." he thought. "I will follow his tracks, and help him to bring it back."

He started out, following the imprints in the snow, then realized that it was already so late in the day that they would not want to backtrack to this camp, so he went back, and picked up both his and his uncle's bags of supplies and the gifts from the festival. Thus loaded down, he again plodded to the south, in his uncle's tracks.

A small boy, carrying both packs, cold and hungry, he walked with his eyes to the ground, staggering under the load. Before he realized it, the ground under his feet had changed. It was open and cleared! He looked up suddenly, and realized he was standing in the middle of the roadway, unhidden. He dropped to the ground and dragged his burden back out of sight at the side of the road. There were other tracks ahead of him, following the roadway. People had been through here this morning. Then, in horror, he saw that the tracks he had been following, his uncle's, showed signs of an encounter, of fighting or scuffling, and then merged with the others, turning to the south.

"I must find him." Paho thought. "They were going toward the village at the foot of the Great Mountain. That is where he will be." He carefully followed his tracks back out of sight, trying not to make any new imprints that would tell of his detour. He then hid the packs under a pinon tree and covered them with pine needles and a scattering of snow. Now ready, he retraced his way to the road and boldly ran down it, in the old and confused tracks, which told no story of his having been there. Soon he came to a place where there was a drop-off from the side of the road to a grassy snowless area. He leapt across, leaving no footprints, and continued away from the roadway until he could follow it visually, but left no tracks in the snow that could be noticed by someone traveling the road. Then he stealthily made his way to the south.

The village at the foot of the Great Mountain was primarily a lumber camp. Many logs were needed for the roofs and floors of the hundreds of rooms being continually built and rebuilt in the massive cities of the canyon. Dozens of men spent their days on the slopes of the mountain, cutting the logs with stone axes, trimming them, and then sliding or carrying them to the village. From there the log carriers would transport them to the canyon.

They did grow some crops in the fertile valley below the pueblo, but this was neither their main job nor their livelihood. Much of what they needed was sent to them from the large storage facilities at the Canyon. They were certainly not slaves. They worked for the canyon in order to receive both necessities and luxuries in exchange for the logs they provided. They chose this life. They could, if they wished, give up logging and only live off the land. The canyon, however, could provide them with a more reliable food supply, could send them fine jewelry, precious stones and shells, pottery and fabrics.

There was little cover as he neared the village. Open fields led up to it on all sides except the back, the side toward the Great Mountain. Paho decided to make a large circle to his left, staying below the small hills in that direction, and reaching the somewhat safer brushy foothills. Then he would be able to come toward the pueblo from the back, with the protection of the trees. This took him over an hour, but he eventually found himself in a stand of young cottonwoods, just above the pueblo, where a small stream came out of the mountains and provided the water for the inhabitants.

He was able to approach the area easily now, since the storage buildings were ranged in a line between him and the clan kivas where he knew the people would be. Looking around the corner of the building and into the open plaza area he saw that there were only a few people visible, and no children. His uncle must be in one of the storage rooms, but all the doors faced the plaza, in plain view. He realized, then, that adults would be suspicious of another strange adult in their midst, but would pay no attention to a small child like himself. Therefore, he boldly stood up and sauntered into the plaza area, staying close to the row or buildings. No one seemed to pay any attention to him as he checked doorway after doorway, looking quickly inside each. They were mostly work areas in the front rooms, with storage rooms behind them, some open, but most walled closed with mortar and rock. At the fourth door, however, he saw that it was a cooking area, and the door into the interior room was open, and the room beyond seemed empty. He entered, and slipped into the interior room. In the dimness of the light that penetrated from the small doorway he could see that another door led to the right into another interior room, and that door had been covered with a stone slab, but it had just been placed there, and not mortared in place. It was evidently a room in which the grain had already been used or was now being used. He grasped the top edge of the large rock, which was serving as a door, and pulled it toward him. First it did not move, but slowly it came toward him, and finally it toppled away, and the room was open to him.

"Uncle," he whispered, "Are you in here?"

"Over here, behind the corn stalks."

He had been tied, and was in the corner of the room. By now Paho's eyes were more accustomed to the dark, and he could see that the room was still over half full of corn stalks with the corn still on them. The corn would be food, and the stalks fuel for the cooking fires and warmth for the kivas. Of course, this settlement, being located as it was, near the mountain, and surounded by forested area, had little need to hoard the corn stalks for fuel, but the traditions of the people dictated that the corn should be stored on the stalks, and that no fuel be wasted, so of course that is what was done.

Paho quickly untied his uncle. "There are people in the plaza who would see you." he said. "Maybe I can get their attention, so you will be able to slip away." He then went back out to the central area of the village and then ducked into the brush behind the buildings. He noticed that the people had built a pen out of sticks and brush. It was also in the direction of the mountain, but to the west, whereas he had approached the pueblo from the east. In it were about twenty large fat turkeys. He pulled aside the woven framework which served as a gate and entered, trying to be as quiet as possible. Next he managed to corner and catch one of the largest turkeys. Leaving the gate open, he shooed a number of the birds out into a grove of saplings, before carrying his one captive turkey back to the edge of the plaza, where he released it in a flurry of feathers and gobbling. The reaction was instantaneous. Turkeys were food and clothing to the people. Every available person rushed to the grove, helping to recapture the valuable fowl. In the excitement no one noticed the small boy and the young man who disappeared to the east, circling back toward the place where Paho had hidden their possessions.

"What happened, Uncle? Who caught you and tied you up?"

"I had gone to get firewood, just as it was starting to get light. I thought to let you sleep since we had walked so long in the snow yesterday. I looked carefully before nearing the roadway and saw no one, but did not realize that a group of log carriers had just passsed by, on their way from the canyon back to the pueblo for another log. They had left the roadway, just beyond where I was, following a deer track in the new snow. They saw me before I saw them, and called for me to stop."

"And, did you not run away?"

"No, I feared leaving you, and yet did not dare to run toward your sleeping place for fear that they might capture you also. It seemed best to speak to them, hoping they would be friendly. Such was not the case. They saw that I was a stranger and did not have the clothing of a log cutter. They forced me to go to the village with them, and soon saw that no one knew me. They had enough log carriers in their group, and knew that I would run away from their company at the first opportunity anyway, but they knew also that there was always a need of more strong young men in the tree cutting work, so they turned me over to the villagers, in return for a supply of dried elk meat which they could take back to the canyon and use for trade. The villagers could have kept me there easily, with no way of escaping. It was brave of you to do what you did, Paho. You are still a young boy, but you think like a man. When we return I will tell the story in our villages, so that they all may know.

"Now, let us find the provisions you hid, and return to the safety of our own people."

CHAPTER SIX

Ours is a dry land and a thirsty land. The rains must come each summer, so that the crops may grow. It is for this reason that we sing the rain songs and dance the rain dances. We ask the gods to bring the moisture, which gives life to our parched fields. When the gods withhold that blessing the crops cannot grow, and the people suffer. When our people were few they could wander across the land, and search for food in other areas where the rain had visited. But by the time of Paho the people were many, and they had long abandoned their wandering ways. They had been forced to stop in fertile valleys and grow crops. Nature could no longer provide for them, so they had to provide for themselves.

The act of settling, of ceasing their wandering, was not a step upward. Our people were not evolving to a higher plane of civilization, as is often said. It was a change that was forced upon them in order to survive; and it was a change that brought both blessings and curses. Abandoning the nomadic ways of their fathers brought a permanence, which allowed the building of better homes. Instead of tents of animal skins or burrows in the backs of rock overhangs, they could now live for many years in the same location. Starting first with primitive shelters dug into the ground, they eventually developed the fine stone cities whose ruins you marvel at today. Instead of carrying what little food they could as they wandered from place to place, they could now store their surplus against the times of need. Instead of suffering in the weather, they could warm themselves by a fire, out of the wind and snow.

But each of these advantages was in itself also an evil. The cities of stone could not be loaded on a man's back and carried to another place. Our people could not follow the rain clouds that peeked over the horizon; they had to wait for the clouds to come to them. Their fields were established, their seeds planted, their runoff systems in place. Only could the gods of the rain determine their destiny. They had lost the ability to control their own survival. The fact that there were too many of them to any longer live off the unattended crops of nature denied them the ability to be their own masters.

They created large storage areas in which they saved the extra food from the good years, knowing that the bad years would come. They were then unable to move away from these hoards easily, so they stayed, even when the gods failed to bring the rains. They farmed the same fields year after year, and watched the crops become less and less as they depleted the strength of the soil. Their cities of stone were hard to leave.

Warm fires in the round rooms were comfortable, but they also needed to be fed, and the firewood necessary for them became scarce. Especially in the canyon, the firewood had to be brought great distances, and was a luxury. Only the rich could live in a large kiva and have a fire when they wanted. The others crowded into the smaller underground chambers and relied as much upon accumulated body heat as on glowing embers to eliminate the winter chill.

In time they forgot the old ways. The nomadic wanderings of their ancestors were nothing more than tales told in the legends of their storytellers. They had gotten into the habit of permanence. Even in the worst of times it was inconceivable that they leave their cities of stone in search of better conditions. In time, they knew, conditions would improve, and they needed only to work and wait.

When enough rain did not come in a year, the people were ready. They had stored food for the bad times, and they could survive without too much difficulty. When the rains were insufficient for two consecutive years the people were no longer as well prepared. Then they would begin to suffer. When the drought extended into a third year our people starved.

Paho was in his thirteenth year when the rains failed for the first time in his short memory. There had been little snow during the winter; so that by the time it came time to plant the crops the ground was already cracked and powdery. Not only the adults, but also the children were kept at work many hours each day, carrying jars of water to the crops. It was over a mile to the nearest spring, and the path crossed a ridge, which made it a hard climb in both directions. As dry spring became dry summer our people watched the horizon, waiting for the clouds, which gathered there to sweep over the land and bring new life to the parched earth. Occasionally the sky would darken, the wind would gust around the bluffs, and the rain would begin, only to move on after dropping barely enough rain to settle the dust.

In the fields the corn was dry and stunted. The ears that formed were few, and those that did form contained small kernels scattered on the stunted ears. The Squash did better, since the people were better able to keep them moist, and the beans produced quite well, even without enough water. The people, when they were not carrying water to the crops, walked many miles to the mountains in search of berries and of game. Even there, however, the lack of rain had taken its toll. The berries and seeds were few, and the people covered vast distances in order to find enough to justify the journey. Even the animals seemed to be scarce. Deer and elk had moved to higher and wetter lands, also in search of food. The hunters soon found themselves pursuing game to the high meadows of the Great Mountain, in the region where the spirits of the dead were said to reside. Here they were afraid of violating the home ofthe dead, and often had to turn back empty-handed.

By the end of the growing season it was evident that the food supply for the coming winter would be meager. But some of the back rooms of the pueblo below the red sandstone bluffs were still full of grain stored from the prior year. It had been walled in tightly with closely fitted rocks; every possible opening or weakness filled with chips of rock. No mice would find an opening that would cost our people their carefully hoarded supplies. The walls had also been covered with a smooth, unclimbable plaster veneer. This made sure no vermin could find a place to start digging. After the rooms were filled, each doorway had been painstakingly sealed in the same manner. Only when the food was needed would each room be unsealed.

It was in this dry year that Paho was to make his first entrance into the Great Kiva; the day he had dreamed about. It was a sad and difficult time for the people, but the traditions and ceremonies were not to be ignored. He was, by now grown tall, and he was a fast runner and a good hunter. He had learned the chants and ceremonies of his clan, and carried in his head the many legends that had been repeated to him time after time. His early show of initiative and bravery in rescuing his uncle had been a help. It had singled him out from among the many boys who were waiting to be called to the Great Kiva.

It was a day in the late fall. The weather should have been cold and the wind should have been gusting around the bluffs. Instead the air was quiet and the sun was warm. The people sat in the sun grinding meal on the flat rock metates, or went to the mountains, in search of food. The time, they knew was nearing for the harvest dance; the thanksgiving for the food the gods had sent them. When the time came that the gods declared the start of the ceremonies they would be ready.

As the sun was setting, a cry was heard from the gap in the sandstone rocks to the east, the pass near Paho's home. A shouting, and then a man appeared, loping with the steady pace and easy swing of a long distance runner; a messenger. In his hair were raven feathers, the symbol of the messenger, and on his arms were the woven bands of cloth with symbols of the kiva clan from the cities in the canyon. Everyone knew, of course, why he was there. A similar runner had appeared each year for as long as they could remember. But the formalities must be observed.

The runner was greeted by the elders of the pueblo, and taken to the Great kiva. All the male leaders of the various clans descended to the depths of the dark room, leaving only the runner outside. A deep murmuring could be heard from within, and then a drum began to slowly beat. Voices chanted to the rhythm, the sound drifting upward through the entryway. As the tempo increased the voices became louder. Soon the beat was loud and rapid, and the voices could be heard reverberating throughout the pueblo. The chant increased in intensity for a number of minutes, and then suddenly and abruptly ended. A voice within, which all recognized as Melolo, the priest of the Snake clan, summoned the runner, who slowly descended the ladder. All was silent, both inside the kiva, and among the people who waited in the plaza above. Even small children sensed the solemnity of the moment and sat quietly in the dust at the feet of their mothers.

A distant drum began to sound, seemingly coming from above the sandstone cliffs. Another was heard to the east then, answering the echoes from the north. Next the south responded, and finally the drum of the west echoed briefly across the village. After a moment of silence the drums of the four directions began again, in unison, and were joined by the deep resonance of the drum within the Kiva. The elders filed slowly out of the Kiva, toward the plaza, stamping their feet in time to the drums, and singing the song of the harvest. The line of elders made a corridor, then, two rows of men leading from the Kiva to the beaten earth of the plaza. As the song continued, and the elders stamped their feet in a complicated rhythm, first the runner, and finally Melolo emerged from the dark depths of the Great ceremonial chamber, and solemnly strode between the rows of men to the plaza, where they stood facing the people.

"The day of the harvest festival is announced." Melolo shouted suddenly. "The runner has come from the Canyon. Our highest priest, he who watches the sun and the stars and talks with the gods, has been told by Spider Woman herself that in four days we must be ready. Every member of The People, in every village, will give thanks for the food that the gods have sent. The runners left last night to all parts of the empire, that everyone might know and be prepared. For three days all must work to prepare, and on the fourth morning the fires will be lighted and all will give thanks.

"Then also, the deserving youths will be tested." he continued. "The people will now give thanks to the gods and their messenger, and then begin the preparations. All youths who are of the age to be called will go to the cave on the west and wait."

It was dark by this time, and the people lighted a large fire in center of the plaza, and danced the dance of the welcome. The runner was fed and given gifts by the people, and offered his choice of sleeping rooms. Then the drums began again, and the dancing continued well into the night, the chanting and the drumbeat echoing back from the sandstone cliffs.

Eleven boys of Paho's age joined him in the walk to the cave. This was not one of the great caves above the village, but a small cave which ran more deeply into the rocks, further to the west. There was little talk, now. Each boy was lost in his own thoughts, wondering if he would this year be called to the Great Kiva. It was anticipation and longing, certainly, but mixed with a great deal of fear. No one ever talked of the initiation ceremony, but the lack of knowledge in itself lent a terror to the anticipation. Each boy knew that he would, if called, be tested by the elders, and each wondered if he would be brave enough, strong enough and wise enough to pass the tests. They knew of youths who had been called to the kiva and then had never again been seen. It was thought that they must have been killed trying to pass one of the challenges, but no one ever was allowed to mention the names of the missing boys from that day onward.

Once having reached the cave, the boys filed inside and crouched along the walls, not looking at each other and watching the doorway. Below them they could hear the drums and the singing, and they could see shadows passing between them and the fire as the people danced. Off to the right they could make out the dark shape of the Great Kiva, and knew that inside it they were being discussed and considered.

"I hope," Paho thought," They will come for me. I have learned my lessons well. I can do the chants of the morning and of the evening and of the hunt, and am learning the songs for curing and the songs of the seasons. I have tried to be brave and, even when scared, to appear brave." Then he sat in the dark and saw the other boys, some bigger and older than him, and wondered if they were more worthy than he of being called. "Perhaps," he thought, "They are stronger and braver than I, and could pass the tests, where I might fail." Then he began to be concerned, and thought about the boys who never came home, and decided he wished he would not be called. Fear and courage replaced one another many times during that night; a night in which he was sure he would not be able to sleep.

He awoke to the sense that someone was standing near him! The moon had set, and the cave was very dark. The dancing and drumbeats had ceased in the village below, and all was quiet. He could hear the heavy breathing of the boys around him sleeping. Suddenly a voice was near him in the darkness; a deep whisper. "Come, you are chosen. Follow me."

CHAPTER SEVEN

Three boys, about to be tested as men, now too excited to be sleepy, stumbled down the rocky path toward the village. Paho had been aware the other boys had awakened, sensing the change in their breathing, but they all lay silently around the perimeter of the cave, waiting to see if they would be similarly roused. In the end only two others had heard the deep whisper in their ear. They were both older boys who had been expected to be called the year before but had been passed over. The boy from the water clan was almost as tall as most of the men of the village, and very strong. His home, in the valley to the west, was a long distance from the main pueblo, and Paho barely knew him, but remembered that his name was Yahoya. Paho knew that this boy would be able to meet all of the physical challenges of the tribal elders. He wondered if he would do as well.

The other boy Paho knew very well. He was a year older than Paho, and had grown up with him; a member of the snake clan, the dominant clan of the village. He was named Kolello, and was the nephew of Melolo, the high priest of the snake clan, who was therefore the most powerful man in the region. This made Kolello a boy who might expect to assume a dominant position when he was older; a fact that Kolello never forgot, and never let the other boys forget. The prior year all the people had expected that Kolello would be called, and were amazed when he was passed over. It was rumored that the other clan chiefs had opposed Melolo, feeling that Kolello was not ready, and that this had led to tensions in the leadership. It had also embittered Kolello, so that he was even more arrogant, and tried to show his disdain for the people who had insulted him by bullying the smaller children.

Paho was one who Kolello had tried to intimidate. Paho had been recognized by the people as a clever and resourceful boy, ever since his freeing of his uncle, and their escape from the village of the tree cutters. It was believed that Paho would be a leader of his people some day. This had always bothered Kolello, but it was even more irking when he was not called out for initiation in his first eligible year. As a result, he went out of his way to insult and ridicule Paho, trying to precipitate a fight, but had met with such disdain that now the two boys had only contempt for one another. Paho, therefore, was far from happy to see that one of his fellow initiates would be this longtime adversary.

By the time they reached the houses the three boys, accompanied by a silent man who they had known all their lives but who said nothing and treated them as strangers, their eyes had become more accustomed to the dark. They could see the glowing coals of the fire of the evening before, and then a faint light from the entry of the Great Kiva. There was no sign of dawn yet, but the cold air gave the feeling that night was about to end. In the distance they could hear a coyote, soon answered by another much closer. The turkeys were bunched together for warmth in one corner of their enclosure and a dog slept near the door of one of the work rooms. The man who had summoned them now led them to another of the plaza facing rooms and beckoned for them to enter.

It was dark and quiet inside, but they could feel the presence of a number of people, waiting in the darkness. Each boy was pushed roughly to a different section of the room, where he found himself surrounded by a group of people.

Paho was at first terrified, with dark shapes pressing in on him, but he made no sound that might show that fear. Then a smell came to him, which he recognized. It was the distinctive odor he had known all his life that came from the combination of cooking smells and weaving smells and fire making smells. It was the woman odor of his own home and his own people. He then knew that those who were about him were not enemies but his own people. In the dark he soon knew that his mother, his aunts and his grandmother were all there, but no word was said.

Silently the women worked over him, preparing him for the ceremonies. First they bathed him, and he could tell from the sounds that the same thing was being done to the other two youths in their respective corners. Then he felt feathers being put in his hair, and a loop of feathers and beads placed around his neck. One of the women came close to him and he felt her finger making lines on his face and down his neck and shoulders. He knew this would be the black and white paints which were used for placing the clan marks. Finally someone brought a pot full of corn meal, dry and powdery and another, who he sensed was his mother, mixed it with some water to make a thick paste, which was then daubed on his exposed skin everywhere except his face. Now he was properly purified by the ceremonial bathing, marked with the clan symbols, and wore the hair feathers of a man. The corn symbolized his maturity and ripening to manhood, that he might be a keeper and producer of corn, and also that he might be a fruitful producer of other worthy clan members. In the corn symbol was both survival and fertility. The women, as was customary, had prepared him for his manhood. In this act they were continuing what they had done since his birth, but symbolically, they were doing it for the last time. He was now to enter the realm of men, and women would no longer minister to him.

He was the last of the three to climb down the long ladder into the interior of the Great Kiva. As he gripped the pine poles, polished to a lustre by generations of hands sliding over them, he felt a thrill of excitement. This was the scene he and Tokchii had tried to imagine for years as they sat in their cave in the warm sun. But now it was really happening, and he was gripped with a fear. A low fire burned in the center of the large round chamber. Around the room were seated about thirty men, their bodies glistening in the heat and closeness, lit by the firelight. The highest ranked men, usually the oldest of each clan were toward the north, and the newer initiates were nearer the entrance ladder. As one gained maturity and prestige he progressed toward the warmer and less drafty section. At he north end, flanked by two very old men was Melolo, chief of the Snake clan! His eyes were dark and shaded, and he stared unsmilingly at the three, showing no recognition even to his nephew, Kolello. All waited for a time which seemed to

Paho to be interminable, with each boy carefully scrutinized by the elders. Then Melolo rose to his feet.

"Are you ready to become men?" he intoned slowly.

"We are ready"

"And can you prove your bravery?"

"We will try to be worthy of our people, our clan and the gifts of our gods." The three repeated the phrase they had been taught since childhood.

"We will see." rumbled the deep voice of Melolo. "You are not now men, and will only be men in name, even if you pass our tests. The feathers of men, which you now wear in your hair are symbols of your coming manhood, only. Deeds, not time or ceremonies can truly make you men. You have only three days, before the dance of the harvest, to perform the necessary acts. Each of you will have a teacher who will stay with you for these three days and oversee your testing. At the end of those three days we will judge whether you have been worthy of our selection.

"Now, the light is starting to appear in the east. We will all sing the morning song, and then the trials will begin."

The next two days were a blur to Paho. He was allowed no sleep or food for the entire time, and water was only given to him twice each day. His mentor never left his side, suffering exactly as he suffered, and doing, seemingly with ease, all of what he was required to do. During the days he was required to perform physical feats, which would prove his ability to provide food, shelter and protection for the tribe and his clan. During the night they met again in the Great Kiva, where the sacred stones were unwrapped and placed before them for the first time. Then they heard the stories of their ancestors and sang the songs of their people.

The young initiates were not placed in competition with one another, but with their mentors. They were expected to do everything the older men challenged them to do. This included endurance tests in which they ran continuously with the swinging lope of the distance messenger. In this way they covered a great distance, never stopping for many hours. At the end of the run, at a spring far to the north, they filled water jars, and resumed their run, returning to the village with the full jars, proving they had not spilled any nor drunk any of the precious liquid. Next came a trial to show their ability to provide shelter for their people. They were required to climb the high cliffs, using the familiar hand and foot holds they had used since children, and select building stones of the correct type, size and shape. Then they carried these stones, one at a time, back down the cliffs and across the lower hills to a new building site. Next they went to the clay banks and brought back the dry earth, which would be their mortar. Finally, they mixed the mortar, using the water they had brought from the spring, and painstakingly fitted the rocks to one another, using as little mortar as possible, and filling every gap with smaller pieces of flat stone, which they had also brought down from the cliff tops. Each boy built a section of wall.

They were required to demonstrate their marksmanship with bow and arrow, equalling the challenges set by their mentor. They ran to the area where the smooth hard rocks were to be found and brought back well selected pieces, which they then broke and chipped until they had fashioned arrow points. They showed their accuracy with spears and with thrown rocks. They followed the tracks of animals, identifying them and finally encountering them.

They also were required to track and find their mentors who went ahead of them and tried to elude them.

At the end of the second day Paho was so exhausted and hungry he felt himself weak and dizzy. The pace had continued without cease for two days and one entire night, not counting the night spent in the cave waiting to be selected. He knew he had done well on the trials. All of his boyhood had been aimed at this goal, and he had learned the lessons of survival, awaiting this moment. A few times during these days he had wondered if it was worth it. The man assigned to test him showed no weakness, setting almost impossible examples, which he had been required to equal. But each time he had thought of the days he had dreamed of this, and had summoned additional energy to keep on going. One time, when he had been especially discouraged he had been carrying a very heavy log back to the building site, and had passed near the main pueblo. Here, he knew, the people could see him and judge how he was withstanding the trials. He was almost ready to give in anyway, when he saw a person at the edge of the plaza, watching him over the low wall, and realized it was Tokchii. He had seen little of her during the past few months, and had not realized that she was no longer a little girl, but was fast becoming a young woman. He lifted the log higher on his shoulder and stepped out with his burden, acting as though he was not at all tired or discouraged.

At the end of the second day they again were returned to the Great Kiva, to face the elders. The glow of the firelight and the warmth of the closely packed people brought out all the weariness, which had been building for the last two days. Combined with his lack of food, he felt very sleepy. Yahoya and Kolello were there with him, all allowed now to be seated on the packed clay floor. They were, of course, at the furthest point from the center of authority, the north side where Melolo and the other most powerful chiefs sat. As warmth and weariness almost overcame him, he saw, through half closed eyes, that Melolo had now risen, as he had the first night, and was standing before the elders, the light of the fire reflecting upward and making his face seem to glow ethereally in the center of the Kiva. Then he was suddenly wide-awake as Melolo's voice shattered the silence.

"Rise! Face the elders without weariness!" They jumped rapidly to their feet. "You have done well, I am told. Each of you has passed the tests and is now worthy to be a part of this gathering. From this day forth you will be welcomed in the midst of men, and will be providers and guardians of the people. Only if you bring dishonor to the group will you be barred from your seat among men. Never will you be without help if another of us is nearby, and never will you refuse anything to another of the group.

"As the smoke rises through the smoke hole, so did our people rise from the third world into this the fourth. Sotuknang told us to follow his laws and put his needs before our own. He ordered that we sing the songs of praise as the seasons came and went, showing him our thanks for all he has provided. Then he told us we must honor his fruitfulness with our own fruit. Our finest men would be dedicated to him at each harvest time. You three have been chosen to honor Sotuknang. Deeds of courage will be expected of you in every day of your life, that Sotuknang will know that we have chosen well. Perhaps, someday, one of you will stand where I now stand, choosing, as I have had to choose. Therefore, be sure that you do not make a lie of the choice that I have made."

Two of the younger men now rose and went to the niche high in the kiva wall, behind where Melolo had sat, and extracted two cloth wrapped bundles. They took them to the center of the round room, and unwrapped them slowly, laying them at the feet of the high chief. One was a large smooth rock, black and shiny, with figures carved in its surface. It was, the youths knew, the powerful stone of the people, which had been given to them by Spider Woman when they had arrived at the shores of the new continent, after the destruction of the third world by great floods. It contained the strength of the gods, and bestowed those strengths on the people. This was the source of power for those who held it. The second object was a carved piece of wood, as long as a man's arm, and painted with grey and brown triangles. It was the snake stick, the power symbol of the snake clan. It was this object that represented the position that Malolo held in the region. As long as the snake stick was allowed by the gods to stay with the black stone of Spider Woman, the Snake clan would hold the power. None of the youths had ever been allowed to see either of these before, but had been told many times of their existence and power.

"Come forward, and place your hands on these objects." Malolo commanded. "Now, swear, each of you, in your heart, to be worthy of the honor we bestow upon you. The power of our ancestors who made the migrations and founded the empire in the canyon is now your power. The future of our people is now your responsibility. If you do well they will prosper, if you fail them, they will starve and die.... Swear!"

And they swore.

"Now," Melolo resumed, "There is one more duty you must perform. Each of you has one more day before the festival begins. You will go out from the pueblo, alone, each in your own direction, and show your ability to feed your people. In this bad year food is scarce. You will return at nightfall and show us what you have brought to the festival. First, you will be allowed food and rest, but in the morning you will be gone from our sight. Go now to the upper rooms, that you may be fed and allowed to sleep. We will wait to judge your gifts. We will see which of you best serves your people."

CHAPTER EIGHT

Paho awoke. The bright triangle of stars, which had been directly over his head when he had lain down were over his right shoulder now. He knew only a short time had passed, and his body still begged for more sleep, but he forced himself awake. He had determined where he must go if he was to prove himself the best hunter, and that was a great distance away. The village was dark and silent. He rose stiffly, and went into the closest room, where he had recently been fed by the women. The coals were still glowing under the pot, and he found there was a little food remaining. He ate this quickly and then hurried the quarter mile back to his clan rooms, where he found his canteen; an earthen jug with a small neck. He filled this with water, forced a cloth stopper into the opening, and placed its woven fiber strap around his neck and arm so that it hung behind him. He picked up his bow and arrows and started to walk rapidly through the darkness, toward the east.

Paho was not the only one to rise early, however. The other two initiates were just as anxious as he to hunt well, and had also gotten just enough sleep to clear their heads and had then started out. Yahoya had gone to the west, following the face of the cliffs, knowing he would find water in this direction, and that the game would, in this dry year, be near water. He was of the water clan, and would therefore use his clan symbol to show that their strength came to the aid of the people. Kolello had gone to the south. The high country above the lava flows was well wooded and watered, and game could often be found there. Being of the snake clan, he had been taught that there were snakes to symbolize each of the directions. He had chosen the direction of Palulukang, the water snake, for Kolello knew, as had Yahoya, that in this dry year his success would be found where the animals found water. Paho had gone East because that would lead him to the high country of the Great Mountain. As an Eagle he sought his hunting in the upper air, the realm of his clan.

For the two days during which the three young men had undergone their trials, the people had been preparing for the ceremonies. Each clan group had hung corn stalks from the outside of their work and storage rooms. Gourds had been painted with harvest symbols, and were gathered under the shelter of the ramadas. Men had gathered firewood, which had been placed in stacks at the end of the plaza, awaiting the night of watching. Even in this year of few crops the pots were filled with corn and squash. Beans were also prepared for the feast, and dried berries and fruits had been brought forth. Only meat was lacking, and the three new hunters would provide this.

During these two days it had not only been the initiates who had gone without food and sleep. All of the elders who had sat in judgment of them had undergone the same deprivation. Now, on the third day, they continued the denial ritual. The three hunters had been given food, that they might be strong enough to provide for the people, but the others ate nothing, fought off sleep, and sang the songs of the hunt. The low beating of the drum and the sound of their voices could be clearly heard by the people at work in the plaza. The elders were praying to the gods that their hunters would do well.

The people had woken to a bitterly cold morning, with a sharp wind from the southwest. High clouds hurried across the sky, colliding with the great mountain and enshrouding its upper reaches in mists that meant snow. The people wrapped themselves tightly in their blankets and darted from shelter to shelter as they continued the preparations. Occasionally they stood in the cutting wind and stared at the mountain, knowing that the snow meant much needed water in the spring, but wondering what it meant for the hunters. All knew that the east was the direction of the eagle, and the high air was the eagle's domain. Paho, they believed, would have gone there. The direction the others were likely to take was less certain.

By late afternoon the wind had died down, but the cold persisted. All was ready for the celebration of the harvest, and the people were only redoing unnecessary chores, awaiting nightfall and the return of the hunters. As evening came, the men of the pueblo brought great armfuls of brush and twigs, and piled them in the center of the plaza. These were lighted and they sent a towering blaze into the sky, lighting every corner of the pueblo. The people gathered near the fire, putting on sticks and then logs, warming themselves in the brightness.

The drumbeat now became louder from the Great Kiva, and the chanting could be clearly heard. The people in the plaza picked up the rhythm, and began to slowly move to the music. Then the elders filed out of the opening, and solemnly walked to the plaza and the fire, where they took their places among the people, to begin the vigil. Another drumbeat now joined the first, from a drum placed near the fire. The elders broke into a loud chant, answered by the others. Soon all were dancing in a twisting chain, in and out of the firelight.

This was the time of waiting. It was a vigil that had been repeated over the centuries, as those who remained waited for the hunters to return. It was the vigil of every worrying wife or mother over the centuries; now it was being ceremoniously enacted for the gods. Dances were done in which each of the animals was personified. The deer dance, the bear dance, the buffalo dance were all performed repeatedly, asking the gods that these animals be brought to the bow of the hunters. It was now very dark beyond the firelight, and a light snow had begun to filter slowly over the village. The people began to glace apprehensively out into that darkness and snow, wondering where the hunters might be.

The first to return was Kolello. He strode out of the darkness, a covering of snow on his head and shoulders which he shook away. Then he removed his cape of feathers and stepped close to the fire, holding up to his uncle, Malolo, his offering. He had shot two large and fat wild turkeys. It was a good omen. The people would eat well of these during the festival. Kolello had shown himself to be an adept hunter. The people were pleased, and he was seated near the fire where he told the story of his hunt.

A short time later another figure was seen approaching the pueblo from the west. He was wrapped tightly in his robe and blanketed in snow. As he entered the firelight they could see that it was Yahoya, and that he also had been successful although perhaps not quite so impressive as Kolello. He carried two large jackrabbits. Again, murmurs of approval rose from the people. In this bleak year game had been scarce, but both youths had brought food for the pots. Only one hunter was still out there.

The fire died down and was restocked a number of times after Yahoya had finished recounting his successful hunt, but still Paho had not returned. The snow had now collected an inch deep on the land. The darkness enveloped the small village below the gigantic sandstone cliffs. The people remembered other long vigils over the years, including some in which the hunter never returned. It was assumed that they had died rather than return and admit defeat. From time to time songs and dances were repeated, as the people tried to maintain the spirit of elation, which had accompanied the return of the other two hunters, soon to be replaced by staring out into the darkness.

It was almost dawn when a lone figure suddenly staggered into the plaza. He was hunched over and covered with snow, but he carried a tremendous burden on his back. He stepped into the firelight and dropped a small elk at the feet of the gathered people. Here was food enough for a great feast. The gods has smiled upon the hunter, bringing them food, and with it the snow, which promised a better year to come. Surely this was a portentous occasion. The hunters had all done well, but the great honor belonged to Paho. In this could be seen that the gods certainly favored him. He would be a leader of his people.

Paho told the people his story. He spoke of the run to the Great Mountain and the grey mists in the aspen forests as he climbed higher and higher. He recounted the biting cold and the deep snow as he watched the sun rise to the east. Then he told the silent audience of the high meadow and the herd of elk, upwind from him and unaware of his presence. Paho glanced around the circle of attentive listeners and saw in the back the face of Tokchii, looking at him as she had on those days when they had been children and he had told her the great things he planned to do. He went on to tell the people of the shooting and tracking of the elk, the final encounter and then the long walk back to the village, burdened with the heavy animal. In his glances he kept coming back to Tokchii, and almost did not see, until his story ended, that another person in the audience stared at him. But this stare carried neither pride nor adoration; it was a look of hate. As he finished his story he suddenly saw that look on the face of Kolello and knew that he had made an enemy.

The people sang again the song of thanksgiving, and then the song of the night, and finally drifted away to their homes, anticipating now the great feast and celebration, which would take, place the next day. Paho soon was alone, by the fire, exhausted, when a figure reappeared from the shadows and came toward him. It was Tokchii. She walked slowly up to him, placed her hand in his and led him away from the firelight.

CHAPTER NINE

That winter was one of much snow. The mountains to the south stayed white all winter, and the Great Mountain carried a heavy crest, which was brilliant in the sunshine. The people were pleased, for this meant water for the land and plentiful crops in the year to come. Much of the good fortune was said to result from the day of the hunt, and the success of the three young men. By early spring the land had a greenish grey haze, which was not usually present. Seeds that had lain for years, awaiting the hint of moisture suddenly sprang to life, taking advantage of the opportunity.

The people also seemed to have suddenly germinated and come to life. There was new vigor that came from the bursting forth of their land, for they were a part of the land. Their ancestors had emerged from the depths of the earth, into the world of the sun god, but their origins were in the earth and they drew their life from the earth. The gods controlled the sun and the rains, but only that the earth might produce, and it was the people who were in charge of that production. When the rains were withheld the land was made to suffer, and this suffering was also the pain of the people, who felt the abandonment of the gods as much as the land did. When the rains came and the snows came, and the gods smiled upon the earth, the land was happy and the people as a part of it were happy also.

The food supplies which had been so depleted during the fall and winter would not be restocked for many months, of course, until the next crop was harvested, but in the meantime, there was game, there were seeds and berries, there were still a few unopened storerooms, and mostly there was confidence. The gods had been appeased and they were once again smiling upon their people. Only Malolo and his closest supporters, including his nephew Kolello seemed to be surly and unhappy in this green and promising time. They went about the village separately, and often were seen standing apart in conversation. There could be no doubt that the Snake Clan leaders were fearful that the people might believe that the leadership was changing; that the gods has sent a message on the day of the hunt.

As the sun moved up the sky, rising further to the north each morning, the people prepared and waited. The most protected and remote back room in the main pueblo was still tightly sealed. They had checked often to make sure that no mice or rats had penetrated the walls, for here was stored the seed corn. Even in the worst of years, the seed was to be preserved, for only in this way could the people be reborn when the good years returned.

They awaited, as they had at the time of the harvest festival, for the messenger from the Canyon. The high priests at the sacred butte would send word when it was time to put the seeds in the ground. It would displease the sun god if they were to plant their crops without the permission of his priest. As the sun crept northward, day-by-day, they watched the horizon, however, and marked its point of rising. When it rose over the left shoulder of the low hill to the east for three days in a row the messenger would come, as he had every year.

This was also a happy time for Paho. He and Tokchii were inseparable that spring. It was understood that they would one day marry, and he would move into the kiva of the Corn Clan. Even the contempt of Kolello could do little to upset their bliss. They were always seen together, doing what either had to do. If she were grinding corn with the women, he would be standing nearby, talking with her. If he were carrying wood for the fire she would be beside him, carrying wood also.

On the expected day the messenger came from the Canyon. He arrived with the word, but unlike the harvest festival, no festivities followed. It was a time of work. The ceremonies would come later, when the seed was in the ground. Then the prayers for fertility would be sung and the dances of the new seeds would be danced.

It happened that Paho and Tokchii were together late one evening, hunting rabbits well to the south of the pueblo, when they saw a group of people coming toward them. It seemed a strange time of day for a group to be leaving the pueblo, as night was almost upon them, so, since they had probably not yet been seen, Paho and Tokchii stepped back behind some pinon trees and watched.

"Look, it is Kolello in front." Said Paho.

"Shhh, yes, and three others. The last one is Malolo!"

"They are carrying a bag, such as is used for seed corn. Perhaps they are planting some fields to the south." Paho said this, but knew it was not true. There were no fields to the south, and the people would never plant a secret field. The grain harvest was raised by all of the people, and belonged to all of the people. It would not have occurred to anyone to raise a private supply.

"I have seen these four leaving the pueblo at other times." said Tokchii. "The first time was the day after the fall festival, and then also, they were carrying a heavy bundle, and leaving in the evening. They did not return until late the next day."

"I wonder," Paho whispered. "If they took part of the elk I shot. I had wanted a piece of the hindquarter as the hunter's reward, just before the festival was to begin, and found that a large part had been removed. I thought, at the time, that it had been taken for the cook pots, but no one was yet cooking."

"No member of the people would ever take food from the others." Tokchii answered.

The four had now passed close to them, and were hurrying toward the southeast. One of the men was carrying a bag woven tightly of yucca fibers. There could be no question this was a seed corn bag. Since the arrival of the messenger the back room had been unsealed, and similar bags of seed corn had been handed out to the planters, that they might put the seed in the ground. Paho noticed also that Malolo was carrying a cloth wrapped object very carefully, almost ceremonially, in his two arms. He had seen this bundle before, on the second night of his initiation. It was the holy stick of the Snake Clan, he was sure. But, he thought, it was never supposed to leave the Great Kiva as long as the Snake Clan was in charge. These were all things that were very strange and unusual.

"Let us follow them." Tokchii suggested.

"No," he answered, "For our families will wonder where we are, and worry. I will follow them, while you return to the pueblo. You must then go to the clan home of my people, and tell them that I was tracking a buck and decided to stay on the trail. I will see what these four are doing, and then return home. The moon is just about to rise, and it will be full. I will have no trouble traveling at night and keeping them in sight."

She reluctantly agreed. He had been making such decisions since they were children, and she had been in the habit of doing what he said. Now, she wondered about the wisdom of his going alone, but decided to follow his suggestion. She turned back toward her home, keeping below the ridge so that the four of the Snake clan would not see her if they were to look back. But she was very worried. The Snake chiefs were powerful, and their contempt for Paho was evident. He had shown up Kolello, the destined leader of their clan. It was not the right of Paho to question their actions; they were the governors of the entire region. He was, however, doing just that. If they were to find out he would be disgraced, and perhaps ostracized from this, his home.

Paho followed at a distance. They seemed to drift through the darkness ahead of him, making no sound as they wove between the cedars and pinons in the moonlight. It was evident that they had covered the route before, as there was no hesitation, and they never stopped to rest or to discuss their path. It seemed, as he saw them ahead of him, that they were only shadows among the shadows that were cast by the moon. There was a ghostliness that seemed unreal, as though he were in a dream.

It was late in the night when they came to the first lava fields; the beginning of the black lands which he had been warned of as a child. The moon had not yet set, and he could look across the jumbled black blocks, with bushes and cacti growing up out of the crevices, and occasional green pathways, which seemed to lead into the interior of the barrenness. There were open meadows, which formed great pools of moonlight in the midst of the blackness, and he twice saw deer grazing in these meadows. The lava was shiny in places, looking like twisted or braided black hair. At other times it was a dull grey, with a surface that could cut through moccasins in an instant.

The four ahead of him followed down the west side of these lava flows for two hours. In this direction it became much more hilly, where the volcanoes had not only poured out their lava, but had raised high cones with their cinders. Paho found that he needed to stay much closer to them in order not to lose them in the blackness. The moon was getting low in the sky, now, and the long shadows made it harder to see. He knew, however, that they were headed south and were restricted by the lava to their left; an area that no member of the people would ever dare enter.

He almost was discovered as he rounded small hill, and hurried forward, trying to see where they were. They had stopped, and were standing together, facing the expanse of lava, only a few feet ahead of him. It was only the sound of their low chant that covered his gasp of surprise. He crouched lower and slipped behind an outlying boulder of lava, from where he silently watched. They had unwrapped the snake clan stick, and placed it against the rocks in front of them. Some of the seed corn had been scattered on the ground before it, and also some corn meal, which one of them had evidently brought, was laid in thin lines pointing toward the four directions. Each of the men now stood at the end of one of the lines, representing the cardinal directions, and faced the clan symbol. They sang a song Paho had never heard before. In rhythm to the chant they raised and lowered their feet in the dust, ethereal in the moonlight. The black lava, which they faced, was a wall, twice as tall as a man, and seemingly uninterrupted and impenetrable. The long shadows of the setting moon cast their figures against the rock, so that there were four other dancers keeping perfect cadence with them.

Each dancer then stepped onto the cornmeal line, which had been his direction, and shuffled toward the crossing point, obliterating the line as he went. They met at the center, whereupon each began to shake his body, perhaps in imitation of the snake they honored, and finally dropped to his knees, at which time all was silent as the ceremony evidently came to an end. Malolo went to the snake stick, and wrapped it again in its cloth, the others following behind him. Then they all walked directly at the lava cliff, as though it were not there, and suddenly disappeared!

CHAPTER TEN

Paho stood transfixed. Surely the magic of the Snake Clan was very strong, but he had not before known that they had the power to become invisible or to walk through rocks. The Snake Clan controlled, he knew, the vibrations of the underworld. The power of their god, as represented in the rattling of the snake's tail was the shaking of the earth. It was the internal life and vibration of the earth, which their god controlled, and it was with this god that the priests of the snake clan spoke. When the earth rumbled deep below, causing the ground to shake and boulders to tumble, this was caused by the vibrations of Tuwachua, who ruled the underworld. Perhaps the ceremony and the dance which he had witnessed just minutes before had asked this snake god to open up the earth that they might go to him.

For some time he crouched in fear behind the outcropping, but eventually curiosity overcame the fear, and he crept to the rock wall where the four had vanished. *It* was black and glassy, with sheer vertical sides dropping to the white sandy area where the dance had been performed. As he came closer, however, he realized that there was a point of rock jutting out from the rest. Skirting this point to the left, he discovered that a narrow passageway went behind it and entered the interior of the black lands. It was wide enough for a man to slip through, and seemed to open up more ahead. It led deep into the forbidden territory. He knew that no one was allowed to enter here, yet there could be no mistaking the fact that the four of the Snake Clan had gone this way; he could see their footprints now, in the sandy entrance. By now they would be far ahead, well into the interior of the twisted black river of lava that stretched for miles to the east and south of him. Dawn would soon arrive, he knew. There was already a barely perceptible grayness on the horizon in that direction.

Paho squatted on his heels at the entrance to the pathway and thought. "What these four do," he said to himself, "Is something bad for our people. They have stolen the food of the village, and taken it for themselves. They even took part of the elk that I killed. This is not as it should be. Malolo teaches the others to plot against his own people. Even Kolello, who has so recently pledged, as I did, to serve the people is now carrying away the food. They even take the seed corn, which has been protected so carefully. The sacredness of the seed is taught to us from birth. In it is the gift of Taiowa, the creator.

"I have pledged to put the good of the people above my own. I do not know whether the gods would punish me for entering the forbidden lands when I serve them. However, the others have already entered and broken the law, while doing evil. Is it not right, then, that I too enter, but only while trying to do good?"

Half expecting instant retribution, but now determined, he stepped across the invisible barrier. Nothing happened. He went further, and still all was quiet. No giant eagle swooped down to carry him off; no bear leaped out to tear him apart; no lightning crashed down upon him. It was cool and dark, surrounded by the high walls of twisted black rock. The sky was starting to grow slightly less dark overhead, and he could hear birds at various distances in the wilderness ahead of him. He followed the now more easily seen footprints in the sand. This pathway had been used by many people for many years. It wound through the lava, always to the southeast, at times skirting grassy areas, at others small stands of stunted pines and cedars in the midst of the rocky tangle of heaved and broken lava.

He crept around a sharp bend in the path, and saw before him the four men. They had descended into a deep hole in the terrain, a sinkhole where the molten rock had once collapsed to form a giant overhang; almost a cave. It was many times deeper than a man is tall, and wider than it was deep. At the bottom, under the overhang, could be seen a sloping ledge of white ice, and flowing out from beneath it was a stream of clear water. The stream formed a shining pool of water at the lowest part of the cave, surrounded by a collar of soft looking grass.

The four were on the near side of the pool, looking across to a shelf of rock under the overhang on which Paho could see five large earthen pots. They were as large as cooking pots, but were decorated on the outside with black and white designs, not blackened by fire. Each would have reached almost to the waist of a tall man. On the black rock above, below and on both sides of the pots were carved many symbols. He could see that some depicted snakes, while others represented rain and clouds. The signs of fertility were there too, in the form of the corn stalk, and earth signs. To the left, but dominating the scene, and appearing to look upon the proceedings was a finely chiseled picture of Kokopelli. He was playing his flute, as always, and watching over the offertory pots from under heavy eyelids, as his hunched back forced his head toward the ground.

As Paho watched, Kolello carried the bag of seed corn around the pool, and poured its contents into the largest of the pots. Meanwhile, the other three, led by Malolo, sang a low chant; the same strange song he had heard them sing before entering the black lands. This was followed by a slow rhythmic dance, which he recognized; it was the dance of the planting, which asked that the corn would grow well. Each dance and song was conducted in front of the Snake Clan stick, which was now planted upright at the edge of the pool. Kolello had rejoined the others, now, and they turned to face the east, to the left of the cave entrance, and sang the morning song, just as the first rays of the sun shimmered over the lava. It reflected in the still pool of clear water, and suddenly lit the shelf of rock with its pots of gifts to the gods. The whole cave glowed with the light of morning, with the shelf of pots brightly shining.

Paho knew now why the Snake Clan was so powerful among the people of the region. It was here, not in their kiva that they spoke to their gods. They must, he thought, be bringing gifts to some very powerful deity who demands a part of the food of the people as a tribute. He now understood why the path had been so well worn. Many generations must have followed this secret route, protecting the people with their chants and prayers, protecting themselves with their sacred clan stick, and entering the forbidden lands to appease the god who dwelt here. It was not to steal from the people, but to protect the people, that they had taken the finest meat from his elk, and the best corn from the storage room.

He knew now that the others of the village must have been aware in some way that such a ritual was being followed. How else could they not notice when the best of the food disappeared? Many others besides Tokchii must have noticed the Snake Clan priests as they carried their offerings away whenever good luck came to the people. Perhaps even his father had known of this, or at least guessed at it, since he had warned Paho so strongly to keep away from the black lands.

The morning song had ended now, and the four had turned back toward the altar, still lighted from the reflecting pool. Paho was crouched behind the rocks at the corner of the entry path, well hidden. Suddenly Kolello turned abruptly, looking directly at Paho and raised his arm, pointing at him.

"He is there!" he whispered in the midst of the silence. "As we thought he would, he has come!"

Paho shrunk back, in terror. They must have known he was following them. He had broken the rules of his people and the religious laws of the clans. He had intruded upon the rites of another clan and learned their secrets. He had even heard their clan song, which was never to be revealed to anyone outside the clan. Could they, then, have lured him here? Was this the result of his greater success in the hunt? Perhaps Kolello and Malolo had made sure he saw them when they left the pueblo, so they could now discredit him. As he thought-all of these things he slid back behind the rock, preparing to rise and run. Just then he became aware of another sound, however, which came from somewhere behind him. It sounded like a shuffling or rustling. Like the far off blowing of leaves across sand. It was barely audible, but there could be no question, something or someone was quietly approaching the shrine from the pathway behind him. Then he knew! It was not he that they were speaking of, but that same sound, which they had been aware of before he was. Perhaps they had been listening for it, knowing it would come, as it had on other occasions when they brought their offerings. Coming down the path behind him must be that deity to whom they had been calling with their songs. He must get out from in between!

Paho quickly got to his feet, staying out of sight behind the corner of rock, and quietly ran back along the path a short distance. There he saw another break in the lava, a path that branched to the right. There were no human footprints in this direction, but it was evidently a well-used game trail leading further into the black lands. He stopped now and listened carefully. The rustling sound could no longer be heard, but he was aware of the sound of the four others, evidently coming along the path behind him. He chose quickly, and darted up the unused path, intending to let them go by and then follow them out of the lava.

The new path was narrow and twisted, and he followed it a short distance until he was well hidden, but could see the fork where the others would pass by. Here he waited and watched, hardly looking behind him until after the four of the Snake Clan had gone by. Then he turned, and saw that he was in a small circular area, surrounded by high walls of lava. The floor was sand covered, and a few dry weeds had gathered at one side. To his right was a dark opening, near the ground, a large tunnel, and in front of it the sand was smoothed from the passing of some animal. Curious, Paho circled to the left, away from the entrance to the area and opposite the tunnel, hoping to see into it. Suddenly, the rustling sound was much louder, and he realized it was coming from the tunnel. He backed against the lava wall, and stared at the hole. To his right was the escape path. Then he saw a head emerge from the dark tunnel, followed by the long body of the largest snake he had ever seen.

The massive body was as large around as Paho's thigh and the head was the size of a man's fist. He was dusty looking, blending into the sand and rocks in which he lived. His back was marked with dull brown diamond shaped markings. At the end of his tail, now vibrating with a dry sound, were many rattles, each counting a year in the long life of this huge reptile. Piercing eyes watched him and the tongue darted repeatedly toward him as the snake moved to cut off any escape. This was, Paho now knew, the god to whom Malolo and his followers brought offerings. He had entered the private realm of that deity, and was now to pay for it. He shrank against the wall and watched the great body slide toward him. The head was held high, swaying slightly, and the eyes were looking into his eyes. It moved ever closer, with Paho transfixed, unable to move in his terror.

As the tiny eyes stared at him and as Paho pressed himself against the rock, he held his hands against the wall beside his body, trying to get as far as possible from the deadly creature. Then he found his right hand was on a fist-sized rock, which was a part of the wall, but loose. He suddenly, almost without thinking, grasped the rock and hurled it at the menacing head. Many years of hunting rabbits with rocks had trained him well. The jagged stone struck the head of the huge snake, knocking it backward and stunning it enough so that he was able to scuttle to the right, and escape down the path.

Paho knew he had not killed the snake, and believed he could not have killed it, since it must have been Tuwachua himself whom he had confronted. Surely Tuwachua would now follow him and kill him. He ran stumbling down the pathway, and turned to follow the others out of the terror of the black lands. Once he fell, his hands catching him as he plunged toward loose glassy lava. He felt the fragments cut into his skin, and later saw the blood running down to his fingers. He was sure he could hear the dry scales on the sand, coming behind him, and he rose and plunged forward. Finally, breathlessly, he emerged from the labyrinth of rock, and into the grassy meadow where he had entered.

Ahead, he could now see the others, as they returned to the pueblo. They were a long distance ahead, so far that he could not distinguish which person was which, but as he stared toward them he saw one of them turn and look backward at him.   Ahead, he could now see the others, as they returned to the pueblo. They were a long distance ahead, so far that he could not distinguish which person was which, but as he stared toward them he saw one of them turn and look backward at him. Then he saw a raised arm pointing in his direction. He knew he had been seen, but probably not identified!

Paho quickly dropped back behind an outcropping of lava and then ran back to a deep arroyo, which cut toward the mountains to the west. He ran as fast he could up this arroyo, keeping out of sight, and finally, when he knew he was well away from the others, climbed out of the arroyo, and circled through the maze of hills and meadows, working his way back toward the village.

CHAPTER ELEVEN

The pueblo was just as he had left it. He had only been gone since the evening before, but somehow he felt that so much had changed that the pueblo and the people would be different. Yet no one took any notice of him. At his home the clan group paid little attention after they found that he had not gotten the deer they had been told he was following.

There were, in all, sixteen others living in the set of rooms huddled against the cliff. They all slept together in the round room. The upper rooms, the small square rooms pressed against the red sandstone cliff were for work or for storage. Here the food was cooked and eaten, the corn was ground, the meat was butchered and dried or smoked. All foods were stored in the upper rooms; the back rooms, in good years, sealed off and filled with corn, beans, and sun-dried squash. The rooms nearer the front had doors of stone which could be tightly fitted into place, and here the meats and forage foods were kept ready to be used. The front rooms contained cooking hearths and corn-grinding bins.

All the food was prepared and consumed either in the front rooms, or in good weather, out-of-doors in front of the square rooms. No food was ever allowed in the round rooms where the people slept, for this would provide a lure for their greatest enemies the rats and mice which roamed everywhere. It was for this reason also that the entry was not from the side, but from a hole in the ceiling. When the people were inside, and the ladder brought down, there was no way that a rat or mouse could climb in with them.

When the people had roamed over the land they had not been greatly concerned with storing food. What they picked, gathered or killed was quickly consumed, and they moved on, looking for another meal. As their numbers grew, however, and food grew scarce, they had been forced to settle in more permanent homes and plant crops. No longer could they wander with the seasons and the game. They now needed to plan ahead, and save food from one crop season to the next. Also, they needed to store seed in order to plant the next crop. Without seed there would be no planting and no food; only starvation.

When the people stopped moving and built permanent homes they first used the methods they had been using for centuries. They built light frame walls and covered them with mud, to keep out the weather. For warmth they dug their homes, into the ground, and built sloping roofs over them. It afforded them protection from the cold of winter and the heat of summer. The entrances were from the side, as was logical, and they kept their food with them in the shelters. They did not, at first, stay in these homes all the time, but moved about, still following game, and supplementing their agriculture with naturally occurring foods.

They would return to the same houses over and over again, since they had planted crops nearby, but crops which needed little or no care between planting and harvest. The shelters were satisfactory for a time.

It was not until they became more dependent upon the crops they raised that the problems with the vermin arose. As they spent more time in one place the rats and mice, which were about in small numbers, began to invade their food supplies, and with more readily available food, they quickly began to multiply. In a single season a few mice could multiply to thousands or even millions. Their population varied directly with the amount of food available, and the people were providing that food. Not only was there stored food, but there were the crops in the fields which provided a new found source. In addition, the people, in settling down, created permanent trash heaps near their houses. These were a marvelous source of nourishment for the burgeoning population of grey marauders.

It was for this reason that Paho's ancestors had developed such fine methods of stone masonry. Only by building thick, tight walls could they keep out the animals that could rob them of their food, and consequently even their life. At first the masonry was crude, using random rocks, held together with large amounts of mud for mortar. Over time, however, it became much more precise, as expert stone masons developed their skills. It became a challenge to build walls with as little mud as possible, compared to the amount of stone. This meant fitting tiny slivers and wedges of stone into every crevice between the larger building stones. It also meant that the stones needed to be broken and chiseled to the desired shape for a close fit. Mice or rats, squirrels and chipmunks, could dig through even the sun baked adobe mortar, but were stopped by stone, so stone was presented as a barricade at every possible nook. Then the resulting walls, beautiful in their precision and intricacy, were plastered over with a layer of adobe mud. This not only made sure every crevice was filled, it provided an unclimbable surface, discouraging creatures searching for a vulnerable spot to start scratching their way toward the all important stores.

The rooms against the sandstone cliff were constructed in this manner, and laid out in the traditional way. Paho and his entire clan group occupied one round room, dug well into the ground. This was the center of all the family activity except that which dealt with food. It was warm and comfortable in winter; the hearth in the center supplemented the body heat, and the warmth was reflected back by every part of the circular structure. Being round there were no cold corners. In the heat of summer the cool surrounding earth made the family kiva a pleasant retreat from the searing sun above. Here the clothes were made, the sandals woven, the hunting tools repaired. Here also the people gathered to talk, to sing, to retell the legends of the people.

Paho lay wrapped in a robe of deerskin, at the eastern side of the room, trying to sleep. On his return he had searched out Tokchii, where she was working with the women at the main pueblo. He signaled to her to meet him later. It was an old sign they had used as children, and she understood what he meant. Shortly thereafter he was waiting for her as she crept into the small secret cave they had hidden and played in as children. It was on the north side of the great bluff which formed the backdrop for the village; a cave about thirty feet above the arroyo bottom, hidden in a dense growth of pinon trees. It would have been only large enough for a grown man to barely fit into, lying down, and the ceiling was low, but it provided shelter from the weather, and had a soft floor of red sand. Here, years before, they had carried rocks up from below, and had built walls in from the sides of the entrance, turning it into a narrow doorway.

At first he had told her very little about his discoveries; he had seen ceremonies which no woman should know about. Before long, however, he found himself telling her more and more about what he had learned, until finally she knew the whole story.

""Do they know, then, that it was you?" she asked.

"I do not think so, but they know someone was behind them, and that they were probably seen coming out of the black lands. They will not want to publicly ask questions, but they will be trying secretly to find out who it was. I made a big circle, after they saw me, knowing they would try to find out who was behind them. When I got back to the pueblo they had not yet returned, but they came in soon after."

"I saw them going from kiva to kiva, visiting the clans. They were probably trying to find out who was missing, or who had been away. I wonder," she mused, "If they checked with your clan, since you are separated from the main pueblo."

"It hardly matters." he answered. "It is not Malolo or his followers that I fear, but Tuwachua, the god of the underworld. I have injured and insulted him. I saw his secret ceremonies, and when he came to punish me I hit him with a stone. He will have his vengeance."

"No!" she said forcefully. "You were acting for the good of our people. You did not know that the Snake priests were also trying to do good. Surely Tuwachua will not punish you for that."

"You do not know the ways of the gods. They are jealous of one another, and each wishes to control the people. I am of the Eagle clan, and eagles have always been the enemies of the snakes. We are able to rise to the heavens, to speak with Taiowa himself, but the snakes must always be deep in the ground, only coming out in the cool of the day when the Creator and giver of life, the Sun, is low in the sky. His nephew, Sotuknang, made the underground the place for Tuwachua, and gave him great powers to control the vibratory centers of the earth, but put the eagle over him. Any time an eagle sees a snake it will swoop down and kill it with its talons.

"Tuwachua will not rest until the insult is avenged. If he does not reach me he will withdraw his favors from the people, and the rains will no longer come. I cannot let all our people suffer for what I have done. Perhaps if I go to Malolo the people will punish me and Tuwachua will be pacified. I will think on this tonight, and decide."

They had parted soon after, and he had returned to his clan kiva. As night fell his family had all descended the ladder and gone to sleep; all except Paho. He had lain most of the night, unable to sleep, even though he had gone through the entire previous night without rest. As morning approached he had decided; he would go to Malolo and tell him everything. This decided, he fell into a restless sleep.

Paho dreamed that he was again in the side pathway in the black lands. His feet were stuck in the soft sand so that he could not move them and the huge snake, even bigger than the real one, was getting closer and closer to him. He could not run and there was now no rock to throw. Faintly first, he could hear the vibration of the rattles. Then they got louder and louder as the snake came closer. The eyes were now only inches away from his face, and the tongue was flicking at him, touching him. The rattle was now a shaking, a vibration, a tremor. Paho awoke with a start. The rumbling sound did not cease. It was all around him, shaking the earth on all sides.

Paho knew now that Tuwachua was coming for him. He rose quickly, staggering against the shaking and rumbling and started to climb the ladder out of the round room. As he emerged into the darkness of night he felt gravel and pebbles pelting him from above. The shaking was raining chips and sand from the cliff, which bent over the clustered rooms. Tuwachua was vibrating the entire earth that Paho might be punished, and the rocks themselves seemed to be flying apart. He grasped the top of the ladder and pulled himself out and away, rolling across the roof of the kiva, and away from the cliff. Inside were his family; he must draw the wrath away from them, and toward himself. A large rock dropped beside him, grazing his arm. Another hit his left ankle; he felt it break.

Paho rolled across the roof, pelted as he went, and dropped over the far edge, a step down only, to the flat ground beyond. The rumbling sound was even louder, and the ground under him was shaking, almost heaving, as though a gigantic animal were under the earth, trying to get out. Waves of motion mingled with the pain in his ankle, as he clung to the ground, unable to move further. Suddenly he heard a deep cracking sound above him, and looked upward. The great slab of sandstone, which had been a part of the overhanging cliff, and which had helped to shelter the rows of rooms was moving! Even in the darkness he could see its shape shift, and then seem to grow larger. It had detached itself, and was dropping toward him and toward the round room. Time seemed to stand still, as he slowly watched the shape become larger and larger as it dropped toward him. Then the whole world was filled with noise and pain and dust, and then nothing.

CHAPTER TWELVE

It was dark and cold when he awoke. Looking straight overhead he could see nothing. He twisted his head sideways and felt pain shoot through his body. It seemed to concentrate in two places, his ankle, and his back. He had twisted to his right, and could now discern a faint lessening of the darkness in that direction. At least he was not blind! He felt as though he was lying on a very large rock, which was just between his shoulder blades. He tried to move slightly to avoid the rock, and was immediately met with a shock of pain in the area where the rock seemed to be, which caused him to cry out. He knew that the pain in his ankle came from the apparent break, when the rock had hit it and he had heard it snap. He could remember nothing after he had seen the great slab of sandstone descending upon the rooms.

He tried once more to get into a more comfortable position, and this time the pain was so great he passed out again. The next time he awakened it was daylight, early morning evidently, and he could now see that he was still huddled against the low side wall of the clan kiva. Over him was a solid mass of sandstone, only inches from his face. It formed a tiny lean-to surrounding his body, and letting in light from the downhill side, where he could see the grassy plains and corn fields, quiet and yellow in the early morning light. He slowly concentrated on moving his head back to the left, toward the kiva. Even trying to move was excruciating, but he managed to roll his head and eyes in that direction enough to see that the rock masonry of the low kiva wall was the only thing that had saved his life. The wall was crumbled and pressed downward by the weight of the sandstone slab, which lay upon it. He could see no more, and only guess at what must have been done to the kiva and its occupants. Surely the great wall of rock, which had been shaken loose, would have destroyed all of the rooms, and come crashing down into the round room. His family, his mother and father, his uncles, his cousins, the old woman, all must have been crushed. He knew that he had been the intended target of the snake god, and that he had brought this vengeance upon his entire clan. He wondered why he had not also been killed.

Then he heard voices, close by, and his hopes soared. The rock fall had been intended for him, and evidently his family had been spared. Tuwachua had tried to crush him in revenge for the intrusion in the black lands, but had let his family live. He could hear them shouting to one another. Then he saw a shadow outside the small opening of his crevice, and tried to call out to them. At first only a rasping whisper came from his throat, which went unheard. He tried again and it was louder. Why didn't they hear him? He strained again and made a loud croaking sound. The shadow outside stopped moving, then grew larger, and finally he could see a pair of legs in the triangle of light. He croaked again. He could see the figure bending, and then a face appeared in the triangle of light; It was Kolello!

He heard Kolello shout to the others, and then go to meet them. He lay in the semi-darkness, staring up at the sandstone over his eyes. There had been a look of hatred, and perhaps fear, in the eyes of Kolello. He had stared at Paho for a long instant, and in that look Paho sensed the truth. They had not expected to find anyone alive in the devastation, and the fact that he had survived was a fearful surprise.

Soon there was a group outside his crevice, alternately bending and looking at him, then talking softly among themselves. They were all from the main pueblo; none of them his own family. He called to them, and begged them to get him out, but they seemed to not be hearing him. He saw that Malolo had been called and was now bending to look at him. Then they all seemed to leave for some time, before just Malolo and Kolello returned. Then Malolo spoke, in the same deep, resonant voice he had used in the Great Kiva during the initiation ceremonies. It was the voice of doom.

"Tuwachua has spared you. All the rest are dead, but you he has only injured. It is his will that you live, so that you may know the evil you have brought upon your own people. It is therefore the desire of Tuwachua that you not die, so we must fulfill that desire.

"Kolello, go and get men to lift away the stones, and free this thing from the rocks which imprison him. He is protected by the gods and we cannot allow him to die. Let every man know that no one may harm him, but no man shall ever join with him. Wherever he goes, let them know that he carries the curse of Tuwachua."

The day was one of agony, physical and mental. The men brought long poles as levers, and rolled away the largest of the rocks which barred the entrance to his cave. They then crawled inside and tried to drag him out into the daylight. The pain was unimaginable! It shot through his back, and down to his feet. He screamed, in spite of efforts not to. The men paid little attention to his agony, until Melolo warned them not to do something that might kill him. They then were somewhat more careful, but still were callous in their attitude. The distaste they felt in what they were doing was evident. No one of the men would look directly at him, even though he had known all of them since he was a child.

In the heat and the dust, with sandstone fragments filtering down from the rocks over his head, he was extremely thirsty, and continually whispered "water" to the men. They ignored him for some time. It was evident they knew he had brought this disaster upon the people, and were only helping to extract him under the orders of Malolo. Late in the day, however, Malolo came by again, and he heard the men tell Malolo of his pleas for water.

"Give him water, then." Malolo said, again in his deep official voice. "This man is not to be tortured or harmed by our people. We must keep him alive and bring him back to health, as the gods have decreed. He must never be denied food and water, or even shelter, wherever he may go.

"Bring him forth into the sun, but do so carefully. He will then be taken away from the village, that we will not need to see him. Take him away, to the round rooms to the east, and place him in one of the abandoned rooms. There he will stay until the gods tell us what should be done with him."

To the east of the main pueblo, in the midst of the corn fields, were clustered five underground round rooms. They were like the clan kivas, but had no storage or work rooms near them. They were used by the field workers when they were tending the corn, so as to not have to return to the pueblo every evening. It gave them a secure and warm shelter. At this time of year they were not being used regularly, since the young corn, just starting to show its dark green shoots, needed little attention yet. It was to one of these round rooms that Paho was moved. After slowly dragging him out from under the rock fall they lifted him onto a litter, made of a deer hide stretched over two pine poles. The pain was agonizing, but now Paho was resolved to give the men no satisfaction. He held his breath, clenched his teeth, and let no sound escape. He felt as though the rock he had been lying upon, and which had been causing him so much pain was dragged out from under the slab with him. He still had a searing pain under his shoulders. When they lifted him onto the litter and raised him from the ground he realized that it must not be a rock, but his own injury, which he was feeling, since it was still there. Every step they took, jostling him as he was carried, was agony. Three miles, to the round room Malolo had decreed as his shelter, and every step he fought to not scream. When they finally arrived he was bathed in sweat, feverish and dizzy. They placed him on the ground, placed a clay canteen of water near him, threw an old robe over him, and left. The whole day had passed in his release and move, and night was coming again. He fell into a feverish sleep.

When morning came Paho was both hungry and thirsty. He found that he could move his arms now, without very much pain, and pulled the water container toward himself. He had been grudgingly given water a number of times the day before, but still craved more. The men had seemed disgusted with the job of holding the canteen to his lips, and he had felt it a sign of weakness to ask for the water, only doing so when he could stand the thirst no longer. Now he lifted the jug, and drank deeply for the first time. There was no food, and he did not know if he had been abandoned here. He tentatively tried to move, wondering if he would be able to take care of himself, and was greeted with a flash of pain in his back. Abandoning this he concentrated on his legs. He found he had feeling and motion in them both, but that the pain was still great in the left ankle. It felt hot and heavy, and he decided not to try to move it again.

A shadow crossed the opening over his head. Someone was there, approaching the ladder that descended into his dimly lighted shelter. Then a pair of youthful, slim legs began to climb down the ladder. He knew instantly it was Tokchii. She came over to him, carrying a pot full of food.

"They sent me," she said, "To take care of you. No one else in the village wanted the job, and they did not, at first, want me to do it. They blame me, also, for the misfortune, because they suspect that I knew what you were doing. Now, however, they have decided that my punishment will be to bring you your food and take care of you."

"Were all my clan killed?" he asked.

"Yes, the rocks have covered the entire clan settlement. When the shaking came, everyone knew that something was wrong, and that someone would be punished. Melolo and his helpers had already let it be known that a great evil had been done, without saying what it was, and had told the people to search for one who might bring bad times to the people. He had also said that Tuwachua was displeased, and of course everyone knows that Tuwachua controls the vibratory centers of the underworld, so when the shaking began all the people wondered who would be revealed as the evil doer.

"Was there any other harm done, besides my family home?"

"None, although everyone was terrified. But the falling of the stone was heard, and after the shaking stopped, many, including I, went to see what had happened. In the darkness it appeared that no one could have lived. I wandered about much of the night, but saw and heard nothing. I too was sure you had been killed. After discovering the rock slide there were discussions in the Great Kiva until dawn. Malolo sent out the word at sunup that it was now known that you had been the bringer of evil, and had brought destruction and death to all of your clan. Tuwachua had been avenged, and prosperity could come to the people. I think that they were secretly pleased to be rid of you, and it was a great shock to find you had not been killed with the rest.

"It was not until morning that I learned you were still alive. I tried to go immediately, but Malolo had forbidden any but his own men to go. Perhaps he feared that you would reveal to others what you had seen in the black lands. It is only because they think it is a detestable job that I have the work of taking care of you. I tried to pretend that I did not want to do it either, which convinced them to punish me in this way."

She helped him to eat, then, and sat, saying little more. She inspected his ankle, and decided that it was straight, and would heal correctly, given time. She went out, and came back later with smooth pieces of wood which she formed around his lower leg and foot, making a splint which she bound in place with strips of yucca fiber. He was able to move enough for her to look at his back, where he said the pain was so bad. She said nothing, except that he would need to rest and wait for it to heal. He pressed her for information as to what damage he had done, and finally learned that his back seemed to be broken. It was oddly twisted into a hump, between his shoulder blades. When she said this he saw her look away, and sensed the truth from the expression on her face. It was a look of pity, but also, he thought, one of revulsion. He was deformed and crippled!

Chapter Thirteen

The next two months were ones of bitterness and seclusion. No one except Tokchii was allowed to enter the underground room. Often he heard voices outside, and knew that they were the field workers, tending the crops. Evidently they continued to use the other round rooms, but were forbidden to enter his. He would call to them, but never got a response.

Tokchii came every day, often twice a day, bringing him food and water. When she could, she would stay with him. talking softly to him, holding his hand, helping him to move on the mats she had gotten for him to lie on. She would tell him of the happenings in the village. It was, indeed, beginning to look like a prosperous year. The crops were developing well; there had been occasional rains, which had returned the greenness to the land. Melolo was being credited with this, and he continually warned the people that the treachery of Paho and his people had been the cause of the drought of the prior year. He had turned the earthquake and rockslide into a sign for the people, that they must never doubt the power of the Snake gods, nor consider a member of another clan as a potential leader, as they had with Paho.

His ankle healed slowly. The splint had to be loosened and retied often, and each time he did this he tried to gently move it. The pain was still there, but he evidently had control and motion, so that he would be able, later, to walk on it. His back was already much better, but he now had a permanent bent position, and he was never without pain from the injury. Within days, however, he had been able to move himself about on the bed, trying to find a more comfortable way to deal with the constant hurt from between his shoulders.

He had a great deal of time to think, as he recuperated. There was little doubt in his mind that Melolo was right; he had been singled out and punished by Tuwachua. The fact that he had not been killed, but only crippled could only be a further curse. He also knew, however, that Melolo and his followers had welcomed the event as a way of consolidating their position. There could be no future for him, now, in this place; he must move away as soon as he was strong enough. He would ask Tokchii to go with him, and they would find a life in some other part of the vast empire that the leaders at the canyon controlled. They were only in their early teens, but were fully versed in the ways of survival. Surely the stigma could be escaped. They would go where no one had ever heard of his dishonor.

He was reluctant to discuss his plans with Tokchii. He had sensed her revulsion when she first saw his humped back, and wondered if she would still be willing to share her life with him, now that he was both a cripple and a pariah. However, he could see that she did more than just the bidding of Melolo when she came to care for him. Her tenderness and concern were far different than the callousness of the villagers who had moved him from the rock fall. She told him of all the village gossip and events, and tried to find out anything she could as to what Melolo and his followers intended for him.

When he became better she would stay with him for hours, nestled close to him as she had before the earthquake. The love of the night of the manhood ceremony had been a love of children, first tasting the pleasures of adults. The love between them now seemed to be different. It had been touched with adversity, and had matured into a deeper, and somehow sadder love. They both knew the love was there, but were afraid to talk of it. He, because he feared a rejection, she because she feared his anger and frustration after the disaster would lead him to push her away. She sensed a self-pity within him that was becoming an anger; a directionless hatred toward the events which had killed his family and crippled him. In one brief instant he had lost his home, his family, his future. There was not even anyone remaining of this branch of the Eagle clan with whom he could ally himself. She could understand and sympathize with this, but his burning hatred, with nothing to hate, she found fearful. She felt it often shutting her out; his long hours of brooding creating a barrier between them.

Tokchii had, indeed, been shocked to see the hunched and twisted back, on that first day, and had recoiled from it, as he had observed. But it had not been a look of revulsion, as he imagined, but one of compassion. This young man, whom she loved, had been suddenly twisted and broken. It aroused in her a need to care for him, which had led to her efforts to be given to job of taking his food to him. Had he asked she would have gladly gone with him, even though it would mean abandoning the only home she had ever known, and renouncing her position in the clan of the Corn. But he did not ask, and she did not suggest such a thing.

After the first two weeks, Paho had tried gingerly to get to his feet. He found that he could do so if he was careful not to try to use the injured ankle. He asked Tokchii to bring him a forked stick, which he could use as a crutch, and with this he was soon able to hobble about the kiva. As time progressed he gained strength, and mobility. His ankle, he knew was mending, but he made no effort to use it yet.

One day, after he had been there nearly a month, he heard voices, as he had many times before, and decided to make his way to the ladder, to see if he could see whom it was. He painfully made his way to the center of the round room and the foot of the ladder. It was near noon, and the sunshine streamed down from overhead, casting a bright patch on the floor. As he stood at the foot of the ladder, clinging to it for support, he looked down and behind him, and saw, cast on the floor, his own shadow! It was a picture of a deformed and misshapen body, curled over beneath the protruding mass, which had once been a back. He turned and slowly made his way back to his bed near the wall.

It was a long time, then, before he again moved about in the daytime. When Tokchii was there he was content to lie on his bed, or sit wrapped in a blanket, so that his form was hidden. Only in the night, when no one could see him, did he exercise his long unused muscles, building his strength. He found that he was now able to move about much more easily, using the crutch, but balancing with a small part of his weight on the injured left ankle. Tokchii continued to believe that he was unable to do more than hobble about occasionally, since he would not let her see him walking, and feigned more weakness than was true.

Then came the night that he was moving about the kiva, and climbing slowly up the ladder to strengthen his legs, when he heard someone coming. Knowing that no one was allowed to enter his hiding place, he worked his was up the ladder until he could see across the mesa toward the pueblo. Someone was indeed coming, directly toward him, walking quietly but not trying to hide. His first thought was one of fear. Perhaps someone had been sent to dispose of him, or perhaps Melolo or Kolello had decided independently that he was too much of a threat. Then he saw that it was a smaller person, a woman; and then saw that it was Tokchii.

She saw that he was not on his bed, but up and around, but made no comment. It was the first time she had come in the nighttime. She silently slipped down the ancient ladder to where he now stood, and took both his hands. She led him back to the darker recess of his shelter and made him sit down.

"They do not know I am here," She whispered. "There is little time. I have heard bad things and have come to warn you. There have been meetings in the Great Kiva the last three nights, and loud voices have been heard from time to time. I have tried to hear what the gossip is among the women, as they grind the corn. They say that the people fear having you here, since the gods may be displeased, and bring misfortune. Melolo still says that you may not be harmed, but no longer wants to keep you here. Some of the others, from other clans have been saying that you should be killed, but Melolo warns that this would displease the snake gods."

"I must know what they decide." he said. "If the others have their way, I must leave here. As you saw, I have regained much strength, and can now walk on the broken ankle. Do they believe I am still unable to move?"

"I have told them little, but, when asked by the elders, have said that you spend all day on your bed. But, there is more. Tonight I crept near the Great Kiva, and could hear the voices within. The chiefs of the other clans were seemingly prevailing over Melolo. I could not hear very much, but it seemed that they were doing most of the talking, and that Melolo was defending his actions. I fear that they will win, and you will be killed."

"Tomorrow night come again as you have tonight, but bring food and water and clothing." He whispered. "Will you go with me?"

He wondered if she paused, but then she answered. "I will go where you go. I feared you would not ask me. I thought that you might not want me, and would go without me if I told you this. I will hurt my family in doing so, but my place is with you.

"I fear that they may have their way and want to kill you soon. Go tonight to the cave where we met as children, and wait for me there. I will gather what is needed and then go there tomorrow night. Can you walk that far?"

"Yes, I have strengthened the muscles and am now healed enough to walk as far as necessary. But think carefully on what you do. Your clan will never accept you again if you choose to go with me. I am despised by all people, and now also a cripple. If you decide to travel with me it will be very difficult. You will not be well fed and clothed as you are now. We will need to go so far that no one will know of my dishonor. Do you think you can do this?"

"Yes," she said, "I am prepared to do these things. I will go to the cave tomorrow evening, and we will start away. Wait for me there."

"Think carefully on what I have said," He replied. "I will wait at the cave, but if you do not come, I will understand. On the next night, if you have not come I will know that you have decided that my life is not your life, and will go alone."

"That will not happen," she said, bringing her body close to his. They fell back upon the robes, which were his bed and loved one another as they had not done since the earthquake.

In the night he awoke once and realized she was awake beside him. Her arms were still around him, and he felt that her hands were slowly passing over the massive hump on his back. He thought, then that he felt her shudder; and in that shudder he suddenly realized what he was asking of her. He could not, he knew then, destroy the future of this delicate and beautiful young girl. If she were to go with him it would only hurt her, and he, a cripple and a pariah, could not do that. She was still so young, he thought, that she could not realize the enormity of the decision she was making.

Before first light they rose together, saying little, each in his own thoughts. They climbed out of the kiva and walked slowly toward the village. When they came near to the gap in the sandstone, and the crushed remains of his clan home they embraced for a long time, and then parted, promising to meet the next evening at the secret cave where they had played as children.

The following evening Tokchii waited until everyone was asleep and stole slowly out of her clan kiva. She had gathered and hidden supplies during the day, which she now retrieved, and made her way silently to the cave where they had promised to meet. She entered the cave quietly and whispered his name. No answer. He had not been to the cave.

Chapter Fourteen

So it was that Kokopelli came to the canyon. We three boys gathered about him, wondering what to do. He looked very old, with his drawn face and tattered clothing, and to young boys he certainly seemed old. In actuality, he was still a young man, although some years had passed since he had run from the village to the south.

His hair was long, and had not been cut from over his eyes, as was the custom, so it draped over his face as well as his shoulders. The broad cheeks and high forehead were dusty and grey, over his dark skin, as though he had been many days wandering, wiping the sweat with grimy hands.

He stirred, then and looked up at us. "What are you staring at? Help me to get back to my feet, and take me to your village." he ordered. "I need food and water, and a place to sleep. Do you have water with you? Give me some, and I will be able to go on."

There was authority in his voice. He expected to be obeyed, and we did so immediately. He gulped the water, then let us lift him to his feet. I walked ahead of him, leading the way, and the other two followed behind. He hobbled along quite rapidly now limping on his left foot, and bowed by his deformity. As we went he asked questions about our homes and our people. He wanted to know which of the cities in the canyon we came from, and which clans resided there. He wanted to know the names of all the leaders, and especially he wanted to know who were the strongest and weakest. He asked questions we had not ourselves considered, and when considering them realized more about our own people.

We were all three of the same massive warren of rooms, constituting one of the great stone cities, which were spotted up and down the canyon floor, and even on the cliff tops which overlooked the canyon. Ours was in the south, near the fields we had been setting snares by. It was the oldest cluster of rooms in the canyon, having started as a block of just twelve square rooms and one round room, when our people first started to raise crops along the sides of the streambed. Our ancestors had built on the side and crest of a small knoll with their backs to the north wind and their faces to the warming winter sun and the towering butte that dominated the valley. Their round room was sunken into the earth, protected by the storage and workrooms that rose to two stories between them and the cold of the north. In stages, over the next two hundred years, the rooms had been added to, until now it was the home for almost one hundred people, belonging to four different clans. The rooms used for storage and work numbered almost one hundred and fifty, and were clustered three or four rooms deep and as much as three stories high in some parts of the pueblo. We even had our own Great Kiva.

As we approached the outer wall, and skirted to the right, to the single entryway into the plaza, we were spotted by the old man who liked to sit in the evening sun outside the wall. He hurried into the enclosure and shouted the word to the people that a stranger was approaching, and by the time we got there a large group had gathered in the plaza, near the Great Kiva. There were many women and children surging forward to see, while in the back, showing little emotion and saying nothing were the men. There was a gasp from many of the children, however, as they saw the strange form and even stranger look of our visitor. A path immediately opened for us, as we, the discoverers, proudly prepared to exhibit our prize.

"Who is chief here?" The stranger suddenly said in a loud voice, so that all could hear. It was not the question of a man who had just been rescued by three small boys, and needed help. It was the voice of a man who was in the habit of being obeyed; who was completely in control of his situation. We three quickly stepped away, and sought the security of our people, being happy to blend into the crowd. He glared now at the people, walking through the crowd of children and women, who scattered before him, and approaching the senior men who stood near the side of the Great Kiva.

"You are the leader of the pueblo?" He asked, approaching Setuana, who was, in fact, the head of the Badger Clan, and the most important man in our city. He had known this, we boys knew, from the answers we had given him on the walk down the valley. "I have come a long way, and need food and rest. Then we will talk. Those three boys who brought me in did well. They gave me water and helped me to walk. I will have them take care of me, and when I have rested there are things which I can tell you which will be of great importance. I have traveled far, in many strange lands, and know things that can bring prosperity to you and your people. "

Setuana now spoke, looking at this curious person. "We are a hospitable people, and give food and shelter to any who come in need. You do not need to demand these things here, nor to promise riches and power, but merely to ask. I will, however, do as you suggest, and ask these boys to see to your needs, since they have, in bringing you here, already made themselves responsible for your survival. Later, after you have rested we will be pleased to listen to what you have to say."

All the people heard this, and were proud of their leader. He was very old, and his deep lined face was one of patience and wisdom. His eyes were still sharp, however, and his manner remained one of dignity. Even in the presence of one who so resembled a god, Kokopelli, he would not be intimidated. He beckoned the three of us forward, and told us to take the stranger to our own clan kiva and see to his needs.

Our clan's home was in the new plaza, near the corner where the two sides of the L shaped series of rooms met. It was lower than the two other round rooms to the west of it, which were raised above the plaza level and built within square outer walls. Ours had no outer walls, but was only a round room, set into the plaza so that just its top showed. Even without having to accommodate this unusual guest, the room was usually crowded. It was the center of most clan activity, and a refuge from the extremes of the weather in both winter and summer. It was only work which pertained to food that could never be done in this room. In the winter there would sometimes be a fire lighted in the centrally located hearth, throwing its light and warmth to all parts of the circle. In summer the cool earth and stones kept out the searing heat of the sun.

On this day the sun had beat down upon the pueblo, heating the sand and rocks, and pressing down upon the land. The bushes along the streambed were grey with dust, and the sand at the bottom was crusted and hard looking. Even where the sand had been dug away so that a pool of water could form there was only a brownish crust of damper looking mud. That was to be expected at this time of year. There was drinking water stored in pots, and soon the thunderstorms would come. But on this day the storms had not yet started, and in fact, very few clouds had even been seen to gather over the mountains. Gusts of hot wind occasionally swirled up the canyon, picking up dust and weeds, whirling them for an instant, and dropping them back onto the sand.

It was stuffy and close in the round room, as we led the way down the ladder. Most of the clan was gathered there, curious to learn more about the stranger. We took him to a place near the bench, away from the ladder, and laid down deerskin robes for him to lie upon. He had already received food from the women in the plaza, who were cooking over a small fire in front of one of the rooms. He had rapidly eaten a great deal of the stew, which was made of cornmeal and beans, with some rabbit meat added. Then he had turned away, still saying nothing to the women, and told us that he wished to rest. He lay down upon the robes and was quickly asleep.

For many days after this he lived in our city. He said little to the people, and walked long distances up and down the valley. Wherever he went the people make room for him, seeing again the Kokopelli of the legends. It had been expected that he would make some explanation to Setuana, as he had said he would do, yet he did little except eat and sleep, and wander by himself. Our rules of hospitality would never have denied him food, as long as there was any, but his attitude was a demanding one. He did not just take our food and shelter, he expected it, and showed no gratitude when it was given. We three boys had been ordered by Setuana to care for him, and he made much use of us.

"Tell me," he said one morning, "Who is the most powerful man in the canyon?"

He had asked this question many times before, and each time we had given the same answer, as we did now. "The chief of the Water clan who resides in the largest pueblo. His is the round room which is almost as large as a Great Kiva. His rooms are filled with corn and beans and also with trade goods. His messengers go to all parts of the empire and bring back precious stones and shells. He has many men who work for him, building more rooms and filling them with his fortune, He is so rich and powerful that he has great stacks of firewood, and can have heat in his round room whenever he wishes. His name is Hopaqa, and he is surely the most powerful man in the valley."

This seemed to make him happy. He smiled at us and nodded his head, as he had before when we had told him of this man. Then he looked up at us and almost shouted, "Take me to him! Now!"

The early morning sun was just starting to heat the canyon as we began to lead him to the north, toward the largest of all the settlements. The dazzling brightness slanted through the gap to the south of our village and lighted the top of the great butte, which dominated the area. The sandstone peak's brightness above the valley floor, and its height made it seem to float over the dusty plain on which it sat. This massive pinnacle rose from the center of the valley, at its south end, a yellow mass of rock, visible for many miles in every direction. Our pueblo had been situated in such a way that the butte was directly before our eyes, lighted from the left in the morning and the right in the evening. In wintertime its noontime shadow cast by the low cold sun pointed directly at our homes.

The butte was sacred to our people. Its steep inclined slopes led upward to a vertical rock wall, then another steep incline to another cliff face, topped finally by a dome of sandstone, an almost insurmountable pinnacle which was higher then the walls of the canyon itself, and rose alone from the valley floor. No one except the priests were allowed to climb this peak. They went there to determine the times for planting and for festivals and for harvesting. They spent many days in their retreat, high above the settlements below, studying the stars and the sun. It was said that the peak was the home of monstrous animals that would devour any person other than a priest who might try to climb up its steep cliffs.

The early morning sun was not yet hot, but the air felt heavy as it anticipated the warming, which would soon come. The dry dustiness under our feet cushioned our quiet steps as we led the way northward, away from the sacred butte and toward the home of the powerful chieftain, Hopaqa. We were fearful of this man, who lived in seclusion in the central pueblo. He was always surrounded by many large and silent men, who were quick to do whatever he commanded. Not only was he rich, but he was the clan leader of the strongest clan in the valley, the water clan. This meant that the priests all were appointed by him, and answered to him. In addition, the very essence of our survival, the water which brought crops and which slacked our thirst, was under his control. When the rains came and the sudden torrents cascaded over the lips of rock, and into our canyon it was he and his men who decided what ditches would receive the precious bounty. In the late summer, when the streambed was not even damp, he said who could carry jugs of water from the sinkhole where a small amount of water was to be found. In the winter months he and his men supervised the building of dams and channels to control the spring runoff, which was to come. The check dams on the mesa tops were placed where he dictated, that seeps and springs at the valley floor would be fed.

In our village Setuana was the most important man, but this importance was small compared to the influence held by Hopaqa. Kokopelli had seen this, and had therefore decided to sidestep the meeting with Setuana, which he had proposed upon his arrival, and went instead to Hopaqa, the true source of power in the valley. He had used our hospitality and never acknowledged his debt, and then had withheld that which he had promised; the valuable information he claimed to bring with him. Keeping it from those people who had helped him. He saw that his advantage lay with Hopaqa, if he could reach him.

The sun had risen over the edge of the canyon by the time we reached the village of Hopaqa, and its light spread across the valley floor. The interlocking rectangular fields were on both sides of us, with their maze of water channels. At places rock slabs were placed in the ditches to divert the flow into chosen fields, should a sudden rainstorm on the mesa above send a brief torrent down this irrigation ditch.

In the fields the corn was now as high as a man's knee and packed into tightly spaced hills. It would be many weeks before it would be ready for harvesting, however, and on this crop rested the well being of the entire region. The numbers of our people had continued to grow over the years, until now it was barely possible to derive enough food from these fields to meagerly feed them all. As it was, much food was brought in from the outlying pueblos, as tribute to the priests and leaders, and as payment for the services the central canyon provided for them.

Should this crop fail, the people would need more food, and would demand it from the richer lands, which surrounded them in all directions. One would have thought that in really extreme conditions the storerooms could be breached, with the hoarded grain from the good years and from the outlying regions. But this was not the grain of our canyon, it was the grain stored there by the people from other parts of the empire. The canyon was, in fact, the central storage area for the people. From all parts of the empire bags of corn and beans were brought, in the good years, to the canyon, where they were held in safekeeping. In the bad years when the outlying pueblos needed food they would come and withdraw food from their stored supplies. It was a trust that could not be breached.

It was men like Hopaqa who controlled that storage, and earned that trust. Theirs were the expert stonemasons who built the carefully sealed rooms. Theirs were the messengers who told the people the exact days when certain crops could be planted, theirs were the tree cutters who provided the wooden beams for the interlocking maze of storage rooms. The roadways which were so important in transporting the grain and logs and which carried their runners to all parts of the empire were built by their men, under their direction, with the holy guidance from their priests.

And among these few powerful men Hopaqa was the most powerful. And it was to see this man that we now took our strange, enigmatic guest.

CHAPTER FIFTEEN

"So, you have now decided it is time to see me!"

"Yes, I have come to tell you of many things. They tell me, Hopaqa, that you are the most powerful man in the canyon, and therefore in the entire empire of the people. I can help you to become even more powerful than you already are. I can show you things which no other person knows."

"I have known, crippled one, of your presence in my valley for many days. My men tell me of your walks up and down the canyon, staring at each village. They tell me of the fear which accompanies you, with the children hiding when you draw near. I am told also that Setuana had fed and cared for you in his pueblo, and that you have done little to repay this kindness. Why now do you come to me?"

He looked intently at Kokopelli as he said this. We boys were still with him, but had moved back away from the men and stood in the shade of the wall that divided the pueblo down the middle. He had been taken into the presence of Hopaqa, but not into the kiva, only outside, in the presence of many people, even children and women. They stood in the main plaza of the large stone city which was Hopaqa's home, and faced one another. Hopaqa looked with disdain at our guest, not asking him to enter the kiva, nor even to sit.

Kokopelli answered. "I have come many miles, from the lands far to the south, where the parrots fill the sky, where food hangs from the trees and where the water runs in great rivers. I have seen many things that our people have never known about, and have brought this knowledge with me. If we may talk in private I can tell you of these things."

"No! Go back to Setuana if he will still shelter you. The story of your clan home to the south reached us years ago. It is only because the gods decided that you should live that we have permitted you to wander amongst our people. There is nothing you can tell me which could be of value. Your humped back and downcast eyes tell us who you are, and your dishonor precedes you wherever you may go."

"Hopaqa," he then answered, "I will go, as you demand, and will serve Setuana in payment for that which he has provided, but do not forget what I have said. It is true that I am the same one who was of the Eagle clan, and whose entire family was destroyed by the gods, now three years ago. I have wandered far and seen many strange things. The gods punished me and continue to punish me, as I carry this burden on my shoulders and limp on this twisted foot. But the very gods who punish me have also opened my eyes and have let me see things which are great and strange. Through the opening at the top of my head they have also entered with their knowledge. I have lain for many nights far from the homes of our people, and seen the skies and learned of their changing ways. In the heat of the sun I have wandered the deserts where no man lives, and watched the ways of the heavens. When no man would have me as a friend I became friends with the birds of the mountains and the animals of the forests.

"A sign will come to you, in just three days time." He now continued in a loud and deep voice. He spoke slowly, that all would hear his words clearly, and in the silence of the plaza they seemed to echo back from the arc of rooms which surrounded us. "Watch for this sign which will tell you that the gods have given me great knowledge. I will return to the village where they have cared for me, and your messenger may reach me there if you so wish."

He turned abruptly, beckoned to us to come with him, and walked away, leaving the people staring after him. No one would ever leave the presence of one as important as Hopaqa without permission, and without backing away while facing him. It was only his twisted form, his resemblance to Kokopelli, which kept the people from falling on him. He hobbled slowly through the gate at the south side of the plaza and continued away without looking back.

We boys now followed well behind him as he returned to our home pueblo. We did not wish to have the people see us with him. He had insulted the leader of all our people. When we finally arrived there the sun had risen high into the cloudless sky, and beat down upon us. The dust, which was disturbed by our walking, seemed to hover a few inches above the ground, unstirred by even the slightest breeze. The people of the pueblo were finding shade wherever possible, as they went about their usual chores. The women who were grinding corn were kneeling at rows of grinding stones, shoulder to shoulder so that they could gossip and joke as they did the work. Children who had been assigned to feeding and tending the turkeys were trying to stay in the shade as much as possible as they brushed out the pens, using bundles of twigs as brooms. Men who were weaving cloth were doing so in the seclusion of the round rooms, where the coolness of the earth around them and over them more than made up for the closeness of the atmosphere and the darkness which made it difficult to follow the pattern in their fabric.

Kokopelli, as he was now called by everybody, entered this scene in a much different manner than he had done only a few weeks before. The people paid little attention to him, other than to quickly look away if he approached them. His godly deformity still brought about an instinctive fear, but it now was expressed as repulsion. The people did not want contact or involvement with this stranger who used their hospitality but gave nothing in return. Such selfishness was the nature of Gods, also, but in their case the people were impelled to respect the Gods, and show that respect, in order to receive favors, or at least avoid retribution. With Kokopelli they felt only a need to avoid this demi-god in order to avert harm.

He now walked more upright than we had ever seen him before, and limped less as he seemed almost to march into the enclosure of the walled plaza. Straight across, in the heavy brightness of the sunlight, to the largest round room, at the northwestern corner of the plaza, he moved, never looking to left or right. The people sensed the change, and looked up from their work, following the stranger as he strode through the dust of the plaza. The other two boys who had been with me now dropped back and joined members of their family, wishing not to be associated with the strange man who acted in such a peculiar manner. I, however, could not now stop, but followed him, filled with curiosity. I slipped into the narrow band of shade cast by the wall to my left, and sat waiting and listening, as he respectfully asked and received permission to enter the kiva of Setuana.

"Setuana," he said, going directly to the point, "I have been to meet with Hopaqa. He has told me I am to return to your pueblo until a sign is given that I am to serve him rather than you. When that sign comes, and it will come in three days time, he will send for me that I may serve him. Until then I am to do as you wish and serve you in any way I can."

"Why, then did you not come to me first, as you had said you would do on the evening of your arrival? These people who now surround us in this kiva are my people. We have extended our hospitality to you, only to have you go to Hopaqa to try to gain his favor."

"What you say, Setuana, is correct. I was wrong in not speaking to you first, but the knowledge I bring will be to your advantage. It is through you that I bring these things to Hopaqa, and I will not forget your kindness. When I go to Hopaqa I will be in a position of influence, and will repay your people for their kindness."

"I know nothing of the knowledge you claim to bring with you, and the influence you believe you will have with Hopaqa remains to be seen. You have now removed our obligation to provide for your well being. Your gratitude and your promises come too late. We have all known, since long before your arrival, of your dishonor to the south many years ago, but we also know that your form is a sign from the gods that you are to be cared for by the people, lest you might die and rob them of their continuing vengeance.

"You may stay in our midst, if you so desire, but you will receive no special favors from anyone. Our food will be made available, so that you cannot starve, but the coolest part of the kiva or the best pieces of meat will no longer be yours. A sign, if it comes will only tell me that the gods have not forgotten you, and wish us to continue to keep you alive for their pleasure. So we were told many years ago when the story of the destruction of your clan reached us. No longer will you have those three boys to do your bidding. They will return to their families where they belong"

From my listening post above I could hear the murmurs of approval from the people in the round room below. Then I sensed a change of attitude, as Kokopelli spoke again. The assurance and arrogance had left his voice, and he said in a softer voice, "When I came here, Setuana, I was close to death from lack of water. I had been wandering for many days, without finding help. Those three boys saved my life. Is it not your custom that a person who saves a life must then assume the responsibility of preserving that which he has snatched away from the gods? Certainly that is what my people to the south believed. I do not need the help of all three boys, but it is plain that without some help, being a cripple as I am, the gods could lose the object of their wrath. If you are the one to take that away from them they may transfer their wrath to you and your people. Therefore, let me have but one of the three, that he may see to it that I continue to live."

"Which of the three, would you then suggest? It does not appear that any of them wishes to be further associated with you, since you walked back alone from the village of Hopaqa."

"There is one, but I know not which, who has not abandoned me. If you will look outside this kiva, right now, you will see him listening to every word we say. I have seen his shadow cross the entryway twice while we have talked. He has wanted to be close enough to know what it is you plan for me. Give me this boy!"

There was no time to run, and I was quickly seized and taken into the kiva, in front of Setuana. In the semi-darkness I could see little, having been in the brightness of the plaza just seconds before, but I could make out forms around the walls. They were not just men, but many other members of Setuana's clan who had happened to be in the kiva when Kokopelli arrived. Some were relatives of mine who had moved to this room when they had married into Setuana's clan. Others were children of my own age who had grown up with me. The boys had the same thoughts and ambitions as I, to be called to the Great Kiva and become leaders of the pueblo. None would have wanted to be committed to slavery to this strange creature.

Setuana spoke. "You have heard what is said. I will not force you to serve this man. What he says is true, that you are now responsible for the life you saved, even though you are only a boy. However, your youth can be an excuse for not being bound by that obligation as an adult might be. If you acted as a man in saving him then you must act as a man now. If you three were only playing a children's game which happened to save him then you are still children and the rules are not the same. You may reject the obligation."

The hunchback spoke then, his eyes looking directly into mine, and unblinking. "I will not have this boy unless he is ready to act as a man. If he follows me he will have hardships but he will gain rewards. I can offer him more than a place in the clan kiva, I can offer him the power and knowledge I have gathered in my travels to places no others could enter. The tribes to the south would have killed any person from our villages if he had not so resembled their god, who is also our god, the humpbacked flute player we call Kokopelli. I am not that god. I was a boy, not unlike this one, who dreamed of leading my people. I was called to the Great Kiva, and I passed the tests. I excelled in the hunt, and I helped feed our people. I was once as straight and healthy as he is now. If he will join with me he may do the things I never was allowed to do , because I insulted one of the gods."

I wanted to run and go back to my family; to be a child still, and wait for the call to the Great Kiva when it should come. I did not want to be a slave to this strange man. He had lied to Setuana about his conversation with Hopaqa, and had no qualms about using and misleading the very people who had sheltered him. I did not know what the great dishonor had been, which the older people had evidently all known about, but it only confirmed my feeling that this man was evil. Yet I knew what Setuana said was true. I could be a man and accept that responsibility or be a child and return to my family. This stranger with his talk of strange lands to the south and promises of power and knowledge had little appeal. I was ready to choose for my family and my childhood, but somehow didn't. I stood and heard myself saying to these assembled people that I would help to keep Kokopelli alive. Had I made a different choice maybe the story I am telling you would have ended differently. As it is, I was there and saw the events as they happened. From that day onward I went wherever Kokopelli went, and learned all he had to tell.

"Come, then!" he said. "Setuana, I thank you for your hospitality. I will not forget these things you have done for me. I will stay in your pueblo and await the call from Hopaqa, and will be here if you wish me to do anything for you. I will treat this boy well, and teach him all the things that I have learned. We will go now."

CHAPTER SIXTEEN

Kokopelli took little time in teaching me what he expected. Before, when all had been readily available to him through the kindness of our people we boys had done little except follow him around, answer his questions, get him his food and make a place for him to sleep. Now he was an outcast, only grudgingly given meager amounts of food, and not welcomed in the round rooms of the clans. He taught me to demand food from a number of different groups, so that we would have enough to eat. He explained the fear that they had of him and taught me how to use this in thinly disguised threats. He had no compunction about using his deformity and his resemblance to the God Kokopelli, if it would help him to survive.

We now slept in an empty storeroom at the front of the pueblo. It had once been used for building materials when the front wall was being built, and there was still a pile of adobe clay in one corner. We chose it from among the empty storerooms because it was far from the rooms which contained grain. There was little reason for the mice to prowl through this room, as it had never been used for food. Nevertheless, we found a large flat rock of layered sandstone which fitted exactly in the doorway, blocking the lower third of the entrance, and discouraging the entrance of the vermin while we were sleeping.

It was in those few days that I was able to finally learn a little bit about him. We spoke for many hours about his background, and he told me the story of his childhood, and his eventual flight from his home to the south. As he told it, it was a sad and pitiful story, not the story of dishonor that our people alluded to. I saw in myself all of the youthful desires which must have led him. As he explained it I could well understand, and knew that I would have acted in the same impetuous way. We talked of the family he had lost and of the love he still had for Tokchii. He was speaking more for himself than for me as he told me these things.

Then he told me of his travels. When he left his home village he had gone to the south, out of the lands of our people. He had been told many times that the people in the south would kill strangers who wandered into their territory, still he went, perhaps not caring if they did kill him. However, his humped back was regarded by these people as a sign that he was a demi-god, and they fed and cared for him rather than harming him. Wherever he went the people seemed to have legends about the hunchbacked flute player, and feared that he was that god or his representative. He, therefore fashioned himself a flute, as he had learned as a child, as we all did as children, and carried it with him. When he approached a settlement, or met strangers on the road he would play his flute, strengthening the impression of Kokopelli, and protecting himself from harm.

In this way he had gone from place to place, always working his way further to the south. He soon learned how to get food and shelter by making pronouncements and predictions. If they wanted to be visited by a god, he would give them what they wanted. He told me that he often would tell the people that they would be receiving good luck because of his visit, and they would look for that good luck. The next good thing that happened would be credited to him and to his power, thereby fortifying the legend which was traveling with him, preceding him often, as he shuffled slowly on his injured foot.

Sometimes he would predict harmful events rather than good ones, and the people would look for those. In the same manner, the next time that a man fell from the cliff top, or the next time a spring went dry his prediction would come to mind, and the people would know that a god had been in their midst. Occasionally he would instead merely tell the people to watch for a sign, which would show his power. He knew that there were many things, which no one could explain, and were therefore attributed to the gods. Any such happening, such as a whirling wind that destroyed crops or a plague that made many people ill would be the sign he had predicted.   For a people who watched the skies they worked under and slept under, the stars and the sun and moon were familiar and predictable friends. The most powerful signs were any events that disturbed the rhythm and regularity of those sky people.

It had even happened that the moon had once been eclipsed after he had warned a village of his power, and the event had been credited to him.   It was a sign that did much to enhance his power wherever he went, as the story was told from person to person.

He never said so, but I often have wondered if his prediction of a strange sign, which he had told to Hopaqa had been the same sort of ploy. If so it had been a desperate gamble to gain the chief's attention, since he had predicted not only an event, but placed a three-day time limit on it.   It was a wild and arrogant move, which had certainly angered Hopaqa, and had, in the process, lost him his status in the village of Setuana.

My new master went on to tell me of the things he had seen to the south. He had wandered for three years among these people, always well fed and housed, and allowed to go where he wished. No other of our people had ever done this, so that all we knew of these people came from the traders, which they sometimes sent to our villages. He had seen the way in which the people built their cities of mud instead of rock, and how they brought water to their crops. He had seen the way in which they made and decorated their pottery, and how they fired it to achieve colors and glazes quite different than those made by our people.

There was a feeling of expectancy in the village in the days that followed. Many people had heard Kokopelli's bold prediction to Hopaqa, and the news had wasted little time in getting back to our pueblo. It soon became a joke, in that any event, no matter how trivial elicited an almost immediate declaration that the stranger's sign had occurred. This was invariably followed by a good deal of laughter.   Underlying the ridicule, however, was a feeling of fear. They joked outwardly, but they wondered inwardly if he could bring about a miracle. Therefore, when he was close by the laughter quickly disappeared. Such was not my treatment, however. The people saw my willingness to serve him as a sign that I was trying to advance myself over them, and they took any opportunity to ridicule my master when I was nearby. I was given the name of "Little Kokopelli" almost immediately, and it followed me wherever I went.

The first day after his pronouncement the people watched anxiously for a sign of his power, but nothing happened. The summer rain cloud gathered over the mountains to the west, and seemed to move toward us, but never got to the valley, and the ground stayed as dry as it had been. That was to be expected, however. Everyone knew that the summer thunderstorms were not yet due, and that they would first try to reach us, day after day, before they finally arrived. The crops were dusty and brown looking in the fields near the center of the valley, but they were slowly growing, as they awaited the rain. They did not wither and die when he passed by. No gigantic walls of rock toppled into the valley from the clifftops to tell us that this man had the power to move the earth; no bears wandered into the valley, carrying a message of his power; no great bird swooped down from the sky to fulfill his prophesy.

The second day was no different than the first, and the people started to find more humor and less fear in the prophecy. The rain clouds came nearer, but still did not reach us, but they sent gusts of wind, which picked up the sand and drove it against our bodies as we stood and watched the sky. Lightning flashed repeatedly in the clouds, and we heard the distant rumble of thunder, as the air cooled slightly, but still no rain fell. The weather had changed to the extent that the nights were not becoming cool as was usual, but stayed hot, and the threatening rain clouds lent a heaviness to the atmosphere which seemed to hold down the day's heat and press it into every corner of the valley. Sleep would not have been as difficult in the round rooms cooled by the surrounding earth, but our storeroom in which we slept seemed to continue to hold all the heat of the day, and we slept but little.

The third day was like the others. The people now sensed their triumph over this man who tried to be a God. His prediction had not come true, and was not apparently going to. As the day drew to a close one could sense lightness in the people, as though someone had lifted a burden from their backs. They could go about their lives now without wondering if a disaster was about to befall them. In the sultry heat at the end of the day they sat and watched the sky to the west, where the clouds hovered over the Chuska Mountains, showing distant flashes of lightning. We sat apart, Kokopelli and I, and he was quiet, looking also to the west. Then he began to tell me of the wonders he had seen in the south, in the place where parrots were everywhere. He told stories of places where great wide rivers of clear water continued all year long, fed by abundant rain; places where massive trees crowded together and obscured the sun. It was a story beyond belief, being told in a land where even the best streams were almost dry at some times of the year; where rain was rare and precious; where trees grew to great heights only in the mountains. He told of a city on an island, surrounded by water, larger than any of our cities, in which the people lived in splendor, adorned by the most beautiful of feathers, the finest stones, the most ornate fabrics. He spoke of stone pyramids built to their gods, towers many times higher than even the great wall of the pueblo of Hopaqa. It was a story which went on for many hours. In the oppressive heat of the night, with no breeze stirring, looking at the clouds slowly building to the west, we journeyed, through his words, to places that our people had never visited.

It was near morning when the crescent moon finally arose over our left shoulders, and we turned to look at it. It had been waning for many days now, and was only slightly more than a thin line of moonlight. In two more days it would be completely gone. We watched it slowly appear over the lip of the mesa, casting a weak glow over the valley, and dimly lighting the towering butte of the star watchers to the south of us. They too would be seeing this moon, we knew, as they studied the heavens from their high outpost. Every evening they could be seen, appearing as tiny dots against the yellow sandstone as they scaled the butte, and went to the narrow ledge where they spent each night, studying the movement of the stars and planets.

We sat, then, looking at the sky to the east, dimly illuminated by the dying moon, as it climbed higher into the sky, a sky soon to be lit by the rising sun. Behind the moon, chasing it across the sky, rose the four stars which we were familiar with, in the shape of a square, the moon not bright enough to wash out their light. Suddenly, in the midst of these stars, well above the horizon now, a new light appeared! First there was nothing there, and then a star burst into existance, a new star we had never seen before, created before our eyes. In only a few minutes it was as bright as the white star, which lay to the north, which never moved like the others. Minutes later it was far brighter, as bright as the planet, which came often in the evening. As we watched it brightened even more, until it was many times brighter than any star we had ever seen!

Even as the sun began to lighten the sky, it was not bright enough to make our new star disappear. In was only later, in the full light of the day that we could no longer see it. We were no longer sitting, we were on our feet and staring to the east at this miracle. I wondered if it I should run and rouse the people, so that they could see this also, but then heard whispered voices to our left, and realized that we were not the only ones who had been watching the rising moon, others had evidently been unable to sleep also, and had now roused the sleepers. Silhouetted against the lightening sky, they were standing on the roofs of the pueblo, motionless and transfixed by the new light in the heavens.

Kokopelli stood beside me saying nothing, but staring at the new star. Then he hobbled back toward the room where we had been living, and I heard him quietly say, "Now they have a sign!"

CHAPTER SEVENTEEN

That day it rained. The clouds, which had been gathering day after day in the late afternoon, now appeared in the early morning, instead, and moved steadily toward our canyon. It began in the morning, with bright flashes of lightning, and rolling thunder to the west. Later the rain began to pelt the pueblo; huge drops falling singly and dotting the dry dust of the valley floor, where they almost dried before the next drop hit in the same area. It stopped then and seemed to be moving on, leaving only a few darker grey pockmarks in the dust, but then suddenly it resumed in the form of large hailstones, which came so fast that the ground was immediately white. The hail beat upon the houses, and upon the corn, and upon the people who had been standing in the plaza watching the storm. As they ran for cover the hail piled up until it was two inches deep before it turned to a deluge of rain, which swept the ice before it.

As lightning crisscrossed the sky, and the thunder shook the valley, the land was transformed from a dry and parched desert to a black and wet land, with water running across it in every direction. The sandstone turned a darker yellow as the rain pounded against it, and the high cliffs were soon dripping with water running over the edges. The sudden flood seemed to turn the entire valley into a great lake, as the water collected faster than it could run off. But rivulets quickly filled, and scoured at the dry undersoil, carrying muddy torrents toward the river valley. As they merged and cascaded into the main stream they carried stones and bushes and debris. In seconds they plunged and rolled into a torrent of black water, rushing through the streambed, cutting at the banks, and carrying away all the trash and debris, which had been collecting there.

The high cap rocks of the canyon are cut by many channels, bringing water from the mesa above down into our farmlands. Our people had built check dams in many places on the cliff tops, so that the scarce and precious rainwater would be held back, and allowed to run into the soil, feeding the springs at the foot of the canyon walls. The deluge soon filled these reservoirs, and ran over or around the dams, carrying away much of the construction and raining not just water, but rocks and mud on the valley below.

Then the rain slowed, but did not stop as it would usually do in an evening thunderstorm. What had been what our people called a male rain changed to what we called a female rain. A lighter, but steady rain followed, which lasted throughout the day and much of the next night. The land drank in the moisture, now. The slow and steady rain was able to penetrate the cooled land, sinking to the roots of the bushes and grass. The corn and the squash seemed to find new life as they filled with the moisture. The dust of months was washed from their leaves and they appeared to turn a darker green.

The people were pleased. It was a good omen that the rain stayed and soaked into the valley. The check dams could be rebuilt, and the hail had not greatly harmed the crops, and the moisture was sinking deep to the roots of the corn. It would be a good year! They went out into the fields, in the midst of the rain, and let the rain run over them also as they worked to channel the flow to the drier areas. The rain washed the dust from their bodies, as it had with the corn, and they looked up into the falling drops, and opened their mouths to drink in the wetness, and they laughed. There could be no doubt that the rain was sent by the gods to show their favor for the people. And that favor must also be a result of the miracle brought about by Kokopelli. It all tied together.

Certainly we often had rains like this in other years, rains that lasted and soaked into the land and fed the crops. But this rain, coming as it did, immediately after the appearance of the star of Kokopelli, was thought to be of special meaning. The appearance of the star had proven his power, there could be no doubt, but that power could be fearful or beneficial, and no one knew which it might be. The downpour, and the steady rain that followed, proved that his power was a good power, one that would help the people.

When the skies cleared at the end of that night, and the sun was about to rise, very few of the people were sleeping. They were waiting to look again to the sky and see if the star had disappeared. Perhaps, they thought, it was only a dream, or an illusion, and that no new bright spot would be seen in the sky. It was still there, as bright or brighter than the night before. It outshone anything else in the night sky except the moon itself. They had not imagined the sight they had seen the night before. A new light had come into the sky, to prove the truth which Kokopelli spoke.

There was a great change in the way in which he was now treated, and this even carried over to me. We were no longer laughed at and ridiculed as we went about the village. People once again made way for this strange stooped figure who could control the skies. However, there was no new show of friendliness either, but rather an aura of fear. Food was now offered freely, and we both had all we wished. But no one invited us to sleep in their round room, or talked with us in the evening. We were still, in accordance with the pronouncements of Setuana, outcasts.

The great event had been seen by many people on that first night, and up and down the valley people in every pueblo had heard the story of Kokopelli's prediction to Hopaqa, and its fulfillment. Each night the people would watch that bright spot in the sky and wonder what other things this man could do. Its brightness stayed the same for many days, and then started very slowly, night by night, to grow dimmer. It was only after twenty-three days that the star finally disappeared completely.

Throughout this entire time there had been no word from Hopaqa or any of his messengers. I had expected immediately to be summoned to the large city, but there was only silence. This did not seem to bother Kokopelli, as we went about our daily rounds of gathering handouts from the people, of talking of the things he had learned, of teaching me of the weather and skies. A calmness had come over him, almost a contentment, which I found hard to understand. I thought that he would now be honored by the people who ruled the cities of the canyon, yet nothing seemed to happen. Surely they would now listen to what he had to say. Instead, the air of tension could be felt wherever we went. As we approached other settlements in our wanderings in the valley the people would disappear into their homes, and the leaders would avoid having to talk to us. Children were quickly called back when they ran out to see what strangers were approaching. Yet, in the midst of this tension Kokopelli seemed unconcerned.

"Why do they not call you to the Great Kiva, and honor you?" I asked. "Does not Hopaqa see the star, and does he not know that you have great knowledge which he can use? Why do the people fear you and ignore you, when you brought the rain also? The crops will be good this year, and the people will prosper. We should not have to sleep with the animals, here in this small room. We should be welcome in any round room in the valley!"

Kokopelli smiled calmly, and said, "I have upset their ways, and have proven them wrong. That is not easy to accept. They would rather I had never come to their valley, speaking of places they have barely heard of and knowing of things that their leaders do not understand. If we wait, they will use me, and even pretend to honor me, perhaps, but they will never like me, nor will they like you, because you are now too much in my confidence. Do not expect them to happily accept a prophet who goes against the ways they have known all their lives. We will wait, and they will decide they need us, but they will never decide they are pleased that we are here.

"There are people in this valley who have been honored and feared for many years; the star watchers who climb the butte. We have hurt their pride by making the prediction, and we have threatened their position with the great leaders like Hopaqa when the prediction was fulfilled. They will even now be trying to turn these leaders against us. They will be saying that they also knew of the coming event, and will remind the leaders of things they said months or years ago, which they claim predicted the birth of the star. We will wait and say nothing."

"Perhaps," I suggested, "They will convince Hopaqa that we are evil, and have us driven from the canyon. That would solve their problem. They have been respected for many years, and the people have prospered and grown during that time. Should we not go now to Hopaqa and gain his support?"

"Certainly that is what the star gazers would like. They will remind the leaders that they have, for all these years, told the people the time to plant their crops and the time to harvest them. They have known when and how to thank each of the Gods, and have asked the Gods to provide for the people. However, the chiefs will value my advice, also, and will eventually decide to use it. This will be done quietly at first, so that the star gazers will not feel threatened.

"If we were to go now to Hopaqa the star gazers would see it as a danger to them, and would double their efforts to get rid of me. Hopaqa, then, faced with a choice, might give in to them. If Hopaqa sends for me, then the choice has been his, and the star gazers will not dare to oppose him or us. No, we must wait."

On the day after the star had disappeared from the night sky Kokopelli and I were walking, as we often did, to another part of the valley. He would hobble along, with me at his side and we would go to all of the major settlements. He said that it was important that the people see him and be used to having him about. It had by now become clear to me that Kokopelli did everything in a planned manner. He did not always explain to me what he had in mind, but he often told me to watch him and study what he did and what he said, since I might have to do these things for him at some time.

On this day our wandering took us toward the towering butte of the stargazers, on our way to the small, very old town, which was to the east of it. As we passed close to the wall of rock we could look straight up over us and feel the immensity of the cliffs which hung over our heads. It was a dizzying thing to try to see the tops of the cliffs, and the ledges above, where the tribal priests, the astronomers, determined the positions of the heavens. With the high wisps of clouds moving across the sky behind the rock, it seemed as though the wall was falling toward us, trying to crush us. Yet the beauty of the butte was such, and the illusion of towering size was so strong that we felt compelled to get even closer, and climbed up the loose rubble until we were right up against the sandstone, at the top of the long and steep talus slope.

Kokopelli was telling me again of his childhood, as we walked beside the cliff, and was lost in his thoughts. The day was cool and the thin clouds were moving fast across the sky. A light breeze was blowing down the canyon ahead of us, and the sun was behind the butte, allowing us to walk in the shade. As we walked I was half listening to him and half thinking of other things, as I glanced upward occasionally at the cliffs to our right. We were about ten feet from the sandstone wall when I glanced upward once more, and became aware of a patch of yellow against the sky which seemed to be a part of the wall which had detached itself from the rest. Before I realized I had done it, I had thrown my body against Kokopelli, and the two of us were sprawling on the sand, against the base of the cliff and seeing an immense block of stone crash into the rubble slope exactly where he had been walking!

The heavy rains of the days before had, we knew, loosened many boulders, and no small number had slid or rolled into the valley in numerous places. Perhaps that is what happened here, and maybe it was only coincidence that we happened to be at that point just as a massive boulder pulled loose and tumbled off the cliff top. We looked upward and could see no one above us, nor any motion in any direction. It was quiet and peaceful as it had been before, with just the thin clouds hurrying past the top of the butte, across the deep blue of the sky. Then a large hawk flew up to the right, as though perhaps disturbed from his nesting place, but perhaps he was only upset by the noise of the falling boulder.

"You have again saved my life," he now said to me. "And risked yours in doing so. Perhaps the first time you three boys were not aware of what you did, but in this there can be no question. You have acted as a man and as a friend. It has been many years since I have been able to call anyone friend. Not since the days before the death of my family have I had anyone who acted to help me out of friendship rather than fear.

"Come, let us go back to the pueblo of Setuana, for I believe we will soon be hearing from Hopaqa. The boulder did not accidentally drop where it did. The priests are feeling pressure, or they would not do this, and that means that they are losing the arguments with the chiefs."

CHAPTER EIGHTEEN

It was not until three days more had passed that a messenger came to us from the pueblo of Hopaqa. He came in the evening, when few people were about, and did not go directly to Kokopelli, but rather to Setuana, as though taking him a message. We were at our dwelling, near the front entrance to the pueblo when he arrived, but he paid us no attention as he went straight to the round room of Setuana. It was only later, as he was leaving the pueblo that he motioned that we should follow him outside the wall. When we were well away from the houses he stopped and looked warily about. Then he turned to Kokopelli and said in a low voice, "You are ordered to go to the Great Kiva of Hopaqa as the sun rises two days from now. You will have all your belongings with you, and will say nothing to any of the people in this village of your plans. The boy will go with you, and will not tell his family that he is going."

We went, as instructed, two days later to the central pueblo. The early morning sun was just about to appear over the rim of rocks when we entered the great plaza and made our way between the many round rooms, which were in its center to the largest of them, the round room of Hopaqa. It lay near the center of the plaza, but on the left side of the wall that divided the plaza into two parts. It was, as we knew, one of the two largest rooms in the pueblo, and seemed large enough and elaborate enough to be a Great Kiva. Only a very rich person could live in such a room, since it was much more difficult to keep warm in the winter. In addition, we knew that only a few other people lived in this round room with him, members also of the water clan. They had many storerooms filled with food and firewood, and had a great number of people working for them.

The pueblo had seemed immense as we approached it. Five stories high, with the rooms stepped back in tiers from the central plaza, it gave a feeling of grandeur. There were many hundreds of above ground rooms here, with their exterior doorways at each level opening onto the roof of the room below, or in the case of the lowest level, opening onto the plaza itself. The plaza looked deceptively like solid ground, until one realized that over three dozen round rooms were hidden under the ground, their flat roofs of clay joining one another to provide the open flat surface which then became the communal living area, and the center of all activity. These round rooms were the living areas of a great number of people, one clan occupying each room, with twenty or more people closely packed into many of them. The larger rooms were, of course, used by the more important clans, and their leaders were the lieutenants of the great chiefs, Hopaqa and Takaselio, his counterpart, who lived in the other very large kiva; the one which dominated the east side of the plaza.

People were already busy in the plaza, preparing food at small fires built in the open, in front of the lower rooms. As we approached the kiva of Hopaqa we heard voices and laughter in one of the rooms which made up the dividing line between the two halves of the pueblo, and glancing in saw a number of women and young girls, kneeling before a row of grinding stones, and enjoying the early morning as they ground corn into meal. Other people were already working at making pots or weaving fabric, sitting in the low rays of the rising sun, which would soon be too hot and which they would then move into the shade to avoid. A group of eight men had just left the large kiva to which we were going, and started toward the gate, passing us closely, and bringing fearfully to mind Kokopelli's story of the log carriers. They were all large and muscular, dressed in the minimum of clothing so that it was easy to notice their sinewy arms and legs, developed by years of heavy work. They had evidently just received their instructions, and were now on their way to carry them out.

Another group of equally imposing men, four of them, were standing before the entrance to the Water Clan kiva. As we came closer they stepped forward and barred our way. "What do you wish, here?" asked the tallest of them.

"We come at the bidding of Hopaqa." answered my master. "We were told to be here at the rising of the sun on this day. I am Paho, of the Eagle Clan."

"You are Kokopelli, to us, and are no longer of any clan. Hopaqa has said nothing to us of your coming. Wait here."

It was some minutes that we stood in the early morning rays of the rising sun, which flecked the pueblo with patches of light as it rose above the mesa top. Finally the man who had first spoken to us, and who had entered the kiva, returned, followed by a number of others who had evidently been in the kiva, and who were now asked to leave. "You may now enter," he said, "You will leave your belongings out here with the boy."

"No," he answered calmly, but without any show of either subservience or insolence. "This boy is my assistant. Where I go he goes, for I need him to help me, crippled as I am. Please tell that to Hopaqa." That was all he said, yet I felt sure that he had now destroyed any chance he might have of gaining favors from Hopaqa. At their first meeting he had insulted the chief by turning his back on him, and now he was questioning his orders.

The four guards looked astonished that anyone would act in this way, and seemed, in fact, reluctant to take this insolent statement to their chief. Finally, however, the one who had spoken before entered the kiva again, and again we stood and waited in the morning sun.

When he re-emerged from the ladder which led down into the underground room he said nothing, but merely looked for some seconds at us, and then motioned that we should both enter the kiva. It was a look of disbelief, which accompanied his waving motion, as though to say that he had now seen everything.

Except for Hopaqa and ourselves the room was empty. I think I had expected to find the various chiefs assembled to pass judgment on my master, who had the temerity to act in such a manner, but only we were there, in the large circular chamber. "Sit. Here in front of me. The boy can go over to the other side of the room. We must talk now of the things we can do for one another."

"Hopaqa," My master now answered, "We are here to serve you."

"All the people saw the sign; the great shining star in the heavens. They now believe you are close to the gods, but they fear you. That is good. You will do nothing to change that, since it can be very useful. I do not, myself, know how you brought about the miracle, but will accept it, and use it. What is it you bring me from the south which you believe so valuable?"

"Hopaqa, what I bring is knowledge. I have traveled to places where none of our people have ever been allowed to go, and seen the ways of the people to the south. There are cities there, which make yours look like nothing. There are chiefs there of great power who have ten times the men working for them as you do. Their fields are full of corn all through the year, and the food even hangs from the trees, where they need do nothing more than reach up and pick it if they are hungry. In their land the rains come often, and the rivers of pure water are as wide as our valley. I have seen their messengers come from all parts of their vast empire, bringing trade goods. These leaders have power far greater than you have ever dreamed of. I know some of their secrets, and can help you to gain that level of power."

"If this is true," Hopaqa mused, "Why is it you come to me? Why do you not use this yourself, and give nothing to me or any other of our leaders?"

"I come to you because we need each other. I cannot do these things alone, but need the influence of a leader who will convince the people to accept what I tell them. What I bring is not a single easy idea, but a large body of ideas, which must be put into actions; actions by many of our people over a long period of time. Even though they have seen my star, and are convinced of my strength, they will not do as I suggest, except perhaps out of fear. On the other hand, the people respect you, and are in the habit of doing what you command. With your strength behind me we can have the people following the things which I will require of them."

"And why do you then not offer this to another of the chiefs? There are others who could also influence the people, and who might give you more. Why did you not go to them?"

Kokopelli lowered his voice, then, and spoke slowly but distinctly. From the other side of the large chamber I was aware of every word; the words he had told me before as we had talked in the evenings while waiting for the summons. I knew now that he was speaking what he believed, and that Hopaqa was being asked to believe also. "Our people are becoming many, Hopaqa, and have spread to great distances. Times have been good, and they have been able to raise enough crops to feed their growing population. In the few bad years they have been able to continue to live well because of the crops which have been stored here, under your protection. The roads which link all parts of our empire make it possible for them to bring in their foods when there is an abundance, and withdraw food when there is a need. This is good.

"Your storage rooms are secure. Few rats or mice ever have been found in the sealed rooms because they are built well and maintained well. Your stonemasons are the best in the canyon. The people know that, and bring their grain to you for protection. They also know that you can lend them food when they are in need, to be repaid in a better year. For these reasons they trust you, and for these reasons you have become the most powerful man in the canyon. They also know that the grain they stored will always be here if they need it; that it will not be stolen or given to others, and that you have many strong men who are loyal to you, so that no one can storm your city and take the food they have entrusted you with.

"Yes, there are others who could have helped me, but that help could not have done as much good for our people. I have seen what must be done to feed our ever growing numbers, and that will take all the strength we can gather. I came to you for that reason, and for one other. You are the leader of the water clan, and water is the basis of our existence and the foundation of my concerns. If the people are to be fed, then it must be done through the judicious use of what little water we receive from the gods. I have seen in the cities to the south how they make better use of the water they have. It is this which I bring back to you.

"You will benefit greatly if the people prosper, and I know that it is that which you desire. I can help you to make the people prosper.

Then they will store their excess with you, and they will trade their goods with your traders. When they cut timber they will send it to you, and when they fashion the finest pottery they will offer it first to you. When they need to borrow seed corn for next years crop they will borrow it from you. When they repay the loan you will profit. Their prosperity will be your prosperity."

Hopaqa nodded his head as he heard this. He glanced over to me, and then back at Kokopelli, staring long at him and saying nothing. At last he stood, and looked down at Kokopelli. "I believe what you say. It is true that our people are becoming many, and that a time will come when the dry years will return. Then they will starve, and they will get desperate. They may then even turn on the people who have protected them over the years. Our clans become larger but our fields stay the same size because we do not have water enough to make them any larger. Our people have spread to many other settlements such as your home to the south, in order to find wet and fertile land. These people are not as closely tied to our central guidance as the nearer and earlier pueblos have been. They only grudgingly give grain to us for storage, and even then they think we are stealing it. When the bad times come it is these people who will first challenge our authority and will first blame us for failing them.

"I believe what you say is true, and I believe you have learned from your travels. It is not for that reason only that I have called you, however. The story of your star has traveled throughout the empire. I know this because I instructed our messengers, our log carriers, our traders and our priests to take this story with them and tell it to the people. The further a village is from here the more awed the people will be by the story of one who can cause stars to explode in the heavens. Surely you learned in your travels how your appearance helped you to gain an audience. The people then feared and respected you because you appeared like a god. How much more will the people in our outlying villages fear and respect you if the not only see your twisted shape, but already have been told the legends of your control of the stars.

"I will send you to our furthest outposts, you and the boy. It will be your job to convince the people that they should rely on our canyon for their guidance. Through their belief that you are a god you will be able to remind them that this canyon was originally chosen by the gods as the center of our empire. You will convince them that the gods still look upon this as the place on which they should place their trust. If you do this well, when the bad years come perhaps they will still trust us. All that we do here is based upon that trust. When the people no longer believe that we have the right, given by the gods, to lead them, then they will lose that trust, and the empire will crumble. Therefore, it is a great responsibility I am placing upon you and your helper!...Boy, come here!"

I rose and went to stand beside Kokopelli, facing the high chief.

He seemed less stern as he looked at me, now. Then he said, "It is a fearsome thing which has been done to you, or rather that you have brought upon yourself. I know that you have saved this man's life, not once but twice. Yes, I was told of the falling boulder by someone who said they saw it from afar. Now you are apprenticed to him at the bidding of Setuana, and this is something I cannot change; something which denies you the right to grow up and be clan leader, as I am sure you have dreamed; as all boys your age dream of. Therefore, the life that I have dictated for this man will be your life also. I will rely also upon you to represent me, and represent me well, as the two of you travel throughout the empire. When we finish here you may return to your people, and tell them that you are doing my bidding, and that they are to come to me if they are in need. While you are in my service your family will be under my protection and will not need for food or water as long as I am able to provide it. Their fields will be watered when the rains come, and their surplus will be stored in my storerooms at no expense to them.

"You, Kokopelli, will, from this day onward, do no one's bidding but mine. You will live in my city, and you will travel throughout the empire representing my interests. Your first duty will be to gain and retain the loyalty of the distant settlements, so that we need not fear their loss of trust if bad years do come. However, you may teach the people those things which can make their life better; which you have learned in the south. You will teach them to me also.

"You will be well rewarded if you can do these things. You will live in my protection, and go anywhere in the empire with no fear, for all will know that you speak for me. You will eat the best food, and never want for it. When trade goods are gained because of your efforts I will see that you receive a fair share. Much turquoise is brought to us as payment for our guidance, and many ornaments from all parts of the world arrive with foreign traders. You will be given some of these when you serve me well. The priests who watch the stars and who foretell the signs of the gods fear and hate you. As long as you serve me well they will not dare to harm you. However, if your work displeases me I can withhold all of these things from you and you will again be a wandering pariah. I can withdraw my protection and the priests will no longer feel restrained. Another time the boulder from the top of the cliff might not miss its mark!... You may go now and seek shelter in the largest of my other kivas. Those who are now there will make room for you because I will let it be known that such is my wish."

He sat again, and seemed to be through speaking, and Kokopelli and I started to move toward the ladder. He spoke again, however. "You insulted me twice before, and humiliated me before my people. The first, when you turned your back on me at our first meeting was done to get the attention of the people, and to emphasize the power of your prediction. I allowed that to pass, waiting to see if your sign would come in the three allotted days. The second time was your refusal to see me without your assistant. Again you made me look weak before my men. I allowed that because I could see that you might be valuable to me. There will be no third time!....Go now and return when I call for you."

CHAPTER NINETEEN

Outside the kiva it was still early morning and the sun was just starting to heat the air. The guards were standing about as we emerged, and seemed to pay us little attention. The same people we had seen earlier were still doing their morning chores, yet it seemed to me as through the entire world had changed, and centuries had passed since we had gone down into Hopaqa's round room.

I did as Hopaqa had instructed, returning to may home kiva and my family the same day, where I told them what he had said. This was a very important thing to my mother's clan, for they would normally have lost their son to another clan upon his marriage, and would have little benefit from his attaining manhood and status within the pueblo. Instead, I was bringing them the protection of the highest placed man in the entire empire. It also meant that within the pueblo, the family, and the more distant relatives, who made up the clan, were a little more influential. They did not in any way challenge or rival the authority of Setuana, who was in total control, but their status was elevated in the minds of the people.

Upon my return we went to the kiva which lay to the north of Hopaqa's, and asked for a place to stay. Evidently instructions had already been given, for room was immediately made for us, and we were told that food was waiting for us in the closest of the workrooms above. Other than us, of course, the occupants were all of one clan, the Bear clan, but all were also in the employ of Hopaqa or were caring for those who did the work of Hopaqa. They numbered twenty-four people, some of them children, and all lived together in a room about thirty feet in diameter. This meant that there was far less crowding than in some of the other rooms. We had a section of our own where we could sleep, and where we could keep our belongings.

We had been waiting for three days without any word from Hopaqa when I found myself, lacking anything to do, wandering about the pueblo. My master was content to sit in the coolness of our new home much of the time, but I was too inquisitive to do the same. The lower level rooms had doors opening onto the plaza; most of these doors were wider at the top than at the bottom, with setbacks half way up that gave them the appearance of a letter "T". I passed one such door, noticing that it was blocked at the bottom with a slab of sandstone which had been leaned into place, but which fitted snugly, allowing no gaps at the lower levels of the door. Above this a network of sapling branches had been woven into a lattice, which blocked the remainder of the opening. Suddenly I saw a colorful movement inside, a flurry of red and green, which reflected the sunlight that filtered in through the upper half of the door. I stopped and went to see what it could be. Inside, on a raised platform that had been built across the entire width of one end of the room, I saw a very large and colorful bird; a macaw, shifting himself across the front edge of the platform, and fluttering his wings as it did so. He swiveled his head back to look at me, and then resumed his gaze, down toward the floor of the room below him.

I had seen these beautiful tropical strangers to our country before. Traders would sometimes be carrying them as they passed by our home when I was a boy. They would be imprisoned in cages made of reeds, suspended on the ends of poles, which the strangers from the south carried over their shoulders, usually two, one on each end. I had marveled at their beauty then, and wondered why they were bringing them, and who could afford to buy such birds. Surely if one wanted the feathers for ornamentation it would have been much easier to bring feathers for trade rather than live birds. Our people had little time for the amusement of owning pets. Our turkeys were kept for food and to eat insects, not for diversion. Our dogs were used to keep down the garbage, which attracted vermin, and some could be trained to catch rats and mice. Also, they were a source of food.

I watched the bird for a long time as it sat on its precarious perch, about three feet above the floor. The room was one that had been used for food preparation, but had now been given over to the bird. Behind it was the smooth wall and the blocked doorway of a storage room. After the room had been filled with dried corn the opening into it had been carefully filled with tightly fitted stones and mud mortar, leaving no possible entries, even for the smallest ants or roaches, much less something as large as a field mouse or ground squirrel. Then, to be certain, the square opening had been plastered over to match the wall, leaving a scarcely discernable rectangle of different looking wall with its raised sill.

The macaw had been shifting back and forth from time to time, but now he suddenly stopped moving, as though frozen. Even his head ceased to swivel, and I could see that he was concentrating on the far corner of the room, where a slight twitch of grey motion could barely be seen. Then, out of a crevice between two rocks in the outer wall crept a small grey mouse. It sidled along the wall, toward the inner wall which contained the blocked doorway, stopping occasionally to nibble tiny bits of corn which remained on the floor of the room. It would stop from time to time as it glanced around, looking for danger, so I remained absolutely still and watched what would happen. Suddenly there was a loud beating of wings and a flurry of motion. The macaw had launched himself at the mouse, and landed between him and the way he had entered. Another flurry and the huge claws had grasped the small furry creature, and the heavy beak had torn into it. Then the bird, grasping his prize, had fluttered back to his perch where he proceeded to eat the meal he had caught. I now knew why the macaws were so prized, and why they were brought all the way from the hot jungles of the south to this unexpected location. On a continent that did not yet have house cats these birds were the best substitute.

The trust given to men like Hopaqa by the people was centered upon the need to have their surplus food carefully stored. The canyon with its dry conditions served well for this, and the tradition of expert stone masonry made the safe storage possible. However, as the population had grown, so had their piles of refuse and offal, and this in turn had encouraged the explosive growth of the vermin population. To the south of each settlement could be found the immense heaps of discarded food, broken pottery, dead animals, human and animal excrement and all the other debris which accumulated when many people lived in an area. As one approached this malodorous mound it often seemed to be in motion, as its surface rippled with waves of furry scurrying animals.

Although it was not the common practice, at times even human bodies were buried in these mounds. This was only on occasions when winter weather and frozen ground made it impossible to take them well away from the pueblos for burial. No one wanted to think of their relatives as food for these masses of rats, mice, cockroaches and maggots, but in the winter the scavengers were not present, and one could almost forget that they would reappear in the spring.

It was also while we were waiting for word from Hopaqa that the importance of the storage areas was again made apparent to all of us. In the other side of the pueblo, the east half which was administered by Takaselio, an older woman, accompanied by a three young girls had arrived from one of the outlying pueblos well to the west of the canyon. Two years before her clan had brought a part of their crop for storage, and had left it in the care of Takaselio. Then, shortly after that fruitful year, her husband and two other of the men had died, and the fields had not been properly planted next season. They were in need of food, and had come to take back part of their deposited hoard of food to see them through until the current crop should be harvested.

The storage room assigned to them had been carefully sealed, and remained untouched. Men now were called to remove the stones and masonry, and to help the woman to take the food back to her clan. The many storage rooms made up an intricate labyrinth, with many rooms having blocked doors in each of their four walls. This meant that it was usually possible to find a pathway to a desired room through others which were already emptied or had not yet been filled. The proper room was soon located, and the men went to work with wooden tools, scraping away the mortar and prying out stones, until they could breach the sealed room. When the rocks were pulled away, however, a scurrying noise could be heard inside the room, and in the dim light a mass of mice and roaches swarmed out through the opening, over the hands and feet of the workers. Somewhere a hole had been found or made, and the stored corn and beans had been feeding generations of vermin! There was nothing now worth saving.

The room itself was a loss. Never again could it be used for food storage, since the people believed a room once so contaminated could no longer be trusted, no matter what repairs might be made. Henceforth the room would be abandoned. No person would even use it as a workroom after its infestation. Such an abandoned room could only be used now as an area in which to dispose of unwanted trash. Such an infestation, although uncommon, meant new rooms had to be added to the pueblos from time to time as old ones were abandoned, so that the pueblos continued to expand even when the population did not.

The woman who had come from the outlying village was not to be blamed for the loss. If the pueblo was to retain its reputation for safety and reliability the woman must have her stored corn. With little comment another room was opened, this time one containing grain belonging to Takaselio, and men proceeded to carry the stored supplies all the way to her clan, many days over the hot mesas. It was important that no one ever doubt the safety of their deposited surplus, a fact well recognized by the people of the canyon.

It was the combination of this trust, and the services that the canyon preformed as a determinant of religious and agricultural knowledge, which guaranteed its continuing leadership. Here the priests watched the stars, the sun and the moon, and sent out the messengers to tell the outlying communities the proper times for their ceremonies and their planting and harvesting. Here the gods were served, that the outliers would be protected. Here the leaders resided, as had been decreed at the time of the great migrations. The gods had told the first clans that they would complete their migrations where the two principal pathways crossed, the one which went from the lands of ice and snow to the lands of the parrots, and the other which extended from one great sea to the other. The first priests had determined that the crossing of the two paths was at this canyon, this dry and forbidding depression, dominated by the high mesa of the sky watchers at its south end. So it was that this place, with little else to make it attractive, ruled an immense region and many thousands of people.

It would remain the center of the empire, and the force that held it together, only so long as the outliers believed they needed it, however. That belief was based upon two things, faith in the priests and faith in the bankers. Neither of these could be allowed to falter or the people would abandon the canyon as their leaders, and such a move would be disastrous to these collected towns, which could not even raise enough food to feed themselves, and needed to import even their firewood.

We had now entered the months of the thunderstorms. They had started the day after the new star had appeared, and had occasionally visited us since then. Almost every afternoon dark clouds could be seem in one direction or another, as they built higher and higher into the desert air. They would sweep by, then, often seeming to surround and envelop us, without dropping any of their valuable moisture. At other times they would seem to drop all of their rain in a matter of only a few minutes, so that most of the water which could have done so much for our crops rolled quickly away, hardly penetrating the dusty surface of the ground before speeding down gullies and disappearing into the sand on the bottom of the arroyo.

It was after one of these sudden downpours, on the third day of waiting, that the two of us were walking through the fields, and my master was explaining the way in which the people to the south trapped and used the water from these storms. We had then spoken of many things, and he had talked again about the village to the south where he had spent his childhood. As he spoke, I wondered if he were not hoping to be sent there by Hopaqa. Having left in disgrace he would now be able to return with dignity, as a representative of the highest chief. He told me again of his childhood friends and of his rivalry with Kolello and his love for Tokchii.

"Master," I said then, "Since you came to our cities you have had no name except Kokopelli. I have called you master because of the position I have been given. When you went to see Hopaqa you told the guard that your name was Paho, however. Shall I call you Paho?"

He was silent so long, as we walked between the hills of corn, that I did not think he was going to answer me. Then he said, "I told the guard that was my name because it truly is my name. Kokopelli is the name of a god, which I am not. It is useful for me to have people think of me as Kokopelli, but I would be pleased if you would call me Paho. It is a name I have not heard used for many years. Remember, however, that we have a job to do, not just for Hopaqa, but also for our people. That duty is best served if they think of me as the returned flute player, and as a demi-god who can even make stars explode. Therefore, when we are together without others about I will be Paho, but when it suits our purposes you must not forget that I am Kokopelli."

That night we were again called to the round room of Hopaqa. This time I was made to wait outside while they talked, and when Paho again emerged from the room he only said softly to me, "Get together food and water and meet me here as the moon rises. We start tonight on our first journey."

CHAPTER TWENTY

South and east, between the sandstone cliffs, following back upstream along the dry wash that had carved the canyon, one soon came to a quite different pueblo. It was only seventeen miles between the two, and to look at the large structure, as it crouched on the top of a bulge in the terrain, one would have thought it was almost identical to the cities of the canyon. And, in fact, architecturally it was. Even the stone masonry, when closely studied, was the same, and the storage and workrooms were clustered around a central plaza, with its many subterranean rooms, just as at the canyon. To look at the people one would still not see any difference, but it was in fact the people that were different; not their clothing or their features, but their attitudes.

The proximity to the main canyon was what made them different. Had they been secluded in a valley, far from the priests and chiefs, they might have been more content and less hostile. They might have accepted a distant authority, and followed the traditions of the people. As it was, they were too close, and felt too strongly the authority that lay just to the west.

As a result these people felt themselves to be subjugated and thus were a constant problem for the leaders such as Hopaqa. To prove that they were not slaves to the canyon they had become the most independent of the pueblos. Any edict coming down from the canyon was a reason for surliness and even refusal.

The independence was not without merit, however. This was a prosperous town, growing more food than their people needed, and not dependent upon anyone else for the necessities of life. Their fields were rich and well watered in the spring, and the their people were hard working and skillful. It was not surprising that they felt themselves superior to the people at the canyon. Whereas the people of Hopaqa depended upon outside supplies of food, these people were self sufficient, and looked down upon the canyon people as parasites. They did not often send their excess food to the canyon, but built extensive storerooms of their own and prided themselves on the skill of their stone masons.

It was only in the area of religion that these people depended upon the canyon, and it was through the astronomer priests that control was at least somewhat maintained. From their pueblo they could easily climb to the top of a nearby rise and, looking to the northwest, see the Butte of the Astronomers, revealed to them through the low pass where the river entered the canyon. It was this butte that was the center of worship, this chiseled mass of rock which loomed over the canyon and which reflected so perfectly the changing sun during the day and the moon at night.

According to the legends, when the first people landed on the shores of this continent, having suffered their way from island to island to cross the great sea of the west, it was this butte, not the entire canyon, which was designated by Taiowa as the center of their world. Here would he communicate to the people through his priests. It was this command which made it possible for the priests to know of the seasons and of the rains and of the ceremonies. When they were on the top of their butte they spoke with the gods, and received the instructions, which they then relayed to the people. Then the people could perform the ceremonies that would bring the rains and snows, which would make the crops grow, which would drive out illness, which would bring the game close to their hunters.

The people had emerged into the fourth world, and had traveled long distances to reach the edge of this landmass, arriving weary and disillusioned. They had received their instructions from Spider Woman, however, and they knew they must obey. Each clan made its migrations, as required, as far as they could go in the four directions. They visited the lands of snow and ice to the north, the lands of the parrots to the south, and the huge oceans to both east and west. This was the requirement before they could settle at the crossroads of these four directions. That point, at which the four paths converged, was the Butte of the Astronomers.

A wide and straight road connected the two settlements, making it an easy walk. This road went over quite level country, so that we had no trouble, even in the faint light of a thin moon, following the track. Roads such as this one radiated in all directions from the canyon, connecting the many pueblos to the center, likes spokes on a wheel. They were absolutely straight, and some were more than thirty miles long. When they met an obstruction they did not veer around it, but went directly over it, never deviating from their straightness. This often meant that steps, or even hand and foot holds had been cut into the steepest sections by the road builders. In this case, however, the road only crossed a number of arroyos before reaching its destination, so our walk was relatively easy.

We traveled at night on this trip for two reasons. First, was the coolness, which made it more comfortable to hike at night. At this time of year the daytime sun was exhausting. Secondly, we traveled at night because Hopaqa had told us to. He wished to have us arrive at the town in the early morning, so that we would not be seen approaching and could surprise the inhabitants. The story of Kokopelli would have already been told throughout the region, and these people would know of it. However, a sudden appearance, in the judgment of Hopaqa, would be more dramatic than to be watched as we slowly hobbled toward the town.

Traveling at night was slower, however, so that it took us most of the night to reach the settlement. When sky began to get grey to the east we were already at the pueblo, though, so that the early risers, when they entered the main plaza, would find us standing there, awaiting them. No one except a few thin dogs had been on guard to challenge our entrance. They dashed at us threateningly but backed off quickly when we showed no fear. Since the people of this prosperous village feared no human enemies they saw no need for posting sentries. The gods would not be stopped by a guard, and the predatory animals in that region were of little consequence. The real enemies were too small and silent to be stopped by any guard. Snares were set for them around the fields and tight walls were built to keep them out of the rooms. The round rooms had only a single entrance in the center of the ceiling, so that when the ladder was moved away even a squirrel could not find a way of defying gravity and crawling in where the people lived and slept.

The dogs had stopped snuffling around us and gone back to their search for something to eat, and the greyness was starting to invade the blackness of the sky, outlining the mountains which lay many miles to the east of the pueblo. A young woman, really a girl, emerged from one of the round rooms, carrying a water jug. She almost walked into us, still sleepy and not seeing well in the dim light. When she suddenly saw the outline of the hunchback she dropped the heavy pottery jug, where it smashed to many pieces on the hard packed earth of the plaza, then she stared transfixed, evidently not knowing if she was still dreaming, or if she was truly confronted with the mythological flute player of her childhood stories. Then she turned and ran to the round room from which she had emerged. It was minutes before another head emerged from the hole in the earth, an older woman, who then ducked back in after looking at us intently for some seconds in the now lightening grayness. Then an alarm was heard to be raised, and the people seemed to flow endlessly from the round room, some standing and staring at us, some running to tell the people in the other sleeping rooms.

In minutes a crowd had gathered in the plaza, all staring at us and saying nothing. Paho spoke first, fixing the people, one after another, as his eyes wandered over the group, glaring from under his bent head. "We will eat first and then talk. My assistant will bring me food and water, and afterward we will then tell you of the reason for our visit. We have traveled far during the night that we might tell you what our priests have told me. While we eat send to the rooms to be sure that all are present. I bring news from the canyon which all should hear."

It was some time before fires could be lighted and food prepared, and when it was ready I noticed that food and drink were brought to both of us. I did not need to go and get it as I had at the home pueblos; boys were given the job of serving us. I was also surprised to see that none of the other people ate, even though great amounts of food had been prepared. They waited to see what my master would do. Seeing this, he first tasted the food, then nodded in an approving manner, and motioned that the others should eat with us. The people quickly filled ladles and dishes with hot corn meal gruel and set to eating, never, however, ceasing to watch us.

When our breakfast was finished Paho rose again, for we had been squatting on flat feet as we ate. The people were still squatting in the dust so that he was over them, looking down. "You saw the star?" he asked, "You watched it for the twenty three days as it hung over our valley?" The people nodded their heads, and a few mumbled words of acknowledgement. "The star was put there as a sign, that the people might know that the gods have not forgotten you. Your priests, those who climb that butte which you can even see from this pueblo, have studied the star. They have spoken with the skies and with me, and have told what they have been instructed. I bring you those words.

"The gods, they say, are unhappy with the people. Three times have they destroyed the earth, first by fire, second by ice and third by water. The gods do not want to destroy the earth again and they want the people this time to save themselves, so that the earth will not have to be destroyed for a fourth time. In the next destruction there would be on one saved and no emergence of a few chosen ones into a fifth world, for there will be no fifth world! The people, all the people, in this village and in all the villages, no matter how near or far from the canyon, must hear the words and must do as is required."

"Should we then be servants to the canyon, as we have been for so many years?" a young man asked in a low voice.

"You must be servants to the gods! The canyon is not your master, but a servant also. Even the priests are but messengers. You must do as the gods command, and the leaders at the canyon are only acting to help carry our the wishes of the gods."

The same man spoke again, "Why do the leaders, like Hopaqa, then prosper at the expense of our people? Do the gods look more favorably upon them than upon us? We have served the leaders at the canyon for many generations, yet we are no better off! The canyon cannot even feed itself so we must help to feed it. They have no firewood but must bring it in from great distances. They have so little water they must carry it great distances, and must drink mud in the dry times. Why do they tell us what we must do?"

Many voices were heard now repeating similar comments, and others nodded their heads in agreement. The crowd seemed to move and sway forward, even as they sat in the dust like children before a teacher. It was not a threatening, but it did reflect a unified belligerence.

Paho answered their raised and quarrelsome voices with a quiet which hushed the gathered crowd. "Look at me. Look at my bent form. Consider the star which you saw in the sky, and which I told the people would come. Remember your legends of the flute player who saved the people, and then ask yourselves if you believe that I am a servant of the leaders of the canyon. Do I come to you because a man in the canyon sent me, or do I come because Taiowa sent me?

"The message I bring to you is the message I take to the canyon. What I say to you I will say to them. Like the messenger Bear who carries news from the gods on his humped back I do the same.I will travel to every village of the people and tell them what I tell you. All must heed the message I bring if the people are to survive."

There were now quieter murmurs, as they absorbed and considered this. We waited until they had had time to accept the viewpoint, and then Paho continued, but in a much louder voice, one of authority. "The people have abandoned the old ways! They put themselves before the leaders, and these leaders speak for the gods. They ignore the teachings of their fathers, and think that they do not need the guidance of the priests. This has come about because the times have been good. There has been much rain and the crops have grown well. The frosts have not come early and killed the plants before they bore fruit, and the hail has not destroyed the crops. The food has been plentiful and the people have had little illness for many years. The old people live longer, and still have food, and the children do not die as often in the first few days of their lives. The numbers of the people grows every year, and there is enough food for everyone. The gods have looked favorably upon their people.

"But now, the people are taking advantage of the gods. They follow the ceremonies as the priest dictate, but they do not do it out of worship or duty but out of pleasure. The festival of the harvest is no longer a tribute to the gods, it is a revelry of the people. The turning back of the sun when it reaches its winter home calls for a celebration, secure in the knowledge that the sun always turns back, rather than a reverence to the god who turned it back. The gods are displeased with this!

"The warning I bring is this: the good times will end, if not next year, perhaps the year after. If my message is not heeded the people will starve, and they will die of thirst and they will fight one another for food and water and a place to live. They will wander the earth and abandon the homes of their ancestors, and the great cities will hold only ghosts, and the fields will be only weeds and cactus. All these things will happen if the gods are ignored.

"You have not heeded the words from the canyon. You build storerooms and save food, which is good, and which is your protection for the bad times. But you forget that you are a part of the empire. Your storage does not help a pueblo, perhaps way to the south or west, which has a bad year in the midst of our prosperity. When food is stored at the center, then all may be helped in bad times. You must send a part of all you produce to the canyon, that it may be there to serve all the people. When the bad years come to this pueblo the food will be there to help you. In this way you have challenged the gods, and made them angry, for you act only for yourselves, not for the good of all our people. The gods will only be pleased when you begin to again act for the good of all the people by sending food for storage at the canyon.

"I have not come only to criticize, however. I know that you work hard here, and produce more than is necessary to feed your people. Your prosperity is due to your hard work, and you feel that you need not share this with those in other villages who may not work as hard. Remember, however, that some do not have the fertile soil and good water supply that you have. They also work hard, but with poorer results. I bring with me a new knowledge, which I will share with you. I will show you how you can raise far more food, by better use of the water you receive. We will stay in your village for many days, and go into the fields with your men. You will be taught how to level your fields, and how to channel the water so that it is used many times. It will allow you to grow more crops in the fields you now have, and expand the area you are planting.

"The numbers of our people have grown in this time of prosperity, but our fields have stayed the same. If we are to survive the bad times, which I tell you are coming, we must prepare for those times. The things we will teach you will help to provide for those many new people. I know that you are thinking, as any successful man would think, that you do not need to change; that the methods you were taught by your fathers and grandfathers have done well for you. Remember that they learned those methods from the gods at a time when those methods were all that was needed. Look again at my bent form and think again about my star, which exploded in the morning sky, and realize who is sending you this new way. If you believe that the gods are trying to help you then you will use the methods they have sent."

CHAPTER TWENTY-ONE

We stayed many days in this pueblo, and I remember it as a time of hard work. Paho was not content to merely tell the people what was to be done, he insisted that we both go to the fields with the men, and teach them how to change the ditches and the dams. In the night, when the people were sleeping we would spend long hours seated in the dust, away from the pueblo, and he would be drawing diagrams in the sand, barely visible in the light of the stars and moon, teaching me the things we would need to implement the next day. It was a system that allowed the water, when it came, to be taken from field to field, and made it possible to plant far more corn, beans and squash than had ever been grown before by these people.

In the darkness I saw him reach down between his knees and fill his hands with some of the parched grey earth of the desert, which stretched away toward the north. He squeezed it in his hands, then brought it up to his face and breathed in its aroma. "This is rich land," he whispered, "And only needs moisture to bring forth crops. Taiowa gave us this land for our use, but we do not fully use it. As our people grow in numbers they must learn to help the land. You must learn everything you can, even though you are young, so that you will be able to teach the people how to use the land."

It was, of course, too late in the season to make any difference to this harvest, but the fields were being prepared for the next year. We worked with the people, day after day, and I can still see Paho, with his walking stick, pointing at the fields and outlining the changes. He could look at a valley and in his mind he knew where every ditch or embankment should be. In his mind it became an organized layout of rectangles, feeding each other down the gradual slopes.

At first the people were more accepting of Paho and his ideas. When they saw that he was not merely a messenger nor a taskmaster, but a teacher who was willing to go to the fields himself, they forgot their surliness, and followed his instructions. We were given a comfortable place to sleep, and food was brought to us by boys given that job.

The man who had first questioned Paho on the day we had arrived at the pueblo, and had made evident the belligerence that pervaded the thoughts of his people, had fields just to the East, rich and productive. His name was Salisim, which meant He who Sings in Winter, for he was of the Singers, the clan which conducted many of the ceremonies. His fields were some of the first we came to, and we knew that his support would be very helpful. Only a few other fields had been reworked when we got to Salisim's area. Paho was very careful to appear to be offering suggestions rather than commands to this man. The suggestions were met, however, with a look of contempt and scepticism.

"Show me," he said, "What it is you think should be done? I will consider it, and do it if I wish. You do not need to help me to ditch my fields as you have the others; I can do my own work as I always have."

"My master will outline the changes," I said, "And you may do as you wish. I am only a boy, and of little use, probably, but I will be pleased to help you if I can."

"No." He answered, looking not at me but at Paho. "I will hear what you say, then you may go on to the others. My crops have been good, and I have always given my share to the gods in offering. I see little reason to change my way of watering and planting."

We did as he suggested. Paho drew lines on the ground, hobbling from place to place in the fields and scratching out a scheme on the ground as he saw it in his head. " A dam of stone here, Salisim, will take the water to the North, and another here will divert it back to the west again. When the heavy rains come a pond can be formed here, so that the water can then flow more slowly through the fields and water the plants rather than tearing the soil from the roots. Over there, where the rocks jut out through the soil you will need a ditch to carry the water away which flows over the rocks, and to bring it back to the place where we now stand."

Salisim nodded as this was said, but did nothing. When we went to the next field, the three men who worked there and who had seen what had transpired with Salisim were reluctant now to do what we said. It was the same with each of the new people we approached, so that now only those who had worked with us prior to our discussion with Salisim had their fields ditched and protected in the new way. We went back to the village that night very discouraged. In the next two days we did little better convincing the people to use our ideas.

It was on the afternoon of the third day that the great clouds gathered to the south, and swept northward toward us. They were black and low to the horizon, and towered upward to where the sun lighted the huge massive tops of boiling white vapor so that they glowed above the blackness below. A cool wind swept in from our right as we watched the storm approach. Lightning now laced the clouds and thunder rumbled over the land, bouncing and echoing from the sandstone ridges. Then the air became filled with blowing sand, and tumbleweeds raced across the land, bouncing against rocks, piling against the walls of the town, seeming to jump over the stream bottoms. The hard grains of sand stung our legs like bees and we turned our backs to the wind. No one wanted to go inside the rooms, however. In this dry land the hope of rain is so strong that only a fool would go and hide when the gods were sending their blessing. We stood in the darkening shadow of that monstrous cloud and waited. Then it came. First, huge drops, each striking the dry dust like a bird that his been shot, and leaving a stain of darker red dust. Then, more and more, and closer together until the ground was brown, and seemed to be alive as each drop caused a small eruption on its surface.

This was not unlike many other storms which I had seen sweep across our plateau over the years, but I remember it still. The people seemed made of stone. They stood in the rain, and it wet their hair and their clothing, and streamed down their bodies, and they did not move. The rain became heavy and the land was a huge pond, only a few raindrops deep but extending as far as we could see. At first it seemed as though the water was motionless even as it collected on the slopes, then it suddenly started to move. Ripples and valleys formed, and the water turned black as it started to carry dirt and gravel with it. It surged down the hills, now, and cascaded into the river bed, which still appeared to be dry, as its sand drank in the first of the flood.

Suddenly it was no longer dry, but filling with the black water which dropped over the sides, and looking upstream, toward the mountains, a wall of black water seemed to be slowly moving down the riverbed. It accelerated as it surged past, carrying away weeds, trash, leaves and even stumps of trees. The black water tumbled and writhed and snatched at the roots of living saplings which grew high up the sides of the river, tearing at them and wrenching them loose, to join the mass of debris which plunged down the stream.

Then, as suddenly as it had started, it was over. We still were standing in the mud of the plaza, our bodies washed clean and our hair in black strings over our faces, when we realized that the storm had passed, that the sky was becoming much brighter, and that the sun would soon come through the clouds to suck up the moisture again. We looked about us and saw that the storm had cut deep furrows across parts of the plaza, carrying away the soil and leaving heavy gravel in its place. It fanned out as it dropped down toward the fields below, covering some of the trash mounds to the south with a new layer of mud and sand

As though a spell had been broken the people started to move again. They wiped away the water and hair from their faces, they squeezed the water from their clothing and they started to look at the damage the sudden deluge had brought. One room wall which had been under construction and had therefore been unprotected had been somewhat harmed as the water washed the mud mortar away from among the building stones, and water had seeped into a few of the round rooms, but otherwise no damage seemed to have been done. However, it was when they went to the fields that they saw the power of the storm, and also the wisdom of Paho's advice.

The first fields, those in which his ideas had been heeded looked as usual, except that there were now large ponds of stored water which was slowly draining into the fields and sending water deep into the soil, to the roots of the food plants, instead of having uselessly roared down the river. Beside these field were the fields of Salisim, and here we could see, even from the pueblo, that a furrow crossed his land, one that had not been there before. When we went down to the field we could see that the cascading flood had broken through one of his ditch banks and gone straight to the river, carrying rich soil and many bean plants with it. Other plants clung to sides of the cut, with their roots exposed. The breakthrough had come at exactly the place where Paho had suggested building the stone dam!

The next day Salisim went to his field and began to build a stone dam and cut new channels in exactly the way Paho had suggested, yet he never said anything more to Paho about it. This was enough though. The other people now accepted our help, and we worked in their fields with them for many days, showing them how to follow the new ways.

It was late in the summer when we left this pueblo. The fields were now all prepared using Paho's methods. Wherever we went we were now welcomed. The people had accepted us, but it still seemed doubtful they had accepted the guidance of the canyon. If they thought of Paho still as the embodiment of Kokopelli they had ceased showing fear or reverence, but rather they had admitted him to their settlement as a friend. This, our first town had been the test. We had arrived as suspicious strangers who represented the authority of the canyon. When we left we were trusted friends.

The day was cold and windy with an overcast sky that promised fall to be close at hand. We were wrapped in our old and torn clothing, which had been in poor condition when we started the trip and had suffered much during our days in the fields. As we started to retrace the road to the canyon a man ran up to us. We knew him to be a promising youth who was the son of Salisim. He had with him two new feather robes, a large one for Paho and a small one from me. He thrust them into our hands, and, turning to go back to the pueblo, said, " Salisim says that you must be protected from the cold so that you may travel far and teach your dams and ditches to all the people."

CHAPTER TWENTY-TWO

Winter came suddenly that year. It had been warm and dry for many days, with the low slanting sun still warming the earth and the sky a deep cloudless blue, so that it seemed as though the warm stillness would go on without end. Even after the crops had been harvested and the songs of thanksgiving had been sung to the creator, still the days were windless and bright.

Then, in a single afternoon it all changed. The sun was first obscured by a thin veil moving in from the northwest, and a colder breeze was felt which stirred the dust and rolled a few small weeds across the open area between the outer wall and the trash heaps. Shortly the sky had become grey and low, and the red sandstone cliffs, which usually seemed to be as sharply traced as if a knife had cut them away from the blue of the sky, now looked soft and indistinct. The people in the plaza looked up at the sky, pulled a cloth over their shoulders, and seemed to shiver, not from the cold but from the anticipation of the winter, which had suddenly announced itself.

There were other sunny and warm days after this, but the spell had been broken, and the people hurried about, gathering in anything that might be burned during the months ahead, and checking the tightness of their storerooms. Not just they, but all of the animals about them would have also felt the message of winter, and would be looking for a warm and well-provisioned retreat. So, like the ground squirrels and pack rats, they lined their nests and stockpiled their acorns for the long nights that lay ahead.

We had, by then, visited a few of the outlying pueblos with much the same results as those achieved on our first encounter. The fear and contempt of the people was usually not as strong as at that first pueblo, but it could be sensed, nevertheless, hiding in the thoughts of the people. Before long, however, the story of our work had spread ahead of us, so that the people were already aware of our efforts, and knew that they had been accepted elsewhere. This made it easier to convince them to listen to Paho and his warnings. Now, however, we had returned to the pueblo of Hopaqa, heeding also the warnings of the weather.

Then winter truly descended upon the stone cities of the canyon, and with winter, and cold, also came the short days, often spent in the clan kivas, listening to tales or singing the songs of the people. Whenever possible work was done inside, and the people congregated in the underground round rooms, where their body heat warmed the darkness. Looms were set up, and tied down to loops in the floor, so that the cloth could be woven. In the dimness of the room it was a difficult task, done more by feel and practice than by sight. But the weavers would sit in front of the framework for many hours each day, talking, laughing, recounting stories of hunts held many years before. Often they would tell the stories many times over, and yet all enjoyed them as though hearing them for the first time.

Firewood was scarce. It had been carried many miles, and stockpiled in pyramid-like stacks outside the pueblo. Only in the bitterest cold would it be used for warmth, and even then it was usually a small fire, in the center of the room, which dimly reflected off the walls, and sent a glow to the dark round faces of the people who sat on the hard packed adobe of the floor and stared toward the embers. The entry door in the ceiling would be partially blocked with woven mats, so that only a small hole remained for the smoke to escape. This made the round room a dark and warm retreat, away from the wind and snow which swirled above.

The women who prepared food were not as comfortable, however. Since no food could be carried into the comforts of the round room they did their food preparation and cooking in the upper rooms, the front rooms built for that purpose. Here they had grinding bins for preparing corn and work rooms for cutting meats and for preparing beans, dried squash and whatever berries and nuts had been gathered and stored during the warmer months. They also had hearths in some of the front rooms. They, of course used the stockpiled firewood, but frugally. Firewood was for cooking, and for firing pottery, not for comfort, unless you were very wealthy.

Unlike the underground rooms with their air ducts and their roof openings, the ventilation system in the cooking rooms was far from pleasant. The smoke curled up from the fires and lingered near the ceiling. Ventilation holes in the sides of some of the rooms let the acrid black smudge escape to a limited extent, but most of it collected until it got low enough to spill out through the top of the doorway. This meant that the women would block the lower part of the only opening, the narrower part in the T shaped door, with a slab of stone, a piece of wood, or woven matting to keep out the cold wind as much as possible, leaving the top open for the smoke to exit through. Unfortunately, the meager warmth of the fire would heat the upper part of the room where the smoke was the thickest, and the lower level, where one could breathe, was still cold. It was a choice between choking and gasping while being somewhat warmer, and shivering inside the tightly wrapped blankets while squatting before the small fire.

Only when the food was ready for eating would the others leave the warmth of the underground room and go to the cooking rooms where they would receive their allotment. This they would quickly bolt down, in order to hurry back to the underground warmth, where the tales and singing would resume.

Winter was a time of little work for us, and we spent long hours talking. Paho would recount his early life to me as we tried to keep warm in the clan kiva, which had become our home. Not being of the clan, nor related to the others, we were usually apart from them, if not actually, at least socially. He told me of the years he had spent to the south, in the land of the parrots, and of the strange people and their customs. Then he would come back to his days in the rooms by the sandstone cliff, when he was a boy. When he told me of this time his voice would lower, so that no others could hear what he was saying, and in fact even I had difficulty hearing him. He was talking for his own ears, not mine. I heard many times the tales of his boyhood, and almost knew the great caverns above the pueblo, so that I could imagine myself sitting in the sun, on the white sand, with Tokchii beside me and the low winter sun heating and lighting the cavern with its pallid glow. When he spoke of Kolello and his hatred, I too felt that I was hated. He even told me of the black lands and of the caverns in the rocks, and the snake-god which dominated the area. When he told of the snake approaching him as he pressed his back against the wall of lava it brought a terror to me which made me glad of the many people crowded into the underground room.

"Why," I asked, "Did you not take Tokchii with you when you left?"

"I did not know, as I still do not know, if she was only pitying me. Many times I have wished that she were with me, but many other times I have been thankful that she has not had to endure what I have endured. Often I have thought that I would go back to the pueblo below the sandstone cliffs and see her. I have feared, until now, to do so because of the wrath of Melolo and Kolello, who would perhaps have me killed or perhaps they would harm her if they thought I went to see her. Now, with the protection of Hopaqa that is perhaps unlikely, but nevertheless, I fear going back. Perhaps I fear what I will find when I see her again. Also, my return might still put her in danger, especially if Kolello and the Snake Clan people believe that she knows of their secret ceremonies."

"We must, you know, go to that settlement just as we must go to all the settlements if we are to obey the orders of Hopaqa." I said. "Let us go there in the spring, and see if Tokchii is there. If she is angry with you then she will be safe from the Snake people because she will show that contempt. If she wishes to forgive then we will bring her back here where she may live with my family at their kiva, and be under the protection of Hopaqa."

"You are but a small boy," he would answer each time I made this suggestion. "Such things are not so simple. Women do not act as one would expect them to. Perhaps she would show no anger but still be unwilling to leave. Kolello is now, no doubt, very powerful, and has the backing of his uncle. Perhaps by now she has married another, and all of her family could be put in danger. Perhaps she would show great anger, and turn the people against both of us , so that we could not do Hopaqa's work. No, there are too many things to consider. To go back would not be wise."

This conversation in many forms was held many times in those long winter discussions. Always they ended in the same way, with Paho saying that I knew too little and was too young to understand. Always afterward there was a long period, perhaps days, in which we spoke only of the weather and of our work. But then he would again start to tell me his stories, and again I would urge him to return to his home pueblo

It was a long and cold winter, which had trouble ending. It would seem as though the spring had arrived and the people would be anxious to start to plant their crops, but still no word would come from the priests so they would wait, and within a few days the cold would return and send the people back to the shelter of the round rooms.

Then, on a day that was cold and blustery, with the wind surging down the canyon toward the sacred butte, drums began to beat from the south and grew louder as they approached. It was a steady thumping as of a slow marching, and we all knew what it meant. The priests had descended from their meditations and studies on the butte, and were moving up the valley, carrying news.

The priests were dressed in heavy cloaks of woven fiber, which had been painted in dark colors of red and brown and black. Around their ankles and wrists were strings of dry berries and thistles, which rattled and rustled with each step that they took. They were walking in cadence with the drum which the last man in the group of ten carried, and the rattling of their ornaments kept time with their firmly placed footsteps. Each of the priests wore a fearsome mask, which covered his head completely. The masks were adorned with bright feathers that extended outward making the priests seem to have huge heads, and each mask was decorated with elaborately painted lines of bright colors. One was an eagle, another a coyote, a third a parrot. They marched into the plaza and straight to the large kiva of Hopaqa. There was a matting placed over the smoke hole of this room, and the first man, the leader, stamped three times on the matting, saying, "Open the door and emerge. It is the time of rebirth."

The matting was flung aside from within, the top of a ladder came into view and then Hopaqa rose into the daylight. "Who calls?" he asked, repeating the litany.

"Prepare for the new world, as our ancestors did. As the people emerged from the earth into the remade world, at the command of Sotuknang, so shall our people emerge from the underground world to serve Taiowa the creator."

"As our people came forth from the home of the ant people, so will we come forth from the bowels of the earth." chanted Hopaqa, and the people in the plaza around him whispered the same words in unison. "We will be reborn with the world, and we will serve Taiowa, the father, the creator, the light. So will we, through him, serve the earth which is our mother, and the corn which is too our mother, as the fruit of the earth."

The priests then increased the tempo of the drum, and of their stamping feet, and the head priest raised his voice and spoke loudly to all of the gathered people. "The time is now here for the planting of the seeds. It has been many days since the Father Sun left his winter home and started to move to the south. He has now told us that his world is ready. Mother Earth is prepared to bring forth new life, and we must help to make her fertile. Tomorrow we begin the planting. Hopaqa, call forth your runners and send them along all our roads to the most distant villages, that they may know it is the time of rebirth."

It only took a few minutes for the people to begin the dances, for they had spent many days anticipating this moment. They had watched the sun and the moon, much as the priests did, and had seen the signs in the weather which said that winter was ending and that the time of planting was close at hand. As the priests had move north up the canyon the people had heard the drums, and all had followed the priests, knowing that they were going to the central pueblo, the city of Hopaqa. Also from the cities to the north came crowds who had heard the drums. It would be a night of dancing, of feasting of singing. Taiowa had again told the people to be fruitful and to help his world to be fruitful. It would be a night of celebration.

It was some time in that night that I was near the priests, stamping my feet, and turning in the firelight, when I saw that Paho had joined the people, and was standing near the firelight, silhouetted by the glow.

Until then he had remained well away from the crowd, unnoticed, but now he had come in close, and his face was turned toward the priests. At just that moment one of the masked priest moved near him. He was unusually tall and broad shouldered, and was a man I did not recognize, even though the priests often were seen about the pueblo when they were not at their butte. As he came near Paho he reached under his chin, and just for an instant he lifted the mask, exposing a narrow face with dark deep-set eyes. The face was unsmiling and fearsome, and he looked directly at Paho before replacing the mask.

I looked then at my master and saw a look of such astonishment that I knew the lifted mask had been meant only for Paho. The look disappeared as quickly as it appeared, however, and I believe I was the only one who saw the episode. The dance went on, and Paho soon left the revelry, although the dancing and singing lasted until dawn.

I had been looking forward to the next three days, which I knew would continue the celebration of the planting. It was one of the great festivals of the year. I had prepared special ornaments to wear at the dances, and knew that there would be great amounts of food to eat, delicacies that had been saved all winter. The sun of the first day had only just risen, and the people had sung the Song of The Creation when my master sent for me. "Prepare food and clothing for us," he said "for we leave today."

"But master," I said, "The celebration is just beginning, and we have been looking forward to it! Can't we wait until the three days have gone by before we start out?"

"No," he said, "We leave as soon as possible for we have much work to do. We cannot remain here playing and dancing when the rebirth calls us to help our people."

Unhappily I prepared to go and do as he said. Then I turned to him again and asked, "Where then are we going?"

"We will go where you have been asking me that we go. We will make our first stop of the season at the village to the south where I came from."

CHAPTER TWENTY-THREE

A green haze covered the usually brown valley, as the moisture of spring fed the seeds, which had lain waiting for the opportunity to send out their tiny green shoots, and dig tenacious rootlets into the unusually moist earth. The bright sunlight warmed our faces as we walked slowly toward the low saddle between the rolling masses of bright red sandstone. From this direction they were not cliffs, but bulges that seemed to look like the backs of gigantic red fish as they rolled out of shallow water in pursuit of some elusive prey.

Paho had said little in the days it had taken us to walk this far. Now he stopped, and I wondered if he would change his mind. He gazed for a long time at the opening in the rocks without speaking, then picked up his string bag and motioned for me to follow. We soon found ourselves passing between high stone abutments, and could see the next valley stretching before us, even greener than the one we were leaving, and very wide. To our right a side canyon cut close to the sandstone, bordered by a tangle of shrubs and sagebrush. Above that I could see the sloping rock, and the pinon and ceder trees which ranged along the top, silhouetted against the sparkling cleanness of the blue, blue sky.

"There," he said, motioning toward the side canyon as we approached it, "Where you can see a clump of cedar trees, a short way above the stream. Behind those bushes is the cave I told you about. It is there where I was to have met Tokchii. Remember it, should we need a meeting place."

The red cliffs grew steeper and higher as we passed into the valley. We kept to the right, walking along a white sandy strip which was below the overhanging sandstone. I noticed that Paho kept looking upward at the rocks above our heads, and slowed as we came closer to a gigantic pile of broken rock, twice the height of a man, with many individual pieces as large as a room. It was not until we had reached this talus that I realized where we were. In the cliffside, facing us I could see three parallel rows of holes cut into the rock, and knew that they had once supported the beam ends of roof supports. They were horizontal rows of holes representing the three floor and ceiling levels of what had once been a settlement. Jutting out from between the broken rocks I could see the cut ends of huge timbers, which had been crushed by the falling cliffside. This was all that remained; yet I knew that under that debris, in a round room which now was completely obliterated, were the bodies of every relative Paho had ever had.

We could have stayed on the other side of the pass and avoided this, but he had wanted to see it again. I stood back, now and waited as he moved forward, stumbling over the rocks and peering into the crevices. Above him I could see the scar on the cliff, the horizontal and vertical cracks, and the overhang that remained after the great slab had dropped away. He groped at the rocks, and seemed to be blindly trying to roll them aside, then he stopped, and sat on the highest slab for some minutes, with his back toward me, looking over the valley. Then he raised himself, climbed back down to where I stood, and silently led the way toward the pueblo.

Soon a dog ran out barking and snarling, followed by a group of naked children who stared at us and ran back to the pueblo, which occupied the slope between the sandstone cliffs and the farmlands below. It was much as I had imagined it in the stories he had told me. The row of stone rooms, the round rooms before them, the wall in front, the great Kiva its low wall standing alone some distance from the pueblo... And dominating the whole scene, looming over the settlement: the gigantic mouths of the caves. It was as if they wished to eat the tiny pueblo, the streaks of black that extended down the back walls looking like fangs, the white sand floor a tongue.

There was no sign of recognition on Paho's part as a middle-aged man with long hair tied back and with a heavy coat of woven fiber approached him. The people who had come forward parted to make a path for the man, indicating he was a chief. The man spoke first "Paho, do you not remember me? I am Sabieto, of the corn clan."

"Yes! of course I remember you well, now that I see you better." Paho said with enthusiasm. "Your family was good to me when I was a boy, and your mother wove sandals for me and fed me many times. Yes, I remember well the years when I used to visit your kiva or watch in the upper rooms when the corn was being ground. I owe you and your family much, and am here to serve you if you have any use for me."

"It is we that must serve you," Sabieto replied. You will be guests in our round room, and you and your helper will eat our food. We have heard strange tales of your journeys and we will wish to have you tell us of them. Your fame has come ahead of you, so that we have been told of the miracle of your star, which even we, this far from the canyon, could see in the sky for many nights.

He led the way for us, and we walked up the slope to the pueblo, followed by a crowd of people.   I could see that Paho was trying to hide his curiosity as he walked beside his old friend, but he would occasionally glance back at the crowd, trying to pick out individuals, and there was little question in my mind who he searched for; Tokchii. Among the people were many younger women, and all seemed curious, but I could not see one who appeared to have the beauty and slimness that Paho had spoken of those many evenings during the past winter. There were few men to be seen, only old ones who could no longer go to the fields to help with the planting.· The runner had arrived only a few days before, and the ceremonies of the planting had only just ended, so the men were all in the fields planting the seed corn and the beans. I knew, also, that the women who did not have very small babies to care for would be helping the men in the fields at this critical time. Perhaps Tokchii was helping with the planting and would be seen at the end of the day.

Below the pueblo, an hour's walk , were the clustered round rooms used by the men when they were tending the crops. I knew this because Paho had told me that it was one of those rooms that had served as his home after the earthquake, when Tokchii had been caring for him. Perhaps the workers would spend the night there in order to get as much planting done as possible, and maybe Tokchii would not appear for a number of days.

In the meantime, we must observe the formalities. As guests we could not seem to be prying by asking questions. We were of the central canyon, and had therefore to not appear to be too curious, since the people in all the outlying settlements guarded against revealing too much to those who represented the Empire, those who might learn too much, and bring down heavier taxation upon them. We knew that eventually we would learn what we wanted to know, but it would have to be at their pace, not ours. Even the fact that Paho was of this settlement originally did not mitigate the need to observe this formality.

Paho and I followed Sabieto, therefore, to the part of the village which was used by the Corn Clan, where we were offered a gourd filled with cool drinking water. This was passed from one to another until it was empty, and then a child was sent to refill it. In the meantime food was brought to us in crockery bowls, with painted ladles for eating. As we ate the others stood by and watched, not participating, but appreciating the pleasure they brought to their guests. We, for our part, had eaten little on the trail, just dried foods which we had brought from the canyon, so the food seemed especially good, and we smiled at our hosts.

It was some time after this that we were resting in the Corn Clan round room, the kiva which Paho must have spent many hours in as a boy, visiting his friend Tokchii. Sabieto, being her uncle, would have been there also, and would have watched as this little boy grew into manhood, and would have known of their love, and of the eventual separation. Yet he said nothing of this, speaking instead of crops, and of weather, and telling us many times of the bad years they had been having, and of the poor crops and the meager existence which allowed them to send but little to the storerooms of Hopaqa and the other chiefs at the canyon. Others would enter the kiva from time to time, usually older people who could not work in the fields, and each would go up to Paho, giving his name, and saying that he remembered him from the early days. Paho would formally greet each of the elders, and they would speak also of the crops and weather, and often reminisce about the days when Paho was a boy. None had forgotten his great success at the time of the initiation, but none mentioned the death of his family or his ostracism.

Then a younger man entered; a heavyset man with a dark face and short legs below a square body. His black hair had been cut in bangs over his dark eyes and he was bare to the waist. Around his neck was the skin of a rattlesnake, fastened loosely over his chest as though the snake were biting its own tail. Below that he wore a girdle of cotton cloth, and below that sandals of woven yucca fiber. He had an air of authority as he stepped away from the ladder and faced Paho.

"Wuchii," exclaimed Paho, "It is you, then, who has taken the leadership of the Snake clan!"

"Yes, Paho. I welcome you to our poor pueblo in the name of the Snake clan. I am sorry I was not here to greet you as was Sabieto, but I was working in the fields with our people. I was sent for, and came as quickly as I could, so that I could welcome you as an old friend."

"I knew," said Paho, "That Kolello was no longer here, since I saw him at the canyon. He is now a high priest and goes to the Butte of the Astronomers each day."

I realized, then, who the priest who had raised his mask had been; the tall man with the fearsome eyes who had revealed himself to Paho. It was then that Paho had decided we would come to this village after all. He had known that his old enemy was no longer here, and that he might find Tokchii without endangering her. It also made me wonder again about the hawk that had been disturbed from his roost on the Butte immediately after we had come so close to being killed by the falling boulder. Had someone been up there, and had that person perhaps been Kolello?

"Yes," Wuchii answered, "Kolello has been gone for three years, now. His grandmother was not of this village but of the snake clan at the canyon, at the cliff top village to the north. It was only shortly after the death of Melolo that he left, although he could well have stayed here and had the position I now occupy. His grandmother, we are told, had sent word that she could help him to become a priest of the Butte of the Astronomers if he would go to the canyon. At first we thought he would stay, but then he suddenly decided to go, and did so in two days time.

"It was strange that he left, because he had always wanted the position of Melolo, as everyone knew, and with Melolo's death he was expected to move into the position. They say now that he is very powerful, and may one day be the head priest. He is feared if not liked."

"So, Melolo has died. He was not very old." mused Paho.

"Oh, he did not just die! His death was a great and a fearful message from Tuwachua, the Snake God. It told us that Kolello would be our next chief. That is why we felt it strange that he went to the canyon.

"It was three years ago, just after you had left us, that Kolello and Melolo went to the south to perform certain rituals. It was felt that Tuwachua was still unhappy, even after the earthquake, and that he must be spoken to. It was usual for four of us to perform such rituals but in this case Melolo said that only the two should go. They went to a secret place of the Snake people, which I am told you might know about," glancing knowingly at Paho, "And were gone three days. At the end of the third day Kolello staggered into the village, carrying the body of Melolo, his uncle. He said that his uncle had been performing a particular dance to Tuwachua, when Tuwachua himself appeared in the form of a huge rattlesnake. Startled, Melolo had leapt sideways, hitting his head against an outcropping of jagged rock, and had fallen unconscious to the ground. As Kolello watched, the great snake had slithered up to the fallen priest and bitten his neck. Then he had make three circles about the body, looked directly into the eyes of Kolello, and finally disappeared into the rocks from where he had come.

"When we looked at Melolo's body it was as Kolello had said, for there was dried blood on the back of his head where he struck the rock, and two holes in his neck which were as far apart as the width of three of my fingers. No one had ever seen a bite of such size before. It had to have been Tuwachua."

"Yes," commented Paho, "And the God, circling the body three times and then looking into the eyes of Kolello would mean that in three days Kolello would take the uncle's place."

"Yes, and Kolello did take the position, but only for a few weeks before deciding to do as his grandmother asked. Therefore I, as next in line, became the leader of the Snake Clan."

CHAPTER TWENTY-FOUR

Many others visited us that day, as we sat in the Corn Clan round room. At the end of the day many of the field workers returned, and all remembered Paho, and came to see him. But still, Tokchii did not appear. The Corn Clan members were very friendly and helpful, and often referred to the early days when Paho came to the kiva, yet none mentioned the missing woman.

That evening all of the clan members of the Corn Clan gathered in the clan kiva, and sat rapt, as Paho spoke for many hours of his travels after leaving the village. They had all known him well in the days before the earthquake, and the death of his family, yet there was now a distance, a gulf that could not be crossed. It was, perhaps, because of his appearance, and the legends that had preceded him, but there was more, too. The people never mentioned the fact that he had been driven from the settlement by the Snake Clan, and that they had done nothing to prevent it, but the fact lay there, in the middle of the kiva, between him and them, like a coiled and menacing viper; like the snake which had caused it. No person would mention the threatening presence, but all knew it was there.

They knew, too that he wished to ask them many questions, but none volunteered information, and all knew that it would be improper for him to pry into the happenings at the pueblo unless they opened the subject. Too much had happened which was not spoken of. He had returned under the wrong circumstances, not as a repentant outcast, but as a powerful emissary from the distrusted and disliked leaders of the Empire. To close the gap, to pass by the snake which coiled between them would mean that they would have to admit that they had wronged him, and this they did not wish to do. So they listened in wonder to the stories of the land of the parrots, and of the great cities, and of the strange customs of the foreigners, and of the games and ceremonies of these people. There was, perhaps, disbelief also, especially when he told of huge lakes of sweet water and of rivers which ran deep and strong all year, and of rain that came almost every day for months, soaking deep into the soil and nurturing gigantic forests.

On the next day we made it known why we were there. It had now become very much the same at each village; the suspicion, the challenges, the reluctance to accept, and finally a grudging acceptance of the ideas and the methods that we brought. Even here it appeared that it would be no different. We would have to do the same job of convincing, but here we lacked the mystique, which accompanied Paho, since the people had known him before he looked like Kokopelli. On the other hand, though, they had known of his prowess as a youth, and of course they knew of the miracle of the exploding star.

We knew we would need to go to the fields with the workers, and work beside them just as we had at the other pueblos, but here we welcomed the opportunity because it gave us chance to go to the work camps, where we might find the woman we were searching for but could not ask about. Therefore, as soon as the formalities of the visit had been observed; the visiting with the people, the feasting, the ceremonies; Paho told the people of the messages he brought from the Canyon, and then about the agricultural methods he wished to teach them. As we had expected, the suspicion surfaced immediately, so that Paho had to explain in detail the way in which the people to the south lived and raised crops. Finally it was arranged that two days later we would go to the work camp and show them what Paho had in mind.

That night was much like the night before, except that now we were in the kiva of the Snake Clan. To have slighted them would have been politically disastrous. Because Paho had already met with their leader, and because his childhood ties had been more with the people of the Corn Clan it had been acceptable that he spend the first evening with the Corn Clan people, but it was expected that the leading clan should not be left out of any news from the canyon. Again, we crouched in the darkened room and again Paho told the people of his travels and of the wonders of the South. He went into a great deal of detail and description, convincing the leaders that he brought wonderful changes from the south not orders from the north. They had already heard, that day, of our intention to go to the fields and show them how to better handle the meager water, which they received. Now Paho tried to convince them that he only came to help them. They listened, and marveled over the things that he said, but, as with every pueblo, were non-committal.

Two days later I was alone in one of the fields. It was a long distance from the five round rooms which were used as a camp for the field workers, to the southeast, where a sandy patch of soil was being planted in the shadow of a sandstone bluff. Here the water from what rain occasionally fell cascaded over the clifftop, briefly filling a steep banked arroyo. Here also, against the cliff, was a seep under the sandstone, which provided a water supply throughout the year. A hollow had been dug, and lined with flat stones and fine white sand, so that the precious water could collect. The area was distant from the pueblo, but frequented by water carriers at times when the closer sources to the main pueblo had dried up during droughts. Now it was being used as a source of water for the people who were staying at the work camp.

Paho had already shown what was to be done to better utilize the water which reached this field, and I was now working alone, placing rocks where the dams were to be built and scraping lines where he had said that the channels should be dug. Later the others would come to this field, and we would all work together to carry out Paho's plan.

I was sitting on the arroyo bank, partially hidden by a creosote bush, and studying the work that was to be done, when I glanced back toward the work camp, and saw a person coming toward me. Being as I was a small boy, and hidden by the bush, which was much the same color as my clothes, she did not see me as she came closer. Those many nights in the canyon when Paho and I had talked, or more exactly, when he had talked and I had listened, I had seen this woman many times in my imagination. It could only be her; Tokchii! He had told me, many times, of her unusual slimness and of her beauty. He had described the clothes she wore, and the jewelry that she had been given by the clan leaders. Especially, he had told me of a pendant which she wore, containing a triangular piece of turquoise, and two shells which had been traded for and which had been brought all the way from the ocean to the west by traders. I could only see that this woman wore a pendant, but was too far away to distinguish its nature.

I waited until she had passed by, and had approached the water hole. Then I crept closer, following the arroyo bottom. I did not wish for her to see me until I was sure. Finally I was close enough, and raised up, to where I could see her clearly, only a few feet away. She had her back to me, but she turned now, and I saw clearly that she was wearing a beautiful pendant around her neck, which rested between her breasts. It was a triangular flat of turquoise as wide as a man's hand, and on each side of it, strung on the leather thong, was a lustrous seashell. It could only be the pendant Paho had described, and this could only be Tokchii.

"What do you want?" she said when she saw me. "You are the boy who comes with Paho. I have been told you were coming. Why are you spying on me?"

"You are Tokchii! I am not spying on you, but was working down below when you approached. You are Tokchii, aren't you?"

"Do not say that name! Do not ever say it again! The person you speak of does not exist in this pueblo any longer. It is forbidden that her name be mentioned. Please leave me alone and do not speak to me of things which are not allowed." She picked up her water jug, and started to turn away, trying to end the conversation.

"Please," I said, "Do not leave me without telling me. My master has searched for you and dreamed of you and spoken of you to me so many times that I know it is you." She hesitated and looked back at me again. "We have come to this pueblo because I asked him to come. He did not wish to come back to so much remembrance, and so much pain, but I wanted him to at least find out if his dreams were only dreams. Please do not leave without at least talking to me."

"I am not the one you spoke of." she now said. "I am the sister of the one whose name may never be mentioned. She has been gone from the village for four years now."

"But, the pendent with the turquoise and sea shells. Paho has told me of it."

"There were two, for the two sisters. Wherever she is, she must still wear the other. Do you not know where she is? We of the village thought she had gone to Paho." The woman had now put down the water jug and was looking wonderingly at me. "We were very close, as sisters, and looked much alike, but she was the younger of us. When the traders came with the seashells my mother had already traded for two identical and beautiful pieces of turquoise, so she then traded a large amount of corn for the strange shells which were brought so far. Then she made two pendants, one for each of us, and told us to wear them always, as a sign that we were sisters, and would always care for one another. Paho will remember this, and will tell you of me. I remember him well, and his love for my sister. He would stand at the door of the workroom for many hours while we ground corn, and speak to us. That was in the last year, after the manhood ceremonies in which he was initiated, and before the death of his family."

"But you say you thought she was with him. Why is she not here, and where has she gone?"

"All the people have probably thought that she was with him at the canyon. They could not ask because it is forbidden to speak of her. You were greeted first by my uncle of the Corn Clan, who hoped to know what had happened to his niece, but could not ask. If you do not know where she is, then neither do we. When she left the pueblo, it was in secret, and no one knew where she was going. It was believed that she went to seek Paho, whom she had loved, and still loved."

"If she left four years ago, it must have been just shortly after Paho was driven out, but he would have been way to the south by then. In the telling of his travels the last two nights the listeners must have known that she could not have found him. If she had gone in search in the same direction she would have been stopped, and perhaps killed, by the strangers. We came to this pueblo hoping she would be here... Tell me why her name may not be spoken, and why she left the pueblo."

"Yes," she said, after some thought, "I will tell you. You can then tell Paho what has happened. She searches for him, I know, and he searches for her.

"After Paho disappeared from the round room where he was being cared for my sister told me of their plans, and of the night when she went to the cave, only to wait in vain. He had left without her. She was bitter and unhappy for some days, and the anger of Kolello and Melolo was brought down upon her. They thought she knew where he had gone, and questioned her many times. They sent men out to look for him, but they could not follow his tracks. She told them she knew nothing but they would not believe her.

"Perhaps it was the questioning sessions which aroused the interest of Kolello. She was taken many times to his kiva, where he would keep her for hours, asking her questions. It may also have been his hatred for Paho which made him fall in love with my sister. I do not know any more, except that he began to insist that my sister see him often, and as the nephew of Melolo, and the heir to the leadership of the pueblo he usually got what he wanted. She told me of this; of his advances and her rejections. He was extremely insistent, and she finally went to Melolo, asking for his protection, for she feared Kolello. Melolo came to her aid, in that he spoke to his nephew, and told him that a leader of his people need not make a fool of himself. I know this must be what he said, for Melolo told my sister that was his opinion, and she told me.

"After that it was better. Kolello often called for my sister, but he was not forceful. Perhaps he feared his uncle. It was then, however, that Kolello and his uncle went to perform the rituals, and Melolo was killed by the huge rattlesnake! That made Kolello the leader, with no one to oppose him. He made it known, within days, that he would marry my sister."

"So she ran away?" I asked, "So that she would not have to marry Kolello?"

"That's right. She told me that night that she was leaving, and I helped her to pack food and clothing. By morning she was gone. She said she would search for Paho, and that she did not care that he was crippled. I told her to climb the sandstone cliffs behind the pueblo, using the hand and foot holds we had used as children. Then she could follow the ridge, staying on the rock and leaving no footprints for Kolello to follow. That is probably what she did, but I do not know where she went from there.

"Kolello was furious! He searched for her for days, and sent others also, but she was never found. Runners were sent to other villages, but nothing could be learned. I have hoped, all these years that she was with Paho, and safe."

"And Kolello forbid that her name ever be spoken again?"

"Yes, he said that the snake god who destroyed the clan of Paho was still angry, and that the disappearance of his bride was also the fault of Paho, who had cast a spell upon her when she was caring for him. He said that the gods would bring a similar disaster to anyone who spoke her name, so her name has not been uttered again until this day, when you spoke it to me."

"You have been very good to tell me this." I said. "I will tell Paho what I now know. Would you speak to him?"

"No!" she said forcefully, "I have told you things which may bring the wrath of Tuwachua upon me and my family, as he did to the family of Paho. I cannot take any further risk. It was only because I did not see you that you were able to talk to me. I have been careful to stay out of sight ever since your arrival."

"Nevertheless," I said, "You have done only good, and I thank you for what you have told me. I spoke to you because you are so beautiful I thought you must be the woman Paho told me of. Your words have shown me, also, that you must be as wise and as kind as Paho has said of your sister. If my master and I can find your sister, we will. If she lives, he will care for her, since he still loves her. Because you have told me these things you may be helping her."

She picked up her water jug, then, and was about to leave. Then she carefully placed it back on the ground, walked over to me and looked deeply into my eyes. "Take care of him," she said. "And search for my sister. If you can, let me know what has happened to her. Paho is fortunate to have a helper like you."

If a boy of nine years could fall in love with a woman of perhaps twenty years, I fell in love with her then. As she carried her water jug back toward the round rooms I watched her in awe. It would be many years before I found another woman like her.

CHAPTER TWENTY-FIVE

There were hundreds of small settlements that made up the Empire. Some were only a few rooms; others were large villages. Our people now numbered in the thousands, growing their crops and building their homes anywhere they could find water and rich land. With the years of good moisture the numbers of people had grown, and with the growth they had occupied areas, which in bad years would not have been suitable. Now they were spread to most of the valleys, and were growing their crops in places that in poorer years would not have supported anything more than cactus. Paho had said we would visit them all! There was no settlement too small or too remote that it could be bypassed. He said that the more remote and isolated villagers needed him the most, since they were the ones who would be the first to suffer when the bad years came.

I knew that Paho believed this, but I also knew that he would search them all as he visited them all. I had told him, of course, what I had learned of the disappearance of Tokchii, and he immediately became determined to find her.

"It is useless," I argued, "To search for her. If she is alive, then she does not wish to see you. Otherwise she would have come to you as soon as she was told the story of the exploding star. We have seen that the tale has been told in every pueblo, and all know where you came from. She could not help but know of you and of your return."

"Yes," he answered, "But I do not believe that she has died. She would not have gone to the south in search of me, because she knew, as everybody knows, the stories of the dangers in that direction. She would not have believed I would go there. I remember, when we were children that we would recount to one another the stories we had heard of the monstrous people to the south, who would kill anyone who wandered into their territory. We would scare each other with these stories, and always said that we would never go in that direction.

"No, she would not have gone to the south because she would not have believed I would have done so. What she did not realize is that I wanted to be killed. When I left my home without her, bearing the curse of the snake, I knew that none of our people would harm me because it was forbidden. I could wander anywhere and be fed and cared for, but also despised. Therefore I went to the south. I did not want to live, so I went where I thought I would be murdered. And it was because I made that choice that Kolello and his scouts never found me. They too knew the stories, and would not venture too far into alien territory. It was a surprise to me when I found that they would not kill me, but feared me because of my deformed shape. My curse had become my protection."

"Why, then, has she not sought you out? If, as you say, she must be alive, and if, as her sister says, she has forgiven you and still loves you, than where is she?"

"That I do not know, but we will search, and we will find her, and we will then know. There are hundreds of settlements, and we will visit them all."

And we did visit almost all of them, over the next eleven years. There was no settlement too remote or too small for our attention. And every time we entered a new settlement Paho would ask if anyone knew of Tokchii. And every time the results would be the same. Nothing. Often they had a memory of a woman who had wandered into the settlement some years back, but they could not be sure if it had been her or some other woman, and they never knew where she had come from or where she had gone. It was this succession of stories that often decided the course of our wanderings. If someone seemed to remember a person who matched the description, then we would visit every person in the district, trying to follow the lead.

Perhaps the strongest clues came to us in the third year, when we were going to the northwest of the canyon. An old woman said that she remembered well a young girl who had reached the single round room she and her family occupied in a remote canyon. It was a winter evening, with snowflakes thinly blowing from the darkening sky, with cold that numbed the face as the wind swirled through the small canyon between sandstone bluffs. She remembered that it had been the last of the good years, and the crops had been stored for the long winter already. A grey sky had been hanging low over the land all afternoon, and now, as the sun disappeared and darkness started to close in, they had seen this girl approach them from the southwest.

"Tell me what she looked like." Paho demanded.

"That is hard to say, for she would not remove her outer clothing, even in the warmth of the round room, but kept herself wrapped in a cloak, covering her head also, so that her face was in shadow. She stayed only that one evening, eating the food we offered, and then slumping down near the fire, and quickly falling asleep. We had tried to ask her questions, but she told us little. Only that she had walked far that day and was very tired. When we told her that we were of the Corn Clan, though, she smiled and told us that she also had been of our clan. She may have only said that in order to gain our favor, however. We learned nothing else from her."

"She must have said more." Paho insisted. "Did she say where she was coming from or where she was going? Did she tell you why she was not at her home on such a night? Surely she must have said more."

"Nothing that I can remember. She spoke, of course, but about the weather and the crops, and of the food we offered her. She was grateful. She spoke of how tired she was, and did say that she had been walking for many days. I remember, too, that she asked if strangers like herself often stopped by our settlement. We told her that it was very unusual, and that we had seen no travelers except herself for almost a year."

"And, did she seem interested or disappointed when you told her that? Do you think she was merely making conversation, or was she trying to find out if others had been by before her?"

"Yes, now that I think back, perhaps she was disappointed. She had been talking freely until then, but afterward she was silent and withdrawn. Soon after she asked if she could sleep in our round room for the night, and we made her a place near the fire. Within minutes she was asleep, still wrapped in her cloak. When we awoke in the morning she was gone."

"Were there tracks in the snow?" he asked. "Do you know which direction she went?"

"There was a little new snow, and she had left tracks out of the mouth of the canyon, but where she went from there we do not know. It was cold and windy, and we did not see any reason to follow her. She had come, now she was gone."

We visited every settlement of any size in the vicinity. No one else recalled the young girl in the cloak. She seemed to have disappeared. But Paho was convinced it must have been Tokchii. He would not give up, and we spent the rest of that season wandering from settlement to settlement. At each we would do our usual work, but always Paho would ask about the girl, and also ask about remote settlements, which we might not have yet visited. Each visit would lead us, therefore to another, more obscure, hidden in some small valley, perhaps only a few people struggling to grow enough food to survive, gathering berries and nuts in the hills, and hunting rabbits, prairie dogs, birds, and deer. Often they were suspicious and threatening when we arrived, fearful that we came to take their meager stockpiles of food. We then would have to win the trust of these people. Paho did this in order to learn what he could of his missing Tokchii, but also to convince them that he could help them to survive better, and to get through the bad times, which he believed would come. As a result he also, perhaps inadvertently, accomplished that which he had been sent by Hopaqa to do; the pulling together of the farthest parts of the empire.

The second result of my telling Paho the things I had learned was to deepen forever the split between him and Kolello. His immediate reaction had been one of rage. He had wanted to go to the canyon and kill his adversary. Luckily we were far enough away at the time that he had time to think it over before we got back to the stone cities.

In fact, I convinced him to stop at a number of settlement on the way back, suggesting that Tokchii might have passed through them. This led to our usual routine in each location, so that it was many weeks before we finally arrived at the canyon.

By then he had thought the situation through. Kolello was in a powerful position politically, and unapproachable physically because he spent his time on the Astronomer's Butte, where no others were allowed to go. Therefore Paho determined to go to Hopaqa and tell him what we now knew. He believed that Hopaqa was a fair man who was interested in the welfare of his people. Perhaps if he knew the truth he would have Kolello removed from his priesthood, and sent back to his village. We both believed Kolello had killed his own uncle, Melolo, and that he had tried to kill us.

Hopaqa listened in silence. The kiva was empty, except for the old chief, the younger hunchback and me, a young boy who stood unobtrusively in the darkest recess of the kiva, lest I be ordered to leave. Paho carefully spoke of all that we had learned. He told of the death of Melolo and the blow that had evidently felled him, putting him at the mercy of the huge snake. He told of the harassment of Tokchii and her rejection of his advances. He told of her flight, and of Kolello's sudden decision to come to the canyon. He told also of the night when Kolello had raised his mask to let Paho know who he was. He spoke of the suspicion we had that someone had caused the boulder to fall from the Astronomer's Butte, nearly killing us.

When he had finished, Hopaqa spoke. "Paho, what you say may all be true, but it is only your suspicion. I know that you hate this man, and so you see every action as an evil plan. Perhaps Melolo did fall and hit his head. Maybe the boulder was loosened by rain and happened to fall just as you passed under it. Kolello is not forbidden from revealing himself by raising his mask to anyone he wishes. Perhaps he was only wanting to let you know it was he."

"Yes, Hopaqa, that is true. But I know this man, and have known him since we were boys together. I know that he is capable of the things of which I speak, and is therefore unfit to be a priest of our people, even if he did not commit these acts. There can be no question of his actions toward Tokchii. If she died at the hands of the aliens, or starved to death in the desert, that is his fault. The man is not to be trusted."

"But see, Paho, that we talk of only a woman. As a leader he has the right to select a wife. Our people would say that she was ungrateful to reject him and to flee. They would say that her rejection caused him to feel himself dishonored in his own pueblo, and bring about his leaving of his home and his position."

"Then you do not believe me, and will not support me?" Paho said quietly.

"I did not say I did not believe you. I believe everything that you say. If I could help you, I would. You do not understand the position that Kolello occupies. I am the leader of the people, but I am only that leader if the gods say so. The priests speak to the gods from their high retreat, and tell the people what they have heard. If the gods tell Kolello that I am to no longer be a leader he may have the power to have me removed.

"Do you not remember the authority of the Snake Clan leaders in your own pueblo? They were only representing what they were told from the priests at the Butte. How much more powerful, then, are these priests! I am not able to oppose Kolello on this, even though I know you are right.

"Let me tell you something. After your star appeared Kolello came to me. He told me then that you were not to be trusted, and that you had brought disaster upon your own clan. He feared you then, and he still does. You, because of your miracle, are more able to oppose him than I am. Mine is a political power, while both yours and his rest upon the signs from the heavens. I can protect you and sponsor you among the people, so that you are able to help our people. I cannot help you when the problem deals with the gods. Your hunched back, your strange knowledge and your exploding light in the sky are of a different sort. That is what Kolello fears, and that is why he will never allow you any peace. The time will come when your power and his power must be tested. It is my hope that you will succeed!"

"What should I do to protect myself, then?" Paho asked.

"Your protection is the reverence, the fear and the knowledge of the people. What you do for me and for them is your best protection.

I knew this when I asked you to represent me in the outlying parts of the Empire. As you go about and teach the people you do two things; you ally me more closely with the spiritual side, and thereby protect me somewhat from the priests, and you ally yourself with the people, making it harder for the priests to discredit you. I was not able to tell you all this at that first meeting, since you were not aware of the threat of Kolello. In truth we need each other, and our common enemy is Kolello. He is only one of a number of priests, now, but he is young and he is ambitious and the leaders of the Astronomers grow old. Even now I see them looking about for a successor, and I see Kolello trying to be that man. To do so he must triumph over a rival, and you have been chosen as that rival. For that reason he already takes any opportunity to speak against you."

"I believe you, Hopaqa. I will do as you say. The boy and I will go to every settlement, and we will continue to tell them that we are there to help them because Hopaqa wishes that we do so. Perhaps you and I will then have the strength of the people behind us so that Kolello will continue to fear us. As we spoke of at our first meeting, I believe that there are to be lean times for our people. If they do not prepare for this, through your storage and through my water management plans, then the Empire will disintegrate. We must not let Kolello discredit us, or our people will be the ones to suffer."

So it was that we continued our travels. We would spend each winter in the Canyon, but as soon as spring appeared we would again search out each small hidden group of farmers and teach them the new ways, always asking questions and looking for the missing Tokchii. As we went to the further settlements we often stopped at others that we had visited in prior years, and were welcomed by people who now knew us and trusted us. They were using the methods Paho had taught them, and their crops were larger and their food supplies were growing faster than their population. These people sent the excess to the canyon for storage, as we asked, and Hopaqa too prospered.

We heard, too, in our travels, that others from the canyon had occasionally visited them, and they came as priests from the Butte. We were told that these men would often speak against Paho, saying that his alien ways were not the ways of our people. They would not tell the people to change, but they did plant seeds of doubt. But the people were hard to convince then they were eating better than they had in many years. To them the star of Paho had been a message that a time of change had come. While they prospered it would be hard to change their minds. Nevertheless, Kolello continued to send his emissaries to cast doubt where they could.

It was in the fourth year after the star that the rains failed. The land lay parched day after day under the clear sky that sucked up all moisture. The crops sprouted and then withered. The people carried water great distances, and the corn tried to raise its head, only to be beat back down by the merciless sun. Some survived and a few ears of corn formed. The meager harvest was not enough, but the people had filled many rooms in their own pueblos during the good years, and they had enough to eat that winter. Those pueblos that had already been visited and instructed by Paho suffered less than those that had not.

That winter little snow fell. It was possible to travel about without worrying about snow. When spring came there was little mud to contend with. The rains still had not returned. The people planted their stored seed corn, and watched for it to sprout. Little did. The people watched the skies day after day, but they remained clear and blue. That fall there was no harvest. The people had eaten the food stored in their villages and there was no more. Even the seed corn was gone. All of Paho's innovations had not been enough to help in this disastrous year. Now the people looked to Hopaqa and the other storehouse owners in the Canyon. It was because of this they survived. The storerooms were opened and the corn and beans were given out to those who had deposited them. So, also, those who had not had any food stored at the canyon were still able to receive foods, which they promised to repay when the good years came back.

The next year the snows and then the rains returned and the land produced great quantities of food. Storerooms were refilled and long lines of men could be seen trudging toward the canyon, carrying sacks of grain for storage or to repay their debts.

CHAPTER TWENTY-SIX

The next few years were ones of great prosperity. The rains came and the snows came, and the crops grew well. The people benefitted as they never had before. Their own storerooms in the outliers were full and the storerooms at the Canyon also were overflowing. An extensive building program was initiated by Hopaqa and his rivals, each wishing to provide sufficient space for the abundance of corn and beans that kept arriving from every part of the Empire. Every stone mason with his many helpers was hard at work adding rooms to the cities, and the log carriers were kept at work from dawn until dark each day, bringing in timbers to roof the new rooms. With the prosperity the people ate well and lived more comfortably. The many logs being brought in meant trimmings that could be used for firewood, and even the least prosperous clans had fires in their round rooms on the cold nights.

Wherever we went, now we were well received. Paho was thought by many to be the bringer of the prosperity. In each village he would warn them that he did not bring the good times, but rather that he wanted to help them to prepare for the bad times, and many heeded him because of the two year drought which had just passed. They knew that they had survived it as well as they had because of the methods and the warnings that we had carried from settlement to settlement.

Kolello, during this time, continued to speak against Paho. He would warn the people that they were abandoning the old ways, and that the gods would be displeased. He said that they were following the ways of the barbarians to the south rather than the ways of their ancestors. Most of his followers were in the main Canyon, rather than the outlying villages. He told them that they would lose their control over the villages if they allowed this hunchbacked false prophet to go out among the people.

"The Gods speak to you through the priests on the Butte," he would say, "And the Gods are saying that you are abandoning them in order to follow the hunchback. Especially, the people in the villages are following him, and ignoring what is decreed through the priests.

"We must bring the people back to the old ways. They must know that the star was foretold by the priests long before this Kokopelli ever appeared, and that he had nothing to do with it. The prosperity which we all share is brought about by the proper observance of the seasons and the ceremonies, and it is we who give the villages guidance, that they may properly observe the ceremonies."

Many of the people listened to him, so that the people were becoming divided between those who supported the new ways of Paho and those who supported the traditionalism of Kolello. It was not a complete rift, yet, but it continued to grow over the years.

By the twelfth year after the appearance of the star many of the younger people did not remember seeing it. It was something their fathers had told them about, and it started to take on the aspect of a myth rather than a miracle. They had begun to listen to Kolello, and to believe that Kolello and his followers might be correct. He had, by then, become far more influential. Only one of the older priest still lived, and was the leader of the priesthood. Among the younger men who were below him Kolello had become the apparent successor.

We were still in the city of Hopaqa in the early spring of that year, awaiting nature's signs that it was time to start to travel again. I was now twenty years old, but still unmarried, having devoted my life to the service of Paho, and through him of our people. Paho was no longer a young man, and Hopaqa was quite old. Hopaqa sent two of his guards and called us to his kiva very early one morning. We entered to see the man, now grey and wrinkled, sitting alone, awaiting us as he had so many times before.

"Paho, sit here beside me," he said. "We must talk as we have talked over the years. But I fear that this may be the last time."

"Why do you say that, Hopaqa?" I asked. "You are still healthy and strong and so are we. Why should we not speak many times more?"

"Yes, I am still healthy. It is not that. Something happened last night, which is of great importance. I have called you here so that you may be warned. The old priest has died, and Kolello is now in power!"

"How does that change things?" Asked Paho. Will he dare to use his new power so soon? Does he have the strength to oppose your authority?"

"Yes, for he will discredit you if he can, and he will attack me if he thinks it will help to harm you. He has been accumulating followers for many months, waiting for this opportunity, and will now try to turn them against you. It may be that he is not yet strong enough, but we will only know that after he tries,and it is best if he is unable to use me to reach you. It is for that reason that you must no longer represent me. You will leave the pueblo immediately, and go very far away. I will say that I do not know where you have gone, and will tell everyone that you are no longer in my employ... Have you ever visited my logging camp in the mountains, many days to the Northeast?"

"No, we have not," I answered, "For we had heard that they did little agriculture, and were loyal to you as your tree cutters. There seemed little reason to spend our time there. We know where it is, though, and have often spoken of going there, but have not yet done so."

"Good, go there then. I will know where you are and send word by runner if I need you. Go there as soon as we finish talking. There is no time for you to gather food and clothing, for people would then see you leaving. My people at the logging camp are loyal to me, so if you can reach there unobserved you will be safe until I can get a message to you.

"Paho, do you remember at our first meeting that I told you that I would share with you the results of your working for me? You have never asked about this, but have continued to do as I have demanded for all these years. You have fulfilled your bargain, and more. You have been a loyal ally, and also a friend. I have not forgotten my promise to you. There are five storerooms, in the deepest recesses of the city, against the back wall, which are yours. In them are corn and beans, but also precious stones which I have received in trade and which I set aside for you. It is not a fortune, but it is enough so that you will be able to live well for many years when you return to the Canyon. I will try to let you know when it is safe to return. This boy, now grown into a man, has served you well, also. I leave it to you to see that he shares in these riches."

"Hopaqa, You are very generous." he said. "I had not forgotten your promise, but I had not felt that it was necessary. You offered me the opportunity to do that which I knew I must do anyway. It was in your name that I was able to teach the people.

"I thank you for your generosity, and will accept it for myself and for my helper. But do not say that we no longer work for you. Let us just tell others that we do not, so that you may be protected. But remember that I will always be a servant to you. You have said that we should leave, and we will do so, that you may no longer be in danger. Kolello is a vindictive man, who will use his new position to discredit me. It is not enough that I disappear, for he will know that you protect me. Therefore, let us make the people believe we now are enemies."

Suddenly Paho seized up a spear with a head of finely formed glassy stone. He slashed the edge across his arm so that a great deal of blood streamed out. He dripped this on the floor and on the ladder that led out of the kiva, and even some on the clothes which Hopaqa was wearing. Then he dropped the bloody spear on the ground and turned back to Hopaqa.

"Your bodyguards know that we are here, for you sent them to get us. We will quietly leave the kiva and climb the stone staircase to the top of the cliff. When we have had enough time to do that you must start to yell and break things, and then call for your guards. When they arrive, tell them that we have had a great quarrel and that I insulted you for the third time. Send them to bring me back, but send them south toward the Butte. Show them that you have wounded me, and say that I will soon die, but that you wish them to bring me back so you can have the pleasure of watching me die."

Hopaqa rose from the floor and embraced us both, something I had never seen a chief do before. Then he went back to his place and sat, looking away from us, and said, "Go, Now!"

When we left the Kiva Paho continued to drop a little blood on the pathway to the south, on rocks where it could be seen. Then we doubled back and quickly climbed the cliff, using the steps which had been laboriously chiseled into the rock, and which showed the wear of centuries of bare feet. Once on top we skirted to the south so as not to be seen by early risers at the upper pueblo, the one used for exchanging trade goods with foreigners when they arrived. We heard many voices as we went by, but were unobserved. Before long the Canyon was well behind us, and we saw no one in pursuit. The early spring air was sharp and cold, and the sun was just rising, shining in our eyes as we made our way eastward. It would take us a week, at least, to reach the village in the mountains where Hopaqa had instructed us to go. On this trip we could not stop in at each settlement and ask for food and a place to sleep. We would have to go in secret.

Chapter Twenty-Seven

Spring was reaching down into the Canyon, warming the earth and stirring it with the first signs of new life, when we started, but winter was still in full sway in the mountains to the north. We could see their whiteness to our left as we slowly made our way toward our haven. The massive peaks were bright in the sunlight, with blurred grey-green patches on their flanks where the stunted trees poked out of the deep snow, struggling to survive at the top limits of their habitat.

We went North and East knowing that we would find a large river, which would be flowing toward us. First, though, we needed to skirt the lone mesa that jutted out of the plain. It was a landmark visible even from the rim of the canyon, many miles away, a block of whitened sandstone, perhaps four times as long as it was high, and topped by two rounded knolls. There were a number of settlements at various points around its base, which we avoided.

Having passed by this danger unobserved, we angled toward the immense dry wash which we had seen many times before in our travels. It was actually at the end of the Great North Road which made a perfectly straight path across the flatness of the plateau all the way from the Canyon to the edge of the broad valley. The road was so long it took a man two days to walk it, and it ended abruptly at the side of a precipice, overlooking the buttes and gullies and the desolate bleakness of the wash. We would have made faster progress if we had followed that broad pathway instead of skirting to the south, but fearing being seen, we made a large detour.

The sky from here is accented to the east by a tower of rock of such unusual shape and size that the eyes are drawn to it. Some say it looks like a man, dressed in a long robe, standing upon a sharp peak. Others say that it looks like a bear. Our legends say that it is one of the four points that hold up the sky. It is visible for many miles in all directions, and lies on the other side of the vastness of the wash as one looks across at it from terminus of the Great North Road. We made for this landmark, and passed to the left of it, skirting the talus slopes which ringed it. Then, angling more toward the snow covered mountains we came upon the river we were seeking.

The water was still quite low, since little snow was yet melting in the high country to feed it. We stayed on the bluffs above the river bed and followed upstream for many miles, always getting closer to the mountains. As we went we watched the river, having been told that we must follow the second big stream that entered it from the north. The ground rose ahead of us, and the terrain became hilly. Now patches of snow were behind every boulder, and we could see ice in places below us where the water at the edges of the river was still. The nights were cold, and we wrapped ourselves in our cloaks, not wanting to show a fire.

On the fourth day after leaving the canyon there were large mountains to our right as well as to our left. Snow lay under the trees, and the hills were white on the north slopes. We hurried onward wishing to reach our destination as quickly as possible. We had taken no food with us, and had found almost nothing along the way. We did not hunt, since we would not want to build a fire to cook by, so we searched for pine nuts as we went. It seemed that the squirrels and chipmunks had searched the same places before us, for few nuts could be found.

We were tired, weak and hungry by the time we reached the place where the second major tributary angled across to the north. It could be seen to enter from a steep walled valley, pointing toward the highest of the snow-covered mountains. Since we had been told that the village we were seeking was to the east of this stream we knew that it would be best to cross the large river above the fork so that we would then not need to cross the tributary stream also. But the river was still quite wide and deep here, even before the heavy spring runoff, and the water was icy cold. It tumbled over and around large boulders on our side, and rushed over a deep smooth stretch in midstream, before shallowing to a narrow gravel bank on the far side.

Being now the stronger of the two of us, I led the way across. The water numbed my feet instantly as I stepped into it and the swirling coldness quickly made my legs ache. Trying to keep my balance against the current I leaned my hands against the closest boulder, chilling my fingers until even they felt numb and clumsy. My first thought was to turn back. My feet were now so cold that I felt the cobbles under them as distant irritations, not a part of me. My feet were someone else's feet, and my body seemed to end at water level. When I took a step it seemed as though I could not control the lower part of my body because it was so cold. I knew, though, that the river must be crossed, and that if I were to go back now another attempt would be impossible. I turned back and saw that Paho was close behind me, doing as I did. If it were difficult for me, with strong young legs, how much more difficult it must be for him! I got beyond the boulders, and looked ahead at the deceptively smooth water between the shallows and me.

As I inched out of reach of the boulders it dropped off quickly, until the water was to my chest. Paho still was gripping the last boulder, and I could see that the deep water would be very difficult for him. I reached back and told him to grasp my wrist, and I gripped back on his in a tight lock. As I edged forward he followed, until he had to scuttle sideways to keep his face out of the water, bent as he was by his injured back. We were both facing downstream and the icy water was pushing against our backs as we clung to one another and painfully edged toward the other bank. I felt like making a sudden lunge, and getting up to the shallows, out of the cold, but of course, with Paho behind me all I could do was inch forward.

The river bottom began to rise under my feet, and I could see that the gravel riffle was just ahead, but Paho behind me had just reached the deepest part of the river. Then a stone moved under my right foot, upsetting my balance.   If I had been warm and dry it would not have meant anything, but the numbness of my legs was such that I felt myself falling to the side. The quick jerk was all that was needed, evidently, to jar Paho's precarious footing, and by the time I had regained my balance I could feel him being swept downstream. I tightened my grip on his wrist, and felt him tighten on mine, but the cold and the numbness were making it difficult. I could sense the two hands being torn from one another, as though they belonged to someone else. I tried to pull him and myself into the shallows, fighting the power of the river, but as I stretched toward the safety, suddenly he was gone!

I lunged up onto the gravel bar and looked downstream, hoping to be able to reach him again and pull him ashore. It was as though he had vanished. The smoothness of the deep water did not show even a part of his clothing, or a clutching hand. It was as though we had never been there. I struggled up the banking and dashed downstream, searching every shallow, and watching the fast water, hoping to see some sign of my master, but there was nothing. I shouted and ran back and forth for some minutes, and then, realizing what I was doing, set to carefully searching the river. I went downstream until I was stopped by the incoming tributary. Cold as I was, I crossed this and continued to look further along the river, but still with no success.

When darkness came I went back up the river and recrossed the tributary. Then, still wet and shivering uncontrollably, I built a fire, careless now if I was detected, and tried to warm myself and dry my clothes. He had died because I could not hold on to him, and because I had stumbled. I would have to go back and tell Hopaqa.

Through that night I did not sleep. The cold of the air was hardly dispelled by the heat of the fire, and my clothes, even when dry, were of little protection. I shivered by the flame, turning to try to warm different parts, with little success. I waited anxiously for morning, to renew my search, hopeless as it seemed.

At first light I started to comb the river and its banks, without hope, looking in most of the same places I had searched the afternoon before. No person could have survived the night of cold, even if they had somehow pulled themselves from the river. But I searched anyway, and as I searched the banks I felt a great fear. Had I allowed him to die? Was he truly Kokopelli, or only a man, as he said? If he had truly been a god, perhaps he had only disappeared, to appear somewhere else. I had not found his body, and in fact, he seemed to have vanished from the moment I lost hold of him. In my numbness maybe I was deceived, and maybe his hand had not really slipped out of mine. Perhaps he just ceased to be there.

As I looked into every recess along the riverbank I thought again of the stories I had heard in the kivas, as a boy. The old woman had fascinated all of us as she told of this god Kokopelli. He was the protector of the people, who needed no mask as did the Kachinas. He went naked, and watered the crops with his urine. It was he who brought the good times for the people. It was also Kokopelli who made the corn grow, and made the people multiply also, for he was a god of fertility.

Best of all had been the story of his flute, fashioned from a hollow reed. He held it to his mouth and blew noiselessly on it. Wherever he went he was always seen carrying the flute, yet it was told in all the stories that no adult had ever heard him play it. But the old woman told us that children, still innocent, were sometimes allowed to hear the high-pitched music that he played. Any child who was privileged to hear the sounds was judged to be pure, untainted yet by the evils of the world. It was also said that when Kokopelli played his flute all of the dogs in the area would join in and howl together, lifting their heads to the sky, and telling the people of the flute player who was among them. The dogs were the sign that he was among them, even when he was not seen. Mothers would tell their children, in the evenings when the moon was full, and the dogs would sit on the hilltops, answering the distant calls of coyotes, "Hear, Kokopelli is out there. The dogs are telling us so. Now, go to sleep, and he will be guarding our pueblo through the night."

According to the stories, however, Kokopelli was known to have saved many of the people from starvation and death. The way in which he was supposed to have done this was again by the playing of his flute. When a pueblo was overrun by rats and mice, so that their food supplies were being invaded and destroyed, the people would say, "Now we need Kokopelli." They would pray to the gods that they would send the hunchbacked flute player to their aid.

If Kokopelli did appear at such an imperiled village, according to the legends, he would wander about the rooms of the people, playing his flute, and wherever he went the rats and mice would flee in terror. Many times over the centuries, he had driven the vermin from the storerooms and then shown the people how to chink and mortar the walls so that the food would be safe.

Was this, then, the strange demi-god who had been my friend and my master, or did Paho merely look like him? If Paho was just a man, why did he try so hard to help the people? Perhaps he truly was Kokopelli and had come to warn of a new danger as threatening as the rodents which were now quite well controlled. If so, had I been responsible for the death of this person, and could he really have died in the river if he were a demi-god?

All of these things were in my mind as I continued to search the banks of the river. Then, looking to my right, away from the river, I noticed a tangle of tree branches and roots which had evidently been deposited by the spring floods of some other year, and saw within their mass a pile of leaves and dirt which had been recently disturbed. I crawled in under the branches and saw there the apparently lifeless form I had been searching for. He had evidently been able to pull himself out of the river and into the partial protection of the debris, scraping leaves and dirt over himself for warmth.

His legs and arms were cold, as I pulled him into the open, and I assumed that he was dead. Then he had made a slight sound deep in his throat. I put my ear to his chest and heard the faint fluttering of life, tenuous but there. My own heart leapt with joy! He was alive, if I could keep him alive!

The rest of that day will always be a blurred memory. I remember taking off my coat and wrapping him in it, and then taking him into my arms and carrying him as one would a baby. I don't know how I found my way. I staggered for many miles, weak from hunger myself, but knowing that I could not stop. I went in the direction we had been going, heading for the village that had been our destination. It was the closest place I could probably find help, and I knew it represented safety from Kolello also.

That evening, still not at the village, I stopped and built a fire. I heaped on the fuel, hoping it would be seen, and knowing that we both must have its warmth. As the flames leapt I continued to add driftwood which was plentiful near the stream, and the heat flooded us, bringing new life. Then he began to stir, for the first time, and his eyes opened.

"So," he mumbled, "They still want me to live. They will not let me die, even yet."

"It is I who will not let you die." I said. "When I found you I thought you had died, but you are very tough. Now, wrap yourself more tightly in that cloak and get some sleep. Tomorrow we will reach the village of the log cutters."

"Yes," he said quietly, but his voice now sounding less weak, "You have again saved my life, as the gods have decreed. They will not let me have peace. Many times I have wished to die, but they have always stepped in the way. It must be as Melolo said, the Gods spared me from the earthquake so that I might suffer more. They placed you with me that they would not be robbed of their pleasure; of making me suffer."

"No, they keep you alive so that you may teach the people. They will not let you die, because there is work that you must do; their work. If it is my duty to keep you alive, then it is for that reason... Now, let us get some rest, for tomorrow we must try to reach the village of the log cutters."

We both slept deeply, with the fire continuing to force life back into his body and energy back into mine. From time to time I rose and piled on more of the driftwood, and the sparks spiralled into the dark night. Paho slept soundly, wrapped in both our cloaks. It was near morning when I lay back down, after having again fed the flames, when, lying on my back, I realized I was looking up at something which I had only hazily seen the night before, preoccupied with my thoughts of the disappearance of Paho. But it had been there at least two nights now, and it was something I had never seen before. In the eastern sky, just above where the sun would soon rise, there was a streak of light. It was a blur, as if thousands of tiny stars had merged together and then been smeared across the blackness. The line of light, like a dim arrow, was so long that I could not, by raising my palm at arms length, completely obscure it.

I studied this new light in sky until the rising sun cast enough light to wash it away, and then woke Paho. He was greatly improved, so that he could hobble about slowly, and was ready to try to go on to the settlement. I told him then about the shaft of silver, which seemed to be pointing away from the rising sun.

"It is a message, from the Sun God himself." He said. "I do not know what the meaning of this is, but the priests will have seen it, and will know what it signifies. All life comes from the sun. It is said that the Sun is the face of Taiowa, and that he watches the people in this way, while he brings them his powers of life. I must see this light in the sky you speak of. I fear that it may be a warning to the people. The arrow of light, you say, points away from sun and at the earth. Perhaps it is saying that Taiowa is again displeased with us, and is ready to destroy the world for a fourth time.

"Let us start for the settlement we seek. You do not need to worry about keeping me alive, now. I must live, and must know what this sign means for our people. Let me just lean upon your shoulder, and we will make our way to the village of the log cutters. The sun is warmer today, and I feel its energy bringing life back into my body."

CHAPTER TWENTY-EIGHT

Our fire had not gone unobserved! We had not walked more than a mile when we suddenly found ourselves surrounded by men with bows and arrows. They had been waiting silently in the brush, and they materialized suddenly on all sides of us. They looked like our people, yet not exactly. Their features were similar, their coloring, their hair. They were, as we are, heavily and strongly built, with short and muscular legs supporting a deep-chested and narrow-hipped torso. Dark eyes challenged us, strong arms kept the nocked arrows pulled to their maximum extent, ready to be loosed at an instant. But their clothes were not the same. They wore animal skins rather than woven fabric.

When they saw there were only two of us, and one a cripple, they relaxed somewhat, and spoke to us, but in a language we did not understand. We answered them in our own tongue, and were surprised to find that they understood. One, in fact, stepped forward and spoke to us, haltingly, in our own language.

"Where do you go, in our country? Your people are not to cross the river just as we are not to enter your empire. We saw your fire in the night, and have waited for you."

I answered, "We are seeking the camp of Hopaqa, where the logs are cut and taken to our pueblos. We come at the direction of Hopaqa, and mean no harm. We know that the river divides our territories, but have been told that you allow our people to live here and cut timber, in exchange for trade goods, which we bring to you. We have not killed your game or stolen your crops; we come in peace, only seeking our own people who are said to live among you."

"If you are from Hopaqa, you are welcome, for he has been a friend of our people. When we have needed food he has fed us from his own storerooms. Come with us, and we will take you to your people, who live with us at our village."

It was a difficult climb, even for me, tired and hungry as I was. For Paho it must have been excruciating, yet he made no complaint, and did his best to keep up. At the end, two of the men helped him to reach the top of the mesa where the village was located. Here we saw the round rooms of these people, dug into the sparse soil at the top of the mesa. The stonework was far less well done than that of our own pueblos and they had few structures above ground level. Theirs was a hand to mouth existence, in which they stored little, year to year, relying on their ability to hunt and to gather seeds and berries from the surrounding mountains. The climate was too cold, and the growing season too short to allow them to grow their food to the extent we did in the lower elevations. Their homes were buried deep in the soil to keep out the winter cold, and huddled together. As clans and families grew larger new round rooms were added, adjacent to the ones of the older members. They had not learned, or did not bother, to chink the walls solidly enough to keep out the vermin, and their homes were overrun by mice, kangaroo rats, chipmunks, squirrels and a wide assortment of roaches and other insects. They even allowed food to be taken into their round rooms, thereby adding to the problem. I couldn't believe our people could be living with them under such primitive conditions!

When I asked where our people were, they pointed up the slope of the mesa, toward the very highest part. From there one could look across to the gigantic pillars of rock, two of them, which dominated the sky and soared above the settlement. They were the most impressive towers I had ever seen, pointing like fingers at the sky. Our people had built their own village at the exact place where the pillars could best be seen. They had built in the ways of our people, using the tightly fitted masonry, filling every tiny hole with a small flat stone, and then plastering the entire structure, inside and out, with a dark mud.

Paho and I started to climb higher, following the trail, which crossed a ridge, with a sharp drop on both sides, and then skirted to the south, before approaching the first of the round rooms. As we came closer the entire village seemed to be deserted. Then I looked over to the right, toward the gigantic towers, to a point of rock that jutted out over the valley.

There, standing on the rock, not looking at us, but watching an eagle as it circled the closer tower, I saw what seemed an apparition. Silhouetted against the sky, wind brushing her long black hair, was a girl. I walked closer, entranced, and realized that Paho was beside me, equally transfixed. We went slowly, as though fearing to startle her as one might a bird. She was as slim as she was small, and looked fragile against the immensity of the landscape behind her. She was, yes, a girl, but almost a woman already. In the chillness of the early spring she wore only a skirt of woven cotton. Even her feet were bare.

I had seen this girl before, somewhere! I remembered then an older woman, walking away from a watering hole, years before. I could see her again as I had on that day, carrying the water jug, and asking me to help to find her sister; telling me the story of Tokchii without ever mentioning the forbidden name. She had been older and more mature, but still it was her, or very like her, a younger copy of the woman who had entranced me as a boy of only nine. Now, suddenly, here she was again, but now she was younger and I was older.

Beside me I heard a sudden intake of breath, and the Paho spoke, loudly, breaking the trance, frightening the bird, returning me to reality. "It is her! The gods have sent Tokchii back to me! She is unchanged, as she was when we were children."

The girl could not flee. She looked in every direction, but the precipice dropped off on three sides and we blocked the fourth. I wondered, at first, if she would disappear, but she stayed there, looking at us as a deer that has been drinking at a watering place and has heard a noise.

"Who are you? What do you want, here?" She asked. Her voice was challenging. We had startled her in her reverie, and she was now alert and fearful.

"I am sorry we intruded," I said. "You looked so much like someone I remembered that I just wanted to make sure you were real. We mean you no harm. You were like a spirit, standing on that rock, and we were wondering if you were a ghost of someone we once knew."

"I am real, I live here." The fear had diminished, " But if you are looking for the men, they are down in the valley, preparing for the spring floods."

"Are you alone here, a young girl?"

" No, there are the two of us. We stay here when they are working. We cook the food, and mend the clothes of the workers. The only other women are those of the village below. They see to some of the needs of the men, but our men will not allow the unclean cooking ways of the women below. So we prepare all the food for the workers. My name is Nuwani."

"You say that there are two of you who take care of the men?" Paho now asked. "Who is the other?"

"She is my mother, and her name is Tokchii."

CHAPTER TWENTY-NINE

Before I was aware he had left, Paho was gone in search of Tokchii. He had gone back into the pueblo, toward the kivas, leaving me still staring at this beautiful girl. The eagle still circled the cliffs behind her, and her hair still stirred in the wind, black and shining in the sunlight.

She was fifteen years old then, and I was twenty. " Only a child," I told myself. "There is certainly no reason for me to feel intimidated by her. I am much older than she, and have traveled to all parts of the Empire. I have seen things, and done things which are beyond her imagination, so there is certainly no reason why I should feel awkward or confused." I backed away from the narrow pathway, which led out to her rock, and sat on a shelf of stone, still looking at her, enchanted and unsure what to say or do, in spite of my resolution. She had said nothing more, but had stared at me, no longer showing any fear, and perhaps a little amused. Then she stepped back onto the mesa top, leaving her aerie, and came over to look down at me.

Her dark eyes were not shy, nor were they challenging. She only looked levelly at me, imparting an illusion of honesty and innocence, which I found confusing and disconcerting. Then she went to another shelf of stone, a few feet away, and facing mine, where she also sat, now looking toward me intently.

"What did you mean," she asked, "When you said you thought I was a ghost? Have we ever met before?"

"No, we are strangers, but I have seen someone very much like you. Someone older than you but also very beautiful. Someone whom I saw but once, and spoke to only briefly, but whom I will never forget...

I will tell you of her in a few minutes, if I may first ask you a few questions."

"If I am able I will answer your questions. It is not often than I have the opportunity to speak to another of our people who is near my age. The tree cutters are older, and they all think of me as their daughter. They have seen me grow, and treat me as a child, still. The village below is full of barbarians. They live in filth, with rats and cockroaches. There is no one there with whom I can talk. So, yes, I will answer you questions, if that is what you wish, but you must promise to tell me more of the strange and beautiful woman whose ghost I am." She said this last with a mocking smile. "Perhaps I am truly that woman, playing tricks on you."

"I thought that at first, but I see now that you are yourself, and no one else. Tell me, Nuwani, have you lived here long, or did you and your mother come here from somewhere else?"

"Oh, no, I have lived here all my life. I was born in this village, and have never been further than the big river. I have wanted, many times, to see other parts, but my mother is content to stay here. She says she likes the privacy. It is as though she does not want to see others, or be seen. Even when someone comes from the Canyon, she only listens quietly to the news, and says little. If your friend has gone to find her he may find that she does not wish to talk to him."

"Is one of the log cutters, then, your father?"

"A log cutter? My father a log cutter? Of course not! My father is an important man. My mother says that he speaks with the gods! She says that I was born a short time after she arrived at this village, and that she was carrying me when she arrived. The log cutters have all been like fathers to me, but they are none of them my father. I have asked my mother why he is not here with us, and she says that he is far too important. He lives at the main canyon, and he speaks with the gods."

"You say," I asked with hesitation, "That he speaks with the gods. Do you mean that he is a priest? Is he one of the astronomer priests who lives at the Sacred Butte, and who foretells the times of planting and of ceremonies?"

" I do not think so," she answered, "For my mother said that he is a teacher of the people. She said that he travels from village to village, teaching them. She says he has great powers. He is even able to make stars grow so bright that they light up the whole sky!"

I looked closely at her, again, and now I could see it. The high forehead and the penetrating eyes were his. In her face I now saw Paho, her father. She was her aunt, but the other was there also. In one person I was seeing the beauty and grace of the lovely woman who carried the water jug and the strength and determination of the man who had been my master, my mentor, at times my responsibility, and always my friend.

"Why has she not gone to this man, your father, rather than stay in this camp and cook for a village of log cutters?"

"I have asked this also. My mother says that he does not know that he has a daughter and that he might not wish to be bothered with a family, because his work is so important. When she first left her home to the south she wished to search for him, but that was before she realized she carried his child. Another man, she said, had become very powerful, and would harm her and the child if he were to find them. She did not want to endanger me, nor to endanger my father. It was only many years later that she heard the story of the exploding star, and learned of the importance of my father."

"You have asked me to tell you why I thought you were a ghost. Let me tell you a story. It is about the most beautiful woman I had ever seen until I saw you today." I went on to tell her the entire history of Paho. I started with the woman at the water hole, and the quest for Paho's missing love, and then went back and told her of his childhood, just as he had told it to me. I told it as a beautiful and tragic story, and she listened intently, not realizing who we were really talking about. When I related the story of the earthquake she was horrified, but had never heard the story before. When I told her of the twisted form and the illusion of Kokopelli, she knew it was my companion I was speaking about, but had not heard of him before. It was not until I spoke of the miracle of the exploding star that she understood.

Nuwani looked at me in wonder. "He is my father." she whispered. "That man who went to look for Tokchii is my father. She has wept many times for him, I know. She has longed to see him, I am sure. Now he is here! My father has been searching for us all these years. That is my father!"

"He is a cripple." I warned.

"He is my father!"

"Yes, and he will now know of you. Let us give them time together. He will be pleased to have a daughter like you, and will not fear that you will interfere with his work. He has thought of nothing other than finding your mother for the twelve years I have been with him."

We spoke for a long time, then, as we waited for Paho and Tokchii to come to us. Nuwani took me to one of the cooking rooms and gave me the first food I had eaten in two days. Someone had come to the room earlier, she said, and taken food. Evidently Tokchii and Paho.

It was evening, and we were back at the upper end of the mesa, overlooking the valley and the pillars of stone, when they came. They walked close together, in the twilight, and I sensed that Paho was happy, at last. Tokchii was just as he had described her those many times over the years, so that I believe I would have recognized her, as I did her sister. They walked to us, saying nothing, and Paho looked at his daughter smiling.

"He has told you?" Tokchii asked Nuwani.

"Yes," she said. "I have found my father! It is something I have always wanted. Father. May I call you that? It will at first be strange, but I will try to be as a daughter to you."

"Yes," said Paho, "And it will take time for me, also. If I had known I had a child, and especially one such as you, I would have searched even in the winters to find you. Now that we are together we will not part again. We four will be a family.

"Your mother and I have talked of plans. We will all stay at this camp for now, as directed by Hopaqa. We will all be safe here. Kolello has become very powerful, so we must not be found. I am told that the log cutters will keep our secret. If we are able, we will go back, when the message comes from Hopaqa. He has put aside riches for me over the years. These riches will now be for all of us when we are told we can return. We will live together as a family at the city of Hopaqa, and we will continue to teach the people the wisdom I learned while living with the southern aliens."

I found myself suddenly flooded with happiness. I had, secretly, feared this reunion. I had known that the day would come when we would find Tokchii, and I believed that on that day Paho would need me no more. I had given up my natural family to follow this strange man. I feared being replaced, and having neither a family nor a friend. Instead, not only had Paho found his love, I had found mine at the same time. He said that we would now be one family. Yes, more so than he realized!

The next three weeks were filled with happiness. In the years I had been with Paho he had rarely smiled. The pain of his back, the difficulty he had walking, were a constant burden. But more than that, he had never forgotten Tokchii, and his thoughts returned frequently to his search for her. In addition, he was consumed with our work. He believed completely in his mission to help the people, and that left little time for pleasure. At this remote outpost there was no teaching to be done, and he now had Tokchii. He relaxed for the first time in the years I had been with him, and he smiled often.

For myself, the days were filled with Nuwani, and we became close. She took me to all of the places she knew, and showed me where the deer lived and where the eagles nested. This forest, reaching toward the snow-covered mountains, had been her playground throughout a childhood that knew no playmates. Now she delighted in taking me to them all, and teaching me the ways of the forest animals, far different that the desert life I had been raised to.

We also went to the base of the mesa on which the village was situated, and watched the log cutters at work. They had spent much of the autumn and then the early spring cutting trees with their stone tools. They had dragged them from the forest and cut away all the limbs, producing logs long enough to roof even the largest ceremonial kivas at the Canyon. With the rapid building program which was going on there, the demand for logs was almost insatiable, and they had prepared many of them for transportation. They were piled by the side of the large stream, which we had followed on our way to the village. There they awaited the heavy spring runoff. At that time they would lash a few together and push them into the rapid water where they would guide them downstream, with a man on each group of logs, keeping to the main current and traveling to the big river, and then to the city which was on the river, directly north of the Canyon. From there the logs would be carried on men's shoulders to the Canyon.

While Nuwani and I amused ourselves Paho and Tokchii stayed at the village, where she prepared food for the log cutters who returned each evening, exhausted from their work. We all lived in one of the round rooms, a very small one which had been the home of Nuwani and her mother prior to our arrival. It was a happy time for us all.

As the weeks went by the strange light in the sky became ever brighter until it spread a third of the way across the heavens. It was a luminous spear which had its sharp point aimed away from the face of Taiowa. No one recalled ever seeing anything like it, and all feared it as a bad omen. The log cutters waited impatiently for some word from the priests at the Canyon, which would tell them what this meant.

We had been there for three weeks, and spring was now starting to reach the mountains. The days were warm and the snow was melting in the higher areas. The streams were starting to rise, and green buds were showing on the bushes and trees. Every small valley now had a stream running through it, so that the ground was soggy when we walked to the many places that Nuwani wanted to show me. It was a particularly warm and breezeless day, and we were at the village, just letting the sun warm us as we lay beside one another looking over the edge of the cliff at the valley below, when the runner arrived.

"I come from the Canyon. I bring word from the Hopaqa and from the Sacred Butte." he announced. The workers below had seen him as he approached the village and had followed him up the slope. Soon they were gathered with us, awaiting the news. "You have seen, have you not, the light in the sky? It began on the day that Kolello was elevated to the highest priesthood. On that night, as the ceremony was being held, Kolello himself pointed to the sky, and all thought that he was calling upon the rising of the sun, but then they saw a glow in the sky. It was as though he had told the sky to glow at that instant. Since then it has grown larger and larger each night, and it is said that it is showing the power of Kolello.

"The people are calling it the miracle of Kolello, and have asked him what the light in the sky signifies. The people are full of fear, for the fire in the sky is brighter each night. Many say that it will grow until it burns the world; that Sotuknang has ordered the end of the fourth world. They await word from the priests.

"Kolello and the other priests have gone back to the top of the Butte, saying that they will descend in five days' time from today to tell the people what they should do. All are awaiting that day. Kolello has said that he will talk directly with the gods, and bring the people the answer. They are to await him on the appointed day, at the base of the Threatening Rock, behind the pueblo of Hopaqa."

After the messenger had been fed and after the log cutters had asked him many more questions, he went off to the side, and beckoned that Paho should follow him. They spoke earnestly for many minutes, and then parted. Paho returned to the three of us and told us to follow him immediately to our round room.

"Hopaqa is ill. He sent word that he needs my help, and that I am to go secretly to the Canyon, and to his kiva, as quickly as possible. However, I will not go without my family. You are all stronger than I am, so you will not be slowing me down. I will need your help, for I cannot deny Hopaqa.

"Let us gather food and warm clothing, and leave as quickly as possible. There is still much time before nightfall, and we cannot waste any of it. Tokchii, you must tell one of the log cutters, so that they will know that we have not come to harm; choose one that you can trust, and ask him not to tell the others we have left until tomorrow. The messenger will be leaving before we do, and has delivered his message but does not know our plans. Let us gather what we need, and meet at the base of the mesa, on the other side from where the logs are stockpiled. We will descend as couples, which will not seem unusual, and then go south by the trail. Tokchii, is there a better place to cross the river than that which we told you of, where I was almost drowned?"

"Yes, I know of the easy crossing the runners use. It is almost within sight of where you crossed, further upstream. But why do we all go? There is danger, and the two young ones are not needed."

"No, we are a family now. We all go or no one goes, for I will not lose my wife, my daughter or my son, even for Hopaqa."

In a very short time we were gathered at the base of the mesa, well supplied for the trip.

Chapter Thirty

Hopaqa had changed so much in the month I had been gone that it hardly looked like the same man. He was wrapped in fur robes and lay near the center of his kiva, where the strengthening light from the overhead entrance shone down upon him. Paho and I had left the women at the foot of the stone stairway, and told them that we would meet them there later in the day. There seemed little to fear for them, since no one knew who they were or that they were with us. A strange man would have been suspect if seen in the canyon, but women went unnoticed. We had crept down those step in the early morning, before sunrise, entirely unobserved, and had then approached the home of Hopaqa. Over our heads the arrow of light dominated the sky, blotting out the stars around it. Hopaqa's guards were not present, and we easily slipped down the ladder, and waited for him to wake.

As the sun rose higher it streamed into the room, and its light moved in a rectangular patch across the packed dirt floor, until it reached his form and illuminated him. When the rays of the sun reached his eyes he lifted a thin hand to brush them aside, then turned away and opened his eyes. The face was thin and lined now, and his hair was grey, as it fell over the side of his face. In a few weeks he seemed to have changed from a vital man, a leader, to an emaciated and weak bundle of frailness, buried already in his heap of fur robes.

His eyes were glassy, and looked opaque when the sun struck them. I wondered if he could see at all, but then his gaze fell upon us, and he smiled weakly.

"Paho," he said, "I knew that you would come. I have wanted to speak to you before I died. It was shortly after you left that the coughing started, and then I could no longer eat. I began to get weaker, and the coughing began to bring up blood. I knew then that I would die, but I wished to see you again, first. It was then that I sent the message."

"Hopaqa," I blurted, " You cannot die. We need you. The people need you. Paho has at last found his love, and I mine. Now, when we see so much ahead, it cannot be that you should die! We came back to the canyon, thinking that we would be able to live here, with you, in this city. Our work is not yet done. We have come back to work for you again."

"Boy, you have served me well, you and your master. I do not choose to die, but there is no choice. I called you back, not to work for me, but to save what we have all worked for. I called you back because Kolello is attempting to destroy everything.

"Even before, when he was a junior priest he spoke against you, Paho, but few listened. As he grew in power more of the people believed him. When the old Chief Priest died he took little time in trying to have you killed as an agent of the southern tribes. That is why I told you to flee. He also attacked me, after gaining that power, telling the people that I had used you in order to become rich. Now, with the sky lighted by the fire of Kolello, as he calls it, he attacks not just me, but all the leaders of the Canyon, all those who store food for others. He tells the people that we are keeping for ourselves food that rightfully belongs to the people. He tells them that we try to scare them with tales of bad years that will never come again. He says that we make them store food that they could be eating, so that we may become rich while they are hungry.

"I have never known, from the day you first entered this kiva, if you are a god or a man. Perhaps you are neither, or perhaps you are a man that the gods are using for their own purposes. I am told that you should have died in that earthquake, and that you never should have survived your travels to the south. You have avoided certain death so many times that I believe you have a special power. That power was seen when your star appeared.

"If you have such a power, now is the time when it is needed. We both know that the rains will not come every year, and that the people must store food, away from the rats if they are to survive. Your methods of planting and of saving our scarce water have increased our production of food. If these are the ways of the southern aliens, so be it. It has helped our people. To change these things would be to destroy all we have worked for, and it would mean the end of this Canyon as the source of guidance for the empire. It could even mean the end of our people. If you have any power to do so, you must stop Kolello!"

"Hopaqa," Paho spoke slowly and thoughtfully, "I do not believe that I am a God, but I do not truly know. Before the earthquake I was a boy like other boys. Afterwards, I was different. It was as though Melolo was right; that the Gods would not let me die. Maybe the boy, here, is right. Perhaps I am not being kept alive as a punishment, but as a servant. Maybe I am here still so that Kolello will not win. I do not know the truth, but I will do everything that I can to fulfill your desire, since I wish the same thing. I believe the Gods want this also."

Hopaqa had been forcing himself toward a sitting position as this conversation went on. Now he slumped back down again, so that I wondered if he was conscious. Then he slowly opened his eyes again.

"The boy said that you have a woman, now? Is that true? Tell me about this." He mumbled.

We spent the rest of the day in the kiva, first telling Hopaqa of our latest journey and its outcome, and then going back and filling him in on the parts of the story he did not know. He was weak, and would stop us from time to time, so that he could doze. But he would then awaken and demand that the narrative continue

As evening came on we left him, and went back to the place where we would meet Nuwani and Tokchii, unnoticed in the dim light. This was the day that Kolello had named, on which he would tell them the meaning of the shaft of brilliance in the sky, and the people from all parts of the canyon and even from other pueblos of the Empire were gathering near the Threatening Rock. Most strangers would go unnoticed, but the unusual shape of Paho, and the fact that he was assumed to be dead, meant that we had to be cautious.

The sun was just setting to the west, and the sky had turned to fire in that direction. The sky was streaked in not just orange and yellow, but subtle shades of green and purple, also. There was a high layer of clouds, which began to pick up the brightness, until the sky seemed to be in flames in all directions, not just where the sun was disappearing. The gathered people, now numbering in the thousands, faced the setting sun, witnessing the daily spectacle of His death and praying for His rebirth. They had their backs to the Threatening Rock.

At some time in the distant past, before the people had lived in the canyon, a large piece of the cliff had cleaved away from the rest, so that it was separated from the canyon wall by an abyss. The remnant was a pinnacle of sandstone, which loomed over the stone city, appearing to be ready at any instant to crash down upon it. It had stood there without moving for many centuries, but the people had always feared its fall, and had even built stonework at its base, in an attempt to shore it up. Therefore it was called Threatening Rock. It was as tall as the cliff itself, and had sheer walls. No wall, however seemed too steep for our people, and someone had hollowed out small indentations on the front side as hand and foot holds, so that a very agile and a very brave person could climb to the top.

There was a loud shout, and the crowd turned to see what it was. Paho and Tokchii were beside us, as Nuwani and I stood, shielded from sight, behind an immense boulder. We all turned our eyes also, as the crowd did, toward the pinnacle of rock. There on its summit stood Kolello! While the people had prayed to the setting sun he had evidently climbed the rock, and stood, spread legged, with his arms lifted, with the blazing sky behind him. He was dressed in ceremonial robes, with a crown of feathers on his head. In his hand he held the carved wooden staff of the astronomers, draped with rabbit fur, eagle claws and the skin of a snake, and hanging from its top was a perfect ear of corn.

"My people," He began, "I have come to tell you of the sign in the heavens. I have gone to the Sacred Butte, and fasted for three days. I have stood in the sun without shade and let the spirit of Taiowa enter through the soft spot at the top of my head. I have spoken with him, and he has told me what my duty is. This is what I come to tell you.

"Taiowa is not happy with the people, and he sends the sign in the sky so that we may know. It is an arrow which has loosed at the earth. It will strike the earth if we do not do as he says. Taiowa says that we have left his pathway, and followed lies. He says that we worship the gods of the southern aliens; that the man you called Kokopelli, was not a servant of his, but an imposter, and that his death proves it.

"I am told that the men who store your food steal from you. They take your crops, which you work to produce, and they produce none themselves. He says that these men are evil, and that they scare you with lies. It is your food, and you should take it back!"

I looked at Paho. He was furious, but he held back, helpless. There was nothing he could do against the power of this man. He stared up at the figure etched against the gold of the sunset. Tokchii held his arm, as though to restrain him, but he was making no attempt to move.

A voice from the crowd shouted. "But what of Hopaqa? He has given us food and has sent food to the villages which were starving. He and men like him have been our friends. To take the storage from their rooms would be to steal from them. And did not Kokopelli work for him, for Hopaqa? And did he not teach us how to grow more and better crops?"

"Speak to me not of Hopaqa." Hopaqa is no more! As the sun set, so did the life of Hopaqa. I saw him dead in his kiva. You have no friend to give you the grain, which was already yours. He is dead."

"No!" A shout beside me. A pained scream. Tokchii tried to hold him now, but he pulled away. "Let me go. I cannot die. The gods will not let me. I have promised Hopaqa."

In the crowd voices were now heard, people who recognized Kokopelli. "He is not dead! He has come back. He is a god, for we saw his star".

Now Paho began to climb the sheer rock wall, using the same foot and hand holds that Kolello must have used. He stopped from time to time, and his form seemed to teeter, so that we held our breaths, expecting him to fall. But he went on, hunched against the rock, fighting the unbalancing weight of his twisted back. At last, he reached the top and pulled himself up beside Kolello.

"Look at me," he said. "Am I dead? Kolello has said that I am not truly Kokopelli because I have died. Do you see a dead man here? No, the dead man is Hopaqa, your friend. Kolello would tell you that you should forget the new ways; that you should break open the storerooms; that you should destroy the dams and ditches which I taught you to build. I say to you that Kolello lies to you. The light in the sky, which you attribute to Kolello, is not his doing. The gods have sent it to tell you that there is danger. They are warning you that the people are once again threatened. Kolello and his ideas are that danger."

"He calls himself a god," Kolello shouted, "But I knew him when we were boys together. He was not a god then and he is not one now. He was then of the Eagle Clan, but because of him all of his people were killed. The Eagle Clan are the messengers to the gods. Our legends say that they are able to fly to the top of the sky and take our prayers to Taiowa himself. If he is still an Eagle, let him go to his fellow gods, and tell them what is done here. If you are an eagle, then show us how you fly!"

Kolello moved quickly. With his staff of authority he reached across the short distance, which separated them, and pushed Paho, upsetting his balance as he stood at the edge of the cliff he had just climbed. For a moment I thought Paho would catch his balance, but then I saw him sway and topple, dragged by the weight over his shoulders. Then he was separated from the cliff and outlined against the rock, his arms seeming to move like the flapping of an eagle's wings. I thought then, for an instant, that I saw him rise, as though to fly, but it was only an illusion, and the crowd gasped as the figure hurtled toward the ground. It was a muted and hollow thump that he made as his body crashed onto the roof of one of the highest rooms, and lay broken and lifeless.

It was only minutes until the mob had broken down the walls of the first of Hopaqa's storerooms and carried away the grain.

About the Author

A newcomer to the world of Fiction, Richard W. Arms, Jr. is world known in the field of Stock Market Technical Analysis, with five published books to his credit. His Arms Index and his Equivolume Charting are mainstays of Wall Street methodology. He has received the \highest awards in the field, including the lifetime achievement award from The Market Technicans Association, and induction into the Traders Hall of Fame. He resides with his wife, June, in Albuquerque, New Mexico.